Wild Oats

MICHAEL EDWARDS

Wild Oats

Macmillan New Writing

First published 2008 by Macmillan New Writing
an imprint of Pan Macmillan Ltd
Pan Macmillan, 20 New Wharf Road, London N1 9RR
Basingstoke and Oxford
Associated companies throughout the world
www.panmacmillan.com

ISBN 978-0-230-71252-2

1 3 5 7 9 8 6 4 2

A CIP catalogue record for this book is available
from the British Library.

Typeset by Intype Libra Ltd
Printed and bound in the UK by
MPG Books Ltd, Bodmin, Cornwall

For Ann

Preamble

All the age-old strictures on imaginative fiction, all the out-pouring of advice to would-be authors time and again stress that before a writer sits down to begin his story he should actually have a story in mind – he should know what he wants to write about, and why – if he's a serious writer then he's got to approach the task with a great deal of thought, and those less serious writers who've a rattling good yarn to tell must have reams of paper with the details of the plot laid out in black and white

and it's exactly the same with characters – these should be precisely delineated, at least in the author's mind if not on paper – after all, before he begins he ought to know his characters fully, know them inside out, from top to bottom – didn't he?

no, no, no, let's cross all that out! – I can't be bothered with those sorts of formalities, I want to get straight on with it, pick up a pen, stare at a blank sheet of paper, and start! – literary critics may have the right idea and teachers on creative writing courses are probably quite correct, but my preferred system of work is just to pick up a pen, is to sit and stare at a nice virgin piece of paper [which, when you consider the matter in an intellectual way, seems to own the propensity of an invitation to violate it], sit and stare until a pale idea presents itself as a possible point of entry to a fantastic work of literature destined to be a certain classic and sell eventually in hundreds of thousands over several centuries – one word is written down, another follows it, and I'm off – as far as characters are concerned I'm quite happy to rattle off their name, their shoe size, the colour of their hair, whether they can tell their left hand from their right, and let genius and instinct take it from there

yes, I agree, this isn't by any means an original approach, in fact it could be said with some authority that it's an idea as old as the hills, nearly a convention in some ways, almost what might academically be called a genre – nonetheless we'll do it, we'll be bold and adventurous, with relish we'll ravish that white paper – I won't have beside me a long route map of the story, no theme, no plan of development, no copious notes of each character's physical appearance or mental state, no idea of what they like to eat – I won't have so much as an inkling of what they're capable of or where they might be going, what they might be doing – they'll be as fresh and new to me as they are to you – all I think I know is how many there might be [but let's face it, that's variable, a lot of people have a habit of turning up when you least expect them] and I might or might not have a rough idea of where the story will lead them, maybe – as for plot and progress, forget it, no idea at all how it'll turn out – no idea either of what each of the characters might end up doing – quite possibly they'll end up the reverse of what I thought they were going to be – it's all a bit like a television soap really, where the characters start out as one sort and end up as another, mutating as they go along

it's a funny old thing, fiction – you start with a character, it comes into your head with enough apparent solidity to make you think you've invented it and you give it things to do, words to say, you put it into certain situations – but without you noticing it this so-called figment of your imagination ceases to be fictional, it becomes a real person with their own ideas about how they should look and act, what they prefer to do, how they prefer to approach life – believe me there's nothing you can do about it, nothing at all, for with no sign of politeness or even common decency they'll take the pen from your hand and in a firm voice say *do you mind? – look here, I'll be the one to decide how I'll react to this ridiculous situation you've put me in, it's bad enough having to wear these awful clothes and do these unusual things* – and what's more galling, what sticks in your creative gullet even more is that they then begin to dictate the plot – *we can't go along that route, we're not that sort of people, it would be so out of character for us – we want to go this way, do this, and if you don't mind we'll do it in our own style –* and before you know where you are the story you thought you were going to tell becomes something else, going off in all directions like a wayward firecracker – they gang up on you, these characters, shoulder to shoulder they stand together and dare you to put them into a straitjacket – *leave it to us* they indignantly declare – *this is our story, you just arrange the words*

so unless you've spent a couple of months plotting out in precise detail every single scene, every single move, every character's distinctive response [as those who write action stories, by the rules of such things, are required to do], unless you act with the arrogance of a dictator and force these subjects to do your bidding whether they like it or not, then these so-called fictional characters will do their own thing, have it their own way – the thing is, and to be truthful, I'm in no way a dictator, not at all, I'm weak when it comes to ordering people about, always have been, 'a defect in my character' said the sergeant who tried to get me some promotion when I was in the army – and what it means is that any upstart so-called fictional character knows it can get the better of me – and the result's not just disorder or disobedience, it's anarchy of course, what else?

yes, I suppose it's an anarchy which has to be directly attributable to my laziness – I might start, and indeed I always do start, with good and honourable intentions but the trouble is I can't be bothered with what you might call classroom preparation – as a result the class riots and before I know it they're throwing things at one another, and at me as well – eventually I'm completely ignored, except as some handy commentator who's prepared to record the shifts and fortunes of the participants as they push their way through the story – in fact, I'm lost before I start, and I can already feel this particular story's characters bursting into life, gathering in the playground they are, nudging their mates at the more than easy time they're going to have – a holiday for them, that's what it is, nothing but a holiday – and they look up, see me at the window, throw me a glance, snort with derision – I look down on them with ever-growing dismay knowing I'm going to have a very hard time

now they're okay when I read their names from the register, this is the easy bit, this is the point where they're more concerned with one another than they are with me, this is where they're just settling into their seats, putting their feet on the desks, sorting out friends from enemies, separating into distinct cliques – it's very easy for me at this stage to lump them together in those cliques, but there's definitely no guarantee that they'll stay in them, no guarantee at all

so we have here the first clique, Mr and Mrs A with three children

and we have a second clique, Mr and Mrs B with two children and a dog

there's also a third clique, a farmer and the farmer's wife with their two children

there might well be a fourth clique, I can see something going on among the desks, it's probably all those sundry characters who are too late for the register

thirteen for sure then, God knows who else might turn up in later pages, and there's a dog as well, all of them determined to go their own way

now I know the name of the farmer, it came to me quite easily, Mr Broadfield, a fairly appropriate name I think and let's face it, Farmer Giles or Farmer Farrow or Farmer Haystack would all be a bit too obvious – Broadfield's by far the easiest character, at this stage anyway, for his distinctive way is to keep out of the story as much as possible, I can tell that just by looking at him – you watch, he'll pass us by on a tractor waving cheerily, and he'll mutter under his breath about the enforced need to let out the cottages, wishing he could get shot of all these visitors and subsist on agriculture alone, but he can't do that, can't survive without subsidies, and even then there's not enough to go round, he has of necessity to put up with these people whether he likes it or not, and if pushed he'll tell us he doesn't like it at all

no, I don't like it – I could have had a golf course, couldn't I? – that's what I thought of, a golf course, but they said I was too far out in the sticks for anyone to bother, they'd never find me, and the land wasn't appropriate, and lots of other reasons why I had to settle for this situation – no choice, what choice have I got?

now you see what I mean? – it was my intention to work into the story gradually and start with the farm's cat but this fellow, this Mr Broadfield's put his spoke in before I was ready for him – I don't intend him to be anything more than a relatively minor character [well, that's the preliminary idea] and he should have kept his trap shut at least until the main characters arrive, that's the decent thing to do isn't it? – so you see what happens, you see how I'm compelled to follow on? – I'm now forced to bring in his wife as well, because if I don't then his side of the story will be unbalanced and right now horrendously out of context, so the cat will have to wait, won't it?

[I might by the way say that it's a patient cat, getting on a bit, sits around a lot, lies happily on any old bit of straw – he's what you might call the guardian of the approaches, has a favourite spot on a wall overlooking the cottages from where on summer Saturdays he can watch the departures and arrivals of the holidaymakers – name of Sammy, been a pet of Mrs Broadfield's ever since he turned up at the farm of his own accord, no one knew from where – there was talk he came over the hill from the duck farm, a place where you never see any ducks, just hear the noise from the sheds – could be Sammy couldn't stand the racket, had to get away]

now here I am again! – I said the cat could wait but just like all of them he's jumped the gun as well and I've started describing him! – Mrs Broadfield now, that's who I was going to bring up because her husband's here, Mrs Broadfield – we have to give her a chance, I suppose, let her put **her** spoke in – no hope whatever of being methodical, absolutely none at all

the golf course wasn't a good idea, now was it, he'd have had people here all the time and if there's one thing he hates it's having people coming to the farm and trampling over his precious acres, he'd have hated that – you'd wake up one morning to find he's ploughed it up and sown it all with peas

peas! – peas! – certainly not peas, you don't know what you're talking about, never grown peas in my life – the nearest the farm's ever come to it was when my father did it once, regretted it no end as soon as he did it, but it was good mulch when he turned it in, I must say, nice bit of wheat we had following – no, it definitely wouldn't be peas, don't be so silly

well, whatever – but you would, wouldn't you, you can't just spend your days looking at grass, however much money it made

I'll tell you what, caravans, that's where the money is – some farmers grow caravans, fields of them, rolling acres of mobile homes – now Nigel Frome, remember him? – he did that, he had caravans

he lived in Cornwall, what do you expect, it's all caravans there

maybe, but still, a couple of fields . . .

hang on, wait a minute! – do you mind? – we haven't properly started yet – it's the cat, remember, it's the introduction that's got to come first, not arguments over peas and caravans – Sammy's the cat, he's where I plan to start, Sammy sitting on a wall watching the new arrivals, giving us a visual preview of the main participants in this story – it's not part of the scheme to give undue prominence to two minor characters, especially if they're arguing, adding nothing to the background – Mr and Mrs Broadfield are supposed to be local colour, not active ingredients

well, all I can say is that he's not very active these days, at least not since we started the cottages – he wasn't happy at first, said the barn was an ancient monument which couldn't be converted, but the architect said it was all right to do so, it wasn't a listed building

it goes back to the seventeenth century, that barn

it had a corrugated-iron roof, not very antique that! – anyway you were glad to start earning from it, now you're talking of caravans – that barn was due for demolition anyway, the architect said you were lucky it hadn't collapsed on top of you

*well, I could only give it as my professional opinion – perhaps with a little structural work it **could** have been saved, I suppose*

hold on, who's this? – what've we got here, an architect

now, coming up and putting himself in the story – anyone else? – do the builders want to say a few words, the electricians, the plumbers? – any chance of me getting back to the cat?

what I said was it had no distinctive merit and would readily lend itself to conversion – I do believe it was Mr Broadfield himself who said he wished it had fallen down so he could claim some insurance

excuse me, are any of you listening to me? – before we know where we are we'll have a whole village of people butting in to this story – let me get back to the cat sitting on the wall or we'll never get started otherwise

my opinion was that no insurance company would have paid out, the barn was far too derelict – what I'd really like to do, and I know Mrs Broadfield's with me on this, is to convert that other barn and create a courtyard of cottages – if they were to let the farmhouse go as well we could have a nice holiday complex of eight or ten units – very popular these days, especially if there's a swimming pool

well, you can stuff that idea – I'm not moving out of the place I was born in just so's a lot of townees can splash about pretending they're in the country – two cottages, that's all we need, not a 'complex' thank you very much – I'm a farmer, my family's a farming family, this stays mainly a farm, not a leisure centre

I wouldn't be so sure Lance wants to follow in your footsteps, he's very unhappy about the spraying – very unenvironmental he says

Lance'll be a farmer once he gets those silly ideas out of

*his head – and if not there's always Tilly, she's close to things
– you can have women farmers too, you know*

*at the moment she only likes horses – she's fifteen with a
pony – wants to be an actress, so don't bank on her – nor on
Lance, he's sensitive, he doesn't really want to follow the
family trade, as you like to call it*

*Mrs Broadfield's quite right, I'm afraid – the present
climate encourages my plans for a holiday centre with swimming pool and gift shop*

shops?

this cat named Sammy, does anyone mind if I get back to
him? – look, he's on a wall, he's poised, if I don't bring him
in now he'll jump down and disappear and I won't have the
beginning I hoped for – if Mr and Mrs Broadfield would
kindly leave the scene, just stand back, give me room to
proceed – and as for the architect . . .

Gregory Price-Masters – rural conversions a speciality

go away, find another story! – I've got thirteen main characters to bring in and we'll go on forever at this rate – 80,000
words, that's all I'm budgeting for, hopefully in some sort of
order that an interested reader could follow – going on like
this it'll be half a million and a complete and utter mess – no
one, but no one, will ever want to read anything as long as
that or as disjointed as this is becoming – it might be that
spontaneity's all very well but this is fast becoming the anarchy I spoke of – please, please, let me get back to the cat!

this is the wall he sits on, it's of red brick, and I don't
mean that sort of plastic-looking red brick you see nowadays
looking all smooth and brittle and somewhat artificial – this
is the old red brick, seventeenth century as Mr Broadfield

claims, a red to make you feel warm and cosy with a texture inviting you to run a hand over its grainy, sandy, dusty surface – it runs from a corner of the farmhouse, pokes out for ten feet or so with no apparent purpose, but it must have been part of something at one time, probably a little outhouse, maybe a store or a privy, with the other walls long gone – in its lee Mr Broadfield's stacked a number of wooden pallets which helps Sammy surmount its seven foot height – been here a long time, these pallets, now they're starting to rot, home to all kinds of insects, slugs, weeds, even mice, despite the presence, the daily presence of Sammy – but he's ageing, perhaps they take advantage of his stiffening limbs – animals can be very quick to spot weakness – ever noticed the careful contempt in which they hold humans? – not only cats and mice but squirrels and birds regard us with disdain for our inability to move as quickly as they can, they play tricks and taunt us – I once used to get pelted with cobnuts on a daily walk I made through some Redditch woods, and everyone knows that birds regularly practise their bomb-aiming, don't they – you think they don't have a sense of humour? – fragile bags of bone and feather will happily make fun of a pregnant cat, daring it to launch an unsuccessful lunge and thus make itself look ridiculous

Sammy with the mice, you see – they know they can escape into any quick crevice of these pallets – the front of the wall's a different matter, it faces across what Price-Masters would make a courtyard, so the mice stay with the pallets, Sammy sits on the moss-topped wall looking down on the scene with feline equanimity – at lunchtime on Saturdays he'll be here, watching and waiting, though he does the same at other times of course, you can't tell me cats know their days of the week and say to themselves today's the first day of the weekend, up on the wall, won't do it on Wednesday, have a day off – some instinct tells him Saturday's the day when one or two lots of visitors go and one or two new ones arrive

Mrs Broadfield again [now she's started you can't keep her out] – *that's only in the summer, mind – there are special out-of-season rates but not many people make use of them, they seem to think the countryside won't be here then – June to August we're full, but other times can be a bit bleak – I keep telling him he should provide more entertainment, get in some sheep so he can make a show of shearing them in May, something like that, put on a bit of a performance – we could buy in lots of produce which he can pretend to harvest in the autumn – none of these visitors would know any different, they think a farm does everything – we tell them we've a thousand acres when we've only got two hundred, but they don't know how big an acre is – sometimes we double it and say hectares*

Sammy doesn't purr much, maybe it comes from having to compete with all those noisy ducks – not a people cat, won't go near a lap if he can help it, hates having to humour Tilly when she wants to pamper him – he scratched Lance some time ago so doesn't get any affectionate approaches from him, just guarded looks – with Tilly he has to tolerate her bouts of sentiment, has to close his nostrils to her teenage experiments in perfume, keep his claws in so's she can delight in his silky paws, put his pads to her cheek – she can't get to him on the wall, has to look up, make irritating sucking noises at him which she thinks he likes – as for the parents he's on reasonably good terms with Her, he knows how to extract the right food and get treated with respect, but with Him there's a dark chasm of intolerance arising from the fact that Mr Broadfield was raised with dogs and thinks cats are effeminate – he hasn't had a dog in years apparently, since before Sammy arrived

she won't let me, will she? – when Ben died she said that's it, no more dogs, what do I need them for she says – it's no good telling her for company, she can't understand that – if I say it's a matter of security all she says is get floodlights

it's Saturday, early afternoon, Sammy in position, can I get going yet? – do we see a car coming up the dusty track, am I allowed to begin this story? – so many interruptions! – just as I feared it would be, I've no control over anything

dusty track, yes – I wanted tarmac, better for everyone, but they all said there had to be authenticity, these architects – holidaying lovers of the country want a dusty track, they expect it, I was told – I had to lay down a load of aggregate, got it from Bill Straw and guess why he was giving it away? – he was putting tarmac up to his place, tarmac, lucky devil, just what I wanted, but these people, these holidaymakers, oh they have to get their cars a bit dusty and muddy or they can't prove anything when they get home

it's a dusty track then, okay, let's emphasize that it's an uneven, freshly potholed stony track with narrow cambers and a scattering of old half-bricks inserted to plug the holes – once they turn off the road the visitors need to feel they're entering a different world, after all this is the country and this is what you get

I told him he should get some pheasants to throw out from that small covert near the gate, that would make them have to brake and get excited – but he couldn't be bothered, no, he said it'd be a devil of a job catching them afterwards

well, I made a warren, didn't I? – spent a week digging holes in the bank – not my fault the rabbits only come out at night, is it?

if you don't want pheasants you could get half a dozen quail to run up and down – they're always a source of wonder to these people

oh yes? – why not a couple of turkeys? – a stray cow? – a stuffed fox?

now you're being silly

all right! – however it is, the visitors come bumping along the dusty track and if they're lucky a rabbit bolts back into its hole – at this the children get excited, the car gets dusty as hoped, anticipation's high, women's spirits low at the thought of having to start work as soon as they arrive

Sammy sees the dust rising in the distance and settles himself on the moss – the other guests left mid-morning, he watched Mrs Broadfield and Tilly going in and out of the cottages with clean linen and welcoming bowls of fruit, vases of flowers

they don't clean themselves, you know – takes me a full two hours to go round with the hoover – the mess some people leave behind – dirty devils

oh dear, now I have to introduce Debbie, don't I – try leaving anyone out in this story and they're all elbows, pushing themselves in, demanding recognition, all belong to the fiction-characters union – this is Debbie who cleans, comes along on Saturdays, earns her wage by dusting and polishing

pittance it is – I work hard – taken for granted, if you ask me – get a fortune from these holidaymakers and what do they pay me? – a pittance – and no one sees me, I'm faceless, a non-person – the leavers of the mess disappear, I'm gone before the new ones arrive – magic wand, that's me, one of the fairies – no one knows what I look like

we don't know what anyone looks like! – and it's not entirely my fault, you will all keep turning up before I've had a chance to say who you are, what you look like – if anyone wants descriptions then I'm supposed to give descriptions – if I'd plotted it out as I said I should have done, made notes on everyone, then at this point I'd pull out a reference card from D and insert a physical description of this Debbie – here she is, I'd say, vacuum cleaner in one hand, duster in the other, a young woman of thirty, dark-haired, medium height, slim build – that do? – satisfied?

hardly! – that could be anyone – sounds like a police notice – 'have you seen this woman?'

she's a bit of a pain really, I can say that now she's gone – the most minor of characters whom we'll never see again [perhaps at the end of the story, if we're that unlucky and if we ever get to that point] – it's back to Sammy then, a medium-haired white cat with black head, black tail, black bits along the sides, makes him look like a domino – kind eyes, thoughtful, you guess he could be a feline philosopher chewing over the great conundrums of life – moves a little stiffly and his undercarriage has slipped to give him what looks like a kangaroo pouch, the joey having left some time ago – a little nick in the top of his left ear suggests that in his younger days he wasn't always a philosopher but a man of action

right, that's pinned him down at last, painted him in – but we're sadly lacking a picture of the others – this Debbie's no more than a caricature really, she talks in stagey worker-speak, nothing true about her – and the Broadfields don't have any originality do they, just two stock figures going through the motions of disagreeing with each other – it would have been all very different if the conventions had been observed, if I'd followed the rules and done some preparation – well, I chose to do it in my own way, so I suppose I can't complain – perhaps it's not too late to recover the situation – the Broadfields will have to develop their characters as we go along, but we can do it right now with the visitors approaching along the dusty track

Sammy's whiskers, ever sensitive to changes in temperature, environmental space or the nature of living creatures, begin to twitch – he senses that these new arrivals are a bit different from the ones who left the cottages this morning – there were the Williamses in Stook Cottage, a late-middle-aged man and his vitally attractive young wife who hardly went anywhere, spent most of their time in the cottage with the curtains drawn, and for all the notice they took of it they needn't have been in the country at all – their neighbours in the adjoining cottage were a total contrast, two youngish, carefully dressed men who every day went out early, came back late, very quietly kept themselves to themselves – they were always polite, these two, no trouble to anyone, you'd think the place was unbooked for the week – when they left this morning they presented Mrs Broadfield with expressions of grateful thanks and a bunch of exotic flowers, a nice touch – the Williamses on the other hand acted as if no one else in the world existed, rushed away without even handing in the key – it was Lance Broadfield who voiced the question as to why they arrived and went home in separate cars

Sammy sees the dust before he can distinguish what's causing it, a cloud bearing a vehicle within, rocking from side to side, bumping in and out of the potholes – this must certainly be an authentic farm track – a flight of rooks picking over the remaining pods of the beans rises into the air from the ten-acre home field that the track skirts – from behind the hedge on the track's other side [and we can reveal that here there's a hidden well-maintained track that anyone not a holidaymaker uses] flies up a corresponding flight of doves, fewer in number but showing more panic, wings flapping wildly while the rooks disdainfully demonstrate their calm stateliness

as the vehicle approaches the farm gate the dust clears and we can now see it's a black estate car with a roof rack holding a blue tarpaulin-wrapped bundle, a nondescript car, made more so by the fine coating of dust – there's no practical reason for the gate to be closed, but it is and the car comes to rest before it, a five-bar, slightly decrepit gate that looks good with the notice beside it warning of the dangers of escaping animals, a contingency the visitors are always wary of – the small herd of milking cows Mr Broadfield has to maintain is always under control, there are no dogs or goats or wandering pigs to come flying out so the notice has no more meaning than the gate, but it all adds to the pleasure received by the visitors as they pause at the gate, get out of their cars, fiddle with the blue nylon rope, swing the gate back [a carefully contrived muddy patch is unavoidable] and tie it up again once they've driven through into the yard – they then feel they've arrived at the pastoral location they imagined and which was indeed stressed in the brochure – Lance's deposits of strategically placed cow dung and the four chickens allowed to roam at will all add to the flavour – and as with certain foodshops where you pick up the invit-ing smells of coffee, garlic or frying bacon as you pass, so Mrs Broadfield's had Lance stack a pile of sour byre-straw nearby, for the smell to waft into the visitor's nostrils

with keen eyes disguised behind a scene-weary appear-ance Sammy assesses the vehicle as it halts at the gate – he's become very astute at determining the relationship of its occupants from the observation of who gets out to perform the gate-opening – a lot depends on the weather, for if it's chucking it down it's nearly always the woman who has to do this, sometimes fighting with an inadequate town umbrella, inevitably unhappy at getting her feet muddy in the puddle – if the weather's fine you can bet it'll be the man who'll get out stiffly to demonstrate the rigours of travelling, stand, stretch, breathe in the air, cast his eye approvingly round the view and effect the opening with an insouciance indicating his long-standing familiarity with such things – but Sammy's noticed it's always the woman who has to go back to shut the gate afterwards

this continual observation's enabled Sammy to discover where the power resides in the family just arriving – by the length of the pause before the gate he gauges the degree of cooperation between the occupants, and in the way the opener conducts themself outside the car he can determine the level of mutuality – he's so expert in this that if he were able to speak he'd tell you whether or not the holiday was going to be a happy one

with his whiskers twitching he's not so sure about this lot – it's a fine day today, sun high, cloudless sky, just the sort of weather when the man usually volunteers for the chore, but this isn't the case with these visitors, it's the woman who gets out from the passenger side after the briefest of pauses before the gate – does this mean she's in charge, she's the one to decide on these things? – in her late thirties or early forties, fair, short-styled hair, not overweight but with a slight round-ness of figure which you'd describe as acceptable and which she no doubt brands a condition she really has to watch lest it leads to portliness – dressed in a simple top and jeans she owns the face of a person cheerful in extremities, you can imagine words like ups-a-daisy, well-it's-all-for-the-best coming from her pleasant lips – a motherly sort? – well, not entirely, there's a good deal of woman-of-the-world about her – she looks approachable, that's the main thing – Sammy knows she's just the type to want to pick him up, so he's fore-warned in that direction

this competent-looking gate-opener's not very good with the blue nylon rope, she fiddles about so long that the man gets out to assist the little woman – after a minute he suc-ceeds in unfastening the gate so that together, with pleasant smiles and unheard words of self-congratulation they coop-eratively push the gate to its widest extent – Sammy's estimate is they'll be the sort whose children could possibly be well behaved, not too much of a pain in the neck

he can see one of the children's heads poking from a window, little bit of blond hair framing a face that could be either girl or boy – when the parents return to the car, conjointly triumphant over their success, the head pops back inside to be replaced almost immediately by another, to Sammy's fading eyesight, identical to the first – twins, he thinks, and inwardly groans at the doubling of trouble, but he's wrong, I've decided for a fact they're not twins

following established custom the woman doesn't get back into the car but follows as it moves through the gate and pulls across the shingle – though she was unable to untie the string she's competent enough at least to tie it up again, doing so with a flourish and a large smile to emphasize her cleverness – and here they are thus prepared to receive the Broadfield treatment

the car parks exactly where it's supposed to, between two marks of Lance's cow dung – the indignant chickens, flustered, run across the concourse with rewarding vocal protests at the manner in which Tilly's ejected them from their roosts at the point of a broom – Mrs Broadfield switches on a fan hidden next to the pile of old straw, the satisfying pong of which duly wrinkles the noses of adults and draws from the children a chorus of poohs! – there was talk in the Broadfield household of playing at this point a tape of a barking dog, but Mr Broadfield wasn't having any of it – want a dog? – get a real one! – so it's just the chickens and the smell which, once it's permeated the fresh air is switched to a more wholesome one of the bread baking specially in Mrs Broadfield's oven – now what could be more truly rural than all this?

I ought to return to being the instigator of this tale, I can't leave it all to the cat whose powers of expression are naturally limited – yes, Sammy can observe, twitch those whiskers, hood those eyes and yawn most cavernously, but it's not right to rely on him as an instrument of exposition, he's just not up to it

now this is that first clique I mentioned, Mr and Mrs A with three children – I suppose this is the point at which I have to give them names, that's the technical bit in any story, naming the characters – sometimes it's a very important process, you can't throw any names at them – imagine Susie of the d'Urbervilles, Gary Bede, Jo Karenina, Fred Shandy – none of that sounds right, does it? – unfortunately they don't come ready-named, prepackaged, so to speak, I have to employ the task of allocation, and I suspect you'll not agree with what I choose – *she's not a Pamela,* you'll say – *more of a Chrissy if you ask me* – well, of course I don't ask you, it's my story [more or less] and I'll give them any names I choose, whether you agree or not – in time, you see, that's the thing, in time they'll grow into their names so that you'll never think of them as anything else – we could well have had Fraser Copperfield or Peter Nickleby and providing they ran well euphonically then we'd never be any the wiser – euphony, you see, that's what it is, does it **sound** right?

how about we call these people, this family just arriving, the Oxfords, how does that sound? – in due course you'll come to love it and think how apt, how suitable, how clever I am to suggest something so easily memorable – and speaking personally I've always liked the name Pansy, ever since I was a schoolboy and miserably in love with a girl in the form above me – it's old-fashioned I know, but Pansy Oxford pleases me as a name for her [have I heard something like it before?] – and what about Martin for him, her husband, a nice square, honest sort of name – Martin and Pansy Oxford then, with their children – Ellen, now I believe she's nine and a bit of a bossy-boots, sweet but going to be a forceful woman one day – Sean [apparently named after Martin's father, who always said he was Irish but no one ever believed it] a boy of seven with such curly blond hair that he's some-times mistaken for his sister [hence Sammy's ascription of twins] – and PS aged two – now PS stands for Penny Saman-tha, but these names were chosen to fit the initials as PS was applied to the embryo once Pansy discovered she was preg-nant again when she didn't expect to be – when they think of it they call the child Penny, but mostly it's PS, as you'll see – of course it's occurred to them that any moment now Ellen's going to cotton on that PS stands for postscript and being an intelligent girl she'll start to think what a coincidence, but the parents are rather set in their ways and console themselves that at least they didn't go for Afterthought or Accident

how do I know all this? – well I'm inventing it, aren't I? – as the author of this work [ha, ha, I hear the characters cry in unison, a grand chorus of derision] as the author I'm supposed to know something of the background of my characters – I may not know what they're going to get up to but I do know, as the current idiom has it, where they're coming from, at least up to a point – I have to qualify this because there are huge blanks in my knowledge of them – certain details such as knowing the derivation of PS's name come to me loud and clear while a staggering eighty per cent of everything else escapes me totally, I've really no more idea in that direction than you or the man in the moon or the Registrar General [who's a person who should know **everything**], I know so little of their life outside the confines of this story that you might say I share with you the expectation of the element of surprise – I'm privy to their present thoughts and current moods, and that's about all

let's get on – we've sorted out the Oxfords, at least cursorily, we'll come to the other lot later

so now this family's arrived at their summer quarters – only for a week, mind you, these places are expensive [which of course the Broadfields would strenuously deny, probably being as outraged as that Debbie with her complaints of a pittance] and in any case a week with friends, especially friends who are not of the bosom sort, can often be long enough – the Waterfords [yes? – do I hear you object? – it seems a logical sort of name to me, if you're going to have one town name you might as well have another] the family of Waterfords who are yet to arrive [and who'll get whichever cottage the Oxfords spurn] are connected through the workplace of Martin and Josh Waterford and whose concomitant partners are friends more by association than by choice – but it must be said that all four have spent a good few happy hours together on various social occasions stretching back over several years, so they all know one another reasonably well – this however is the first time they've ventured jointly for any period longer than a day and who knows how well they'll maintain their companionable relationship – let us just say that Pansy and Beth are friendly enough to go to the hair-dressers together, so there's no reason why on their side anything should happen to unbind them, surely

with Martin and Josh however it could be a different matter – they work in a manufacturing plant where each has the supervision of compatible departments, and ambition being what it is, and men being what they are, a certain spirit of competitiveness resides within their breasts – already evident is Josh's habit of taking the lead when entering pubs or restaurants, a matter which has Martin lowering his brows and scolding himself for never being prepared for that extra step forward which Josh always seems to deploy at the critical moment – a little niggle maybe, but I think we'd better watch this space

Martin dismounts from the car – Pansy, already walking in the yard, faces the homely, homespun figure of Mrs Broadfield emphasizing her farmer's wife waddle as she crosses the yard to meet her – a smile on her lips she has, broad as her name, something perhaps only visitors ever see to that extent – and as you'd expect of someone tearing herself away from her kitchen she's wiping her hands on her apron before extending one a good three metres away from her target – Pansy covers the distance quickly so that they can exchange warm greetings, exchange information – Mrs Broadfield is **so** interested in where they've come from and Pansy is **so** delighted with the ambience – Martin, following close behind, makes a grab for Mrs Broadfield's hand and reiterates the sentiments of his wife – what concord between them!

and Mrs Broadfield can't wait to see the children as they're let out of the car one by one to stand [with the exception of PS who's held in Pansy's arms] looking with cautious interest at everything about them – expressions of delight issue from Mrs Broadfield's lips as she kisses one after the other in ascending order of age, being a teeny bit firm with Ellen as the child exercises her reflexes by leaning away from this unwonted expression of familiarity – Sean watches her resistance, wishes he'd not been such a pushover with this woman who's acting like an auntie, resolves to be more masculine in future

up on his wall, feeling the sun's warmth on his back and particularly on his haunches where of late he's been feeling a few aches and pains [leaping and landing's a devil when you're getting on a bit, and sitting on old damp walls doesn't help] Sammy watches the action, sighs at the formality, the ritual – it's always the same old story, Mrs B putting on her kids-loving act, the visitors falling into the trap of thinking life's always like this, sun always shining, bread forever baking, oh the inevitability of it all – Sammy deigns to tolerate it, would admit to nothing more earnest – but deep down he really wouldn't have it any other way, the procedure consolidates his sense of security, its predictability satisfies that desire in him for everything to remain the same – if he could have a say in this story he'd tell us he'd like the same visitors arriving every time in the same way, then there'd be real continuity, certain stability – in a cat's world the only novelties should be the appearance of suitably sized prey, everything else should be unchanging – that was the trouble at the duck factory, they kept introducing new production lines, new plucking and butchering and packing machinery, lorries in and out all the time – no wonder the ducks made such a racket, anyone would in that world

the visitors enter their chosen cottage, Mrs Broadfield waddles back to turn off the fan and to take the half-baked loaf from the oven for use again when the others turn up – after shooing the chickens into the yard Tilly's already returned to her room to rearrange her rosettes and Lance has gone to help his father watch a football match on television – peace of the kind Sammy likes returns to Upside Farm

so they're settled in, the Oxfords, they've unloaded the car, made a cup of tea, eaten the strawberry tarts thought-fully provided by the farmer's wife [they **must** be home-made, mustn't they?] and strapped PS's booster seat to a dining chair ready for dinner time – Ellen and Sean want to poke round the farm, they keep running in and out, begging for the freedom to be allowed to do so – Martin has to use a stern voice, Pansy a placatory one, promising permission in due course – to Sammy they seem just like any other new cus-tomers, busy, active, curious, full of wonder that another world exists besides their own, even if they but dip their toes into it occasionally

and that's true, isn't it, we live in a world of many worlds, if you know what I mean – there's our own life and circum-stance, the world we inhabit, the familiar daily grind and all that, but we're surrounded by all these others which we only temporarily visit, perhaps for work or recreation – many worlds are closed to us, like Sammy's duck factory which we wouldn't want to visit anyway, not to see a few thousand ducks strung up by their legs ready for slaughtering, or like professional worlds that we enter as clients, as customers, as patients, as electors – or odd worlds like that of royalty, something so artificial and peopled with such strange puppets it's a historical curiosity even while it lives – all these worlds make up the totality of our existence, but they're novelties, not quite real – the Broadfields' farm, to little Sean and Ellen and their parents, is one of those worlds, along with theme parks and overseas resorts that provide a taste of fantasy, some constituent of other people's lives which are composed of other people's rules and therefore carrying the flavour of licence – it's not our world, so to a certain extent we can let our hair down

the Oxfords get a call from the Waterfords – making a conversation out of a message, as women do, Pansy gossips with Beth about when they'll arrive and obtains agreement there's time before then for the Oxfords to go along to the nearest town to buy some provisions to add to what everyone's brought – Pansy also offers to do the evening meal for all of them, a mad impulse of generosity which she regrets almost as soon as she's said it and which Martin's afraid will set some sort of pattern of alternate cooking, a routine to be avoided – already we can see signs of dissent creeping in, can't we, skulking [if Sammy doesn't mind the analogy] like a cat in the shadows

so where are we now? – the story could well do with starting, getting itself off the blocks, that's what you're thinking and I don't blame you for it, not at all, we've wasted too much time already – however I must protest it's not entirely my fault, we have to wait for the characters to turn up first and we haven't yet had the pleasure of meeting the Waterfords – why can't they all come at the same time? – it wouldn't be so bad if they were like those brazen contestants you see on television quiz shows – *hi, my name's Trevor and I'm a toilet attendant from Hull, I'm twenty-six, married to Dianne with fourteen children and I play lacrosse every Saturday morning with my sister Pamela* – you know where you are with that, don't you? – the trouble with my characters [they'd object strongly to the proprietorial claim, so I really ought to whisper it] is that they come when they will and go when they feel like it – in many instances in some stories they don't actually go but hang around like empty seashells on the strand, devoid of content, of no interest but determined not to be left out of things – you can bet your life that cleaner Debbie will come again and again but she's got nothing to offer beyond complaints regarding her employment – *well*, I can hear her saying peevishly *I add a certain amount of colour, don't I – and all for a pittance!* – if it's colour we want we can go to Tilly's bedroom

and what's wrong with my bedroom? – pink and purple complement each other very well – especially with a careful dash of lime green – you're just being picky

yes sorry, Tilly, didn't mean to disturb you – just a small analogy – please stay in your room with your trophies – the last thing we want is any of the Broadfields butting in again

so what we have to do is let the time pass – we can see the Oxfords pile into their car and go off into town for those extra provisions [wherever the town might be, your guess is as good as mine], and we sit on the gate whistling a happy tune to ourselves until the Waterfords eventually come up the track in the same halting, swaying way as the others did, this time in a more rugged vehicle with bull bars on the front, obviously people of intrepidity – they stop at the gate and it's not the mother but the son who gets out, leaps out, anxious to demonstrate not only his agility but his temerity, a youth of fourteen with dark hair all over the place, hasn't seen a comb in years, otherwise pleasant to look at, no spots, frank eyes, clumsy feet [both of which happily find the puddle] and a tendency to keep talking when he knows no one can hear him, as now when he fumbles with the gate, telling the open air what it doesn't much want to know – from a window in the vehicle hangs his sister Abigail, calling to him, urging him to hurry up – girl of twelve, Abigail, long blonde hair getting in everyone's way because she wants one day to tuck it in her belt, though when she's a year older she'll want it chic and French, wants to be Ophelia without knowing who Ophelia was but the name sounds nice – Abigail urges Michael on – mother urges Abigail to be quiet – Josh with stern authority, urges Brewster to lie down [only the dog ever pays any attention to Josh's stern authority] – and all this noisy arrival brings Sammy back on to his wall

a dog? – a dog called Brewster? – any dog called anything's a terrible prospect to contemplate – the last one to come was a long-haired terrier who had to be lured into the deepest and thickest hedge Sammy could find, from where it took its owner an hour and a half to disentangle it – and Mr Broadfield, that erstwhile canine-lover, has been neutered in that respect, no worry there, 'no dogs' is the rule on the farm normally – but obviously there's no bar to visitors bringing one – these visitors have brought one called Brewster – Sammy's going to have to contend with a dog for a whole week!

sitting uncomfortably on the soft mossy top of the wall [think of it, these bricks might have been laid in the Middle Ages!] Sammy muses discontentedly over this unexpected and certainly unwanted new arrival – he's not happy with dogs, Sammy, what cat is? – those noisy animals have no control over their emotions, they're all impetuosity and impulse – and dogs are so wild that they have to be 'trained' – trained! – what self-respecting animal needs training, cats don't? – the trouble with dogs is their rampant immaturity, always the adolescent, always ready for a game – and they ruin any established routine, or try to ignore it – Sammy's in the daily habit of ambling watchfully on regular tours round the yard, doing his duty of frightening off the rats – does the presence of this dog, this Brewster, mean he has to curtail that, change his routine? – well, that's not on at all, he's not having that, things will have to be sorted out!

Lance has done his duty with the new dung and Tilly her act with the chickens, Mrs Broadfield's burnt the remains of her dough in a too-hot oven – if all the visitors could be per-suaded to come at the same time it would certainly make life more amenable – only Mr Broadfield, stalwart at his post in front of the television, sighing over the failure of Chelsea to vanquish Wycombe Wanderers, has nothing to do at the moment – his time will come at dusk, when he's obliged to go out into the fields to discharge his shotgun into the air

Beth Waterford is more than happy to let Josh do the unloading, however much fuss he makes about having no help from anyone – it gives her the opportunity to inspect both the cottages to see if the Oxfords have got the edge on her, and she's able to risk a glance or two at their personal belongings to gauge their level of taste and affluence – young Michael [not so young at fourteen but always referred to as such by his father] takes it upon himself to act responsibly by fixing up a computer game in a corner of the lounge, while his sister follows her mother into the Oxfords' cottage to learn how to make disparaging remarks at the fortunes of others

Brewster's left to himself – this is a dangerous thing to do as far as Sammy's concerned for dogs need chaining up at all times, preferably in stout kennels with double locks on, everyone knows that – this animal, so far quiet, so far a model of propriety, amiably following Josh in and out with the luggage, needs watching carefully for the moment when he senses the presence of his superior up on the wall – it's a beige beast, one of those Sammy's heard described as Labradors, with deceptively kind brown eyes and a hairy tail – he's seen one before, up at the duck farm when he was a lot younger, only just out of kittenhood and unsure of his own power – on that humiliating occasion he turned and ran away, a demeaning thing to do and something of which he's always been dreadfully ashamed – this Brewster will certainly get a different treatment now that years of maturity have passed, the dog may even be the instrument of some redemption – Sammy shifts his position slightly and with wide open eyes stares hard and constantly at the enemy

in due course the Waterfords are settled in and in due course also the Oxfords return laden with shopping – much welcoming is done, kisses and handshakes are exchanged as though they haven't met for ten years – it's the air of excitement which does such things to people, the anticipation that this is something new, something unexplored, something fraught with a soupçon of the unexpected – they are pioneers, banding together to face the unknown perils of a week's holiday in the country – the dangers indeed of uniting as one family instead of two – the uppermost thoughts in the minds of the parents is will the children get on with one another – PS of course is exempt from this worry as she's oh so sweet being only two years old and entirely blameless of the world's sins – one has only to be concerned that her incomplete potty training doesn't lead to any embarrassment

right then, here they all are now, these characters, we have all the ingredients in place, the visitors to the farm are anxious to begin their holiday, the Broadfields eager to earn their income – so let's begin

not all of us are that anxious, I have to say – I know it's money coming in but we have to live here, remember, and it's definitely no holiday for us

sorry, Mrs Broadfield

yes, well – when the football's finished he and Lance have got to get the cows in for milking

you've only got seven, that can't be too much of a chore, can it?

Mrs Broadfield doesn't answer, wipes her hands on her apron, returns inside, sighing and tutting at the ignorance of authors

I

Saturday p.m.

all together now – PS has a new mantra

Pansy, a mother three times over, having heard it all before, is less impressed than she would have been were it her first child prattling, had it been Ellen say [and everyone remembers only too well Ellen's actual first word which was so rude it can hardly be repeated even in the sanctity of the parents' bedroom, let alone in these hallowed pages

didn't get it from me insisted Martin at the time

but she must have got it from somewhere

overheard it going round the supermarket he always prefers to think – *took it into her little head because it was novel*

certainly is says Pansy]

PS now happily and frequently enunciating her *altogether now* or *all together now*, it's not entirely clear which she means, not that it really matters either way, while it's not her first word is new enough to draw everyone's attention

what a clever girl compliments Martin – *isn't she a clever girl, Sean?*

yes – Sean couldn't care less, just lifts his head from his drawing for a split second – he's seven years old, he's not going to be impressed by anything his little sister comes up with – not unless it directly affects him

despite any intentions you may have what is it you do with little ones? – you encourage them, you give them support – and then they reward you – *all together now* she says again, louder this time, with much more emphasis, and once more parents look on approvingly while brother ignores it as brothers learn to do

all together now – PS is well into her stride, getting louder, stronger, more confident – *all together now*

yes, all right, darling – Martin's easily bored

Pansy's more appreciative – [aren't mothers always? – over-tolerant sometimes, if you ask me] – *you're getting a big girl, aren't you – now drink your milk up and you'll be even bigger*

no I won't

Sean – *yes you will*

no I won't!

Sean – *oh yes you will!*

Martin – *all right you two – don't get her going, Sean*

PS goes into a sulk, head down, stares at the drinking cup in her hands, immobile, withdrawn

now look what you've done

*wasn't **my** fault!*

Pansy smiles indulgently, not so much at her children but at the world in general – this is patently maternal heaven, she must be aware of fulfilling herself, the eternal mother with her small brood, a caring husband beside her, food in the larder [so to speak], a break from routine domestic chores in the offing – what more could she want from life? – Pansy doesn't appear to be a woman who spends her time looking for the bad things in life, there's quite enough of them in the world today without going looking for them, thank you – there's such great pleasure to be had in small pleasures, and when those small pleasures are children, especially your own children, then there's very little else to yearn for – Pansy we can see is one of life's hopeful optimists but the residual fear of the pessimist seems to lodge within her breast, creeping up occasionally in the physical form of a dry cough that now and then, when things are going extra well, becomes evident – she's happy now but there it is, a little tickle in the throat to signify an inner apprehension that things may not continue

and Ellen, what of that little charmer, is she quietly part of this scene? – oh yes, here she is, reading a book with her frown pronounced, that little knot of the brows which she's always being told to be careful of in case it sets like that for the rest of her life and no Prince Charming will ever want to marry her – she doesn't believe that nonsense and in any case it's not something she does deliberately, how can you read without frowning? – and how can you read when that irritating baby sister of yours keeps chanting out the same thing over and over again!

apart from the frown, which I personally think makes her more interesting, Ellen's a pretty girl – very light hair, fairly straight but silky with a gentle wave rather than any natural curls, it hangs round her face as she inclines her head to read, arborous curtains implying secrecy and modesty – she has large hazel eyes, her father's, and from her mother inherits the wide forehead and generous lips – that she reads so much at such a young age perturbs her father as he possesses the innate fear that she may read herself out of his intellectual range, but her mother champions anything in her children which may indicate future emancipation – things should always get better, shouldn't they, each generation should improve – so long as she doesn't strain her eyes

they're settled now, the children have had their tea, PS is about to be put to bed and Pansy's keen to get into the kitchen and start preparing the evening meal – the Waterfords will be coming in about eight o'clock and she wants everything ready by then

I can reveal that Pansy's not really the domestic type – oh she's expert at every aspect of it, clean, tidy, efficient, organized, but things domestic aren't really her thing – a day in the kitchen is a day of purgatory for her – keen to start preparing tonight's meal means keen to get it over and done with as soon as possible

and what are they having, what dream delight's on the menu? – after consultation with Martin, who always says a good curry's the best thing to have, Pansy's decided on baked trout stuffed with lemon grass and herbs with braised leeks, green beans and sweet potato – fish is in deference to Beth who doesn't eat meat and keeps telling everyone, well anyone who might be listening, that meat-eating is cruel and you wouldn't eat your pet, would you? – dessert's going to be something from the freezer they bought today, an orange-and-lemon cheesecake to be served with crème fraiche – always a favourite with the men, though given a chance they'd prefer it to be chocolate – Martin gently complains there's no starter but doesn't push this point too far just in case Pansy's a bit tetchy and tells him to do garlic mushrooms or something himself – there's wine of course, Frascati, with a Chianti Classico which Martin's lately addicted to as he claims red wine's good for the heart and men pushing middle age as he is should do everything to ensure sound health

it's story-time for PS, tucked up in the cot across the room from Ellen, a quick burst of expressive relation from Martin about an errant chimpanzee called Constantine – plenty of drama with very authentic animal impersonations – Ellen complains at not being able to get on quietly with her own book – both are kissed and adjured to be good girls, PS not to stand up and lean on the cot sides – and in the next room, alone and put on his best behaviour Sean settles down with his favourite soldier-doll as Martin gives him the all-boys-together treatment in the hope such a call on his loyalty will encourage him to stay where he is

all done – he's returned to the kitchen – *they're tired out, all of them*

her nappy okay? – not loose or anything, you've checked her nappy?

although technically trained and almost trusted to get through the day with pants, PS needs a night nappy just in case, which she's been known to lose in a restless night – *we don't want any disasters*

she's fine, no problem with her – how's the dinner coming?

it's all very much under control so long as you don't bother me – instead of just hanging about why don't you open the wine and pour us a glass?

before they come?

of course before they come – you know what they're like, they'll have been at the bottle for hours and get here all high – I'm not going to be the mouse from the scullery, stone-cold sober

I ought to bring in here the matter of dialogue – the characters are having a conversation and before going any further you may wish to know why one voice is indistinguishable from the other – in real life, apart from Martin's being deeper, there would be other differences, cultural ones perhaps, but there would certainly be a way of speaking, a tone of voice, an accent that would place the speakers in some kind of social context – how can this be represented using written dialogue? – usually you have three types of literary speech – the first is standard tone and composition where everyone uses a voice differentiated only by the attribution of 'he said', 'she said' – the second has the author providing broad indications that the speaker is of a mediocre social class by dropping h's and saying ain't a lot – and the third method is by a garbled series of misspellings where a foreigner has unluckily intruded into the scene

going to the trouble of dropping h's and having people say wot and dunno is a terrible way of indicating they ain't speaking proper, and indicating rusticity by writing long lines of almost unreadable dialogue [*ah bin muckin out yon byre sin crack o dawn, ah bin, n ahm right nackered*] merely irritate the eye and provide obstacles to the smooth reading of the narrative – as for foreigners it's better to have had them educated at an English public school and simply say every so often *they're Latvian*, or else leave them in Latvia or whatever – all in all it's my view that trying to indicate different tones, different accents or dialects in script is a waste of time – have 'em all speak the same, avoid long words if they're semi-literate, plainly tell the reader how they speak and leave it at that

trouble arises where you want to leave out the 'he saids' and 'she saids' – that discussion between Pansy and Martin, because there are only two of them, is fine from the point of view of clarity, but bring in several others and somehow you've got to label the voices – this is the difficulty with radio plays which is why there are so many funny voices in that medium – [I've tried to write radio plays and believe me it's best to create them as duologues] – if you don't label the voices you've no idea what their accent's like, and from that no suggestion of their cultural class – so I shall resort to rather tricky methods and hope to get away with it

the cultural bit first – leaving out long words and intricate sentences doesn't necessarily tell us they're social group D or E – I'm sure lots of old Etonians are inarticulate and can't string a sentence together, whether the fault of laziness or inbreeding it's hard to say – but usually this method does go some way to being of assistance, so long as it's allied to other pointers in the content of what they're saying and doing – we all know the Broadfields' class and accent because they're farmers, and farmers with their families all speak like the aforementioned rustic example, don't they – but the Oxfords and Waterfords? – let me tell you here and now, if they don't object, that advertisers would lump them on the edge of B sliding to C – make of that what you will

arranging the speaking so it's clear who's saying what,

that's another thing – now I'm going to use a variety of ways when there are lots of people gathered together but generally you'll have to excuse the regular use of what you might call stage or screen dialogue – no 'he saids' but just the names of the speakers – this may become boring for you, but I don't care, it's easier for me – I'll give you an example of what I mean

Martin – *what time are they due?*

Pansy – *eight o'clock, isn't it? – you were the one who arranged it, I'm just working to your timetable – let's hope it's all quiet upstairs by then*

Martin – *oh, they're very tired, as I said – they'll be off soon – it's been a long day*

this won't be the style all the way through, now and then I'll forget myself and insert a 'he said' – I may even go so far as to insert a **defining** 'he said'

this is something many writers do to excess I've noticed, they put in adverbial qualifications on every occasion – you'll get something like . . .

hands up said Dick menacingly

no replied Jim defiantly

all right then Dick returned sadly *pretend to hold up your hands*

why? asked Jim stolidly

Dick threatened unequivocally – *because I've got a gun* he growled menacingly

this sort of thing insults the reader, telling you how you should regard the character – I much prefer you to make up your own mind whether or not the speaker's menacing, defiant or sad – treat you like intelligent beings – a lot depends on the situation between the characters and the Mood Prevailing, for which I'll have to provide pointers, of course – [always assuming I've detected the Mood beforehand] – there could even be instances of you getting there before me, sniffing out undercurrents or hidden motives that I'm unaware of – for instance, do you suspect, from this little snatch of dialogue between her and him that there's a certain tension in the air?

of course, you mustn't take anything I've said above as gospel, for I'm just as likely to go against it all and put in plenty of he said defiantlys as I am to make everyone sound exactly the same, and all of them speaking unreal and highly inflated dialogue – just bear with me

Pansy, as I've said, works in a kitchen under sufferance and on this particular occasion, preparing food for guests, she's naturally a little nervous of failing in her duties – Beth's no great gourmet but she is another woman with another woman's critical comparative eye – however laid-back she may appear to be Beth's bound to own that instinctive element of competition, that primeval consideration of Eve as tempter of Man – is Pansy's trout going to lure the men, especially Josh to her side? – primeval fear in the one, a primeval urge to win in the other could well ruin the dinner and its reception

as far as the men are concerned they're oblivious of such things, they only want the nosh and something to wash it down with but they'll naturally give their whole attention to the provider of food, and that's where women's power lies – it's in Pansy's psyche to want to attract Josh and in Beth's to want to foil her – such fundamentally primitive tensions!

Mummy! – this is Sean, calling from upstairs – *Mummy! oh what, darling? – Mummy's busy – go and see what he wants – and you'd better take some water, he's probably thirsty, I noticed he didn't drink much at tea – Daddy's coming, darling!*

as Martin goes to the stairs so the chopped leeks, resting on a piece of kitchen towel now stuck by one corner to a saucepan, get pulled across the worktop and fall one by one to the floor like cascading Houdinis over Niagara – this kind of accident is predetermined and inevitable when in a strange kitchen doing something you'd prefer not to do – a calendar of mishaps could be devised so that such events would be expected and programmed in, thus removing some of the strain caused by the surprise of sudden catastrophe – there might however be more strain involved in the anticipation of the actual nature and extent of the accident, so perhaps that's not such a good idea after all – no calendar then, and every event one of surprise, precipitating impromptu expressions of bad language

Pansy has two bad words only, one of these to describe shocking things and one to be used involuntarily at moments of crisis – the falling of the leeks draws forth this second word, and to identify it as beginning with b doesn't much help as they both start with that letter – to say it has two syllables doesn't help either, for they both do – let us revive an old-fashioned and thoroughly admirable way of writing it thus – b . . . . r – this has the benefit of enlightening those who already know the word, but hiding it from those such as children and persons of a refined nature who will not learn it – I'm of the opinion that the expression of bad language in literature is unnecessary, its inclusion showing a lacking of semantic invention and therefore of art – you'll find none of it herein – go somewhere else if you want sex and violence, crime and bad language – these pages are designed to float happily through centuries of changing fashions, not be fads of the moment

b . . . . r – Pansy raises her hands, fingers extended as though absolving them from having had anything to do with it – hastily she bends, recovers the chopped pieces by pluck-ing them one by one from the floor to put them in a strainer – ever picked up chopped leeks? – they separate, the little rings of diminishing concentricity take the opportunity as you pluck them of slipping out of one another, and they're the very devil to put back again – but you have to do it some-how, and Pansy has to resort to both *b . . . . y* and *b . . . . r* [again] several times before being able to run the strainer under the tap – thankfully no one will ever know, and if someone breaks a tooth on a bit of grit, well, that's what you always get with leeks, don't you

yes, he only wanted a drink, he's all right, very tired though, soon be asleep – the girls are well away – Martin leans against a worktop to watch Pansy, his current duty at an end, successive ones apparently put, as they say, on the back-burner – he's poured them each a glass of wine, there's surely nothing else to do in the short term

the table, you've got to find a cloth, tablemats or some-thing – and I don't know if that cutlery all matches – glasses, napkins, condiments – I've no idea what there is

women just don't like men hanging about a kitchen doing nothing while they themselves are hard at it – they'd rather he sat down with a newspaper out of the way somewhere – but men feel guilty doing that, which is why they stand in the kitchen – they want to give the impression they're keen to help and are only awaiting orders – except that when given orders, as now, they quietly resent it – Martin goes off with a certain huffiness to look for the listed items

we'll stay with Pansy, shall we, now deftly forcing the herb collection into the slit bellies of the four trout, laying in the lemon grass, picking out the odd small bone remaining from the filleting – she's a competent cook rather than a devout one and this is revealed by the expression on her face, one of executive concentration – an occasional sigh when materials don't conform to the will of the fingers handling them is an indication that pleasure's not to be found in her current task – if the truth were known she'd probably much rather be outside in the open air, exploring the farm, walking the Broadfield acres, taking in the beauty of open space, communing with the natural world – I don't know for certain but I presume they must live in a town, suburbia perhaps, the countryside's wideness a car ride away

not many of us get to live the kind of life we'd prefer, and Pansy seems to be no exception – if we were to ask her where she'd really like to live she might tell us about a country cottage with an old English garden and hardly any traffic through the small village – what would she do with herself? – well, lovely things of course, gardening, walking, pottery, painting, walking, occasional horse-riding, cycling round quiet lanes, reading good books in a sunny nook to the sound of friendly birds, daydreaming – ah yes, daydreaming – family? – of course, compliant but exciting husband, absolutely delightful children who never annoy – cheerful neighbours – and preferably someone to come in to do the cleaning and the cooking, in particular the stuffing of reluctant herbs into the bellies of dead trout which keep rejecting the mixture and positively sneer at the idea of having bits of lemon grass stuck in them!

we saw earlier when she got out of the car to open the gate that she was a fair-haired woman in her late thirties to early forties with a figure she has to watch for its tendency to expand – let's elaborate this sketchy view – yes, she's late-thirties, not at all worried at the idea of catching up with Martin at the big four-o, no dread of age, at least not yet – fair-haired? – a soft honey-blonde, natural, no dye, sometimes in certain light it's straw-coloured, usually kept in a style never too long to look dated, never too short to look butch – in its light appearance it enhances the open, honest, trusting countenance which it frames, you couldn't imagine Pansy with dark hair at all – beneath the wide forehead her blue eyes are of a sea-reflecting shade, that colour when the waves are just about to break, the pre-foam blue – she has regular features with a nose unexceptional, ears unremarkable, chin and cheeks uneventful – a generous lower lip with a shapely upper one, in repose her mouth has a slight smile to it, as though she's thinking happy thoughts – an attractive face, one that draws the attention of women by its friendliness, of men by its promise of uncomplicated fun

of her figure Pansy has an ambivalent appreciation – not being vain [for surely vanity's one of those things to be considered ungodly] she'd like to pay no attention to it and providing that physical discomfort isn't the price she'd have to pay she'll let nature take its course – but at the same time a true consideration of one's personal appearance is a duty we should all own, and a consideration also of the duty we owe to our loved ones not to embarrass them by being of exorbitant size – as a consequence of this probable line of thought we can see that Pansy endeavours to watch what she eats, has crispbread instead of nice wholemeal loaf, spurns butter – we can be sure her chief assistant is exercise and though she may only do so intermittently it's likely that she takes herself off to the local gym to work up a good sweat – an exercise bicycle in the corner of her bedroom would be a good bet, but we don't know that for certain

Pansy dresses neatly, she's the type of woman who abhors untidiness and ensures the children are always in clean clothes and with fresh faces – [she might try to discipline Martin in this respect but like all men he'll think there are essential times, such as weekends, when you can let your hair down, muck about shabbily, indeed even go without shaving for a day] – in dressing neatly Pansy dresses plainly – no doubt Martin likes best the crisp white cotton blouse she often wears, tells her he finds it sexy, though she won't see that herself and thinks there must be something wrong with him

a bit of a snapshot this, but you get the basic picture of our dear Pansy, quite a lovable woman with a good heart, to put it plainly – she'll not think bad of people until they prove themselves heinous, and even then she'll make excuses for them – Pansy's the kind of woman who has a natural sympathy with the Salvation Army, but not one for organized virtue – her army's her little family, to which she dedicates herself wholly

the fiddly trout are prepared, there they sit in their deep baking pan with the sprigs of coriander lightly resting on their gills all ready for the oven, while Martin's been successful with the table-laying and is justly proud of his efforts, particularly pleased with having hunted down a pair of candles that now stand, rather insecurely it has to be said, in shallow saucers in the centre of the table – his only fear is that he won't find any matches to light them – none of the party smoke, none will therefore carry means of ignition – short of getting two sticks he'll have to find some matches somewhere

go and ask Mrs Broadfield Pansy suggests, but he's far too shy to do that – *don't want to bother her over a trifle* – so all drawers are investigated, all cupboards searched and Pansy tells him bluntly to stop getting in her way in the kitchen, the most likely place Martin insists, where matches will be found

it's an electric cooker – go and see the Broadfields!

accustomed to taking orders when at home, Martin realizes he'll have to do just that – he sighs deeply [but not so deeply that Pansy's able to hear him] and goes out into the farmyard

for a moment he stands at the door, looking with a serene pleasure at the farmyard, sniffing the sweet/sour smell of hay, watching the day drawing in – the voices of the Waterfords can be heard from the adjoining cottage and he toys with the idea of asking them to search their premises for matches, but the voices appear to be engaged in a mild argument, disjointed differences of opinion reach his ears, such a course therefore being ruled out on the ground of diplomacy – there's nothing worse, is there, than stepping into a family row

it's not yet dusk, the sun still beams delightfully over the tops of the massy trees on the distant hill, the air is warm, balmy, ideal for a barbecue rather than an indoor dinner – but then for a barbecue he'd still need matches – the farm-yard smells have subsided into that aroma of dry hay, the shuffling sounds of some animal in the barn across the yard drifts dully to his ears, the sly, slinky form of a cat disappears round a corner – there's a gentle peacefulness that Martin's reluctant to disturb – he regrets finding those candles – or rather not looking for the matches before telling Pansy he'd found them, in which event he could have lost them again

the conversion of the barn's been done sympathetically, such that the two cottages look as if they've never been anything else – outside each one, beneath the bow windows of the sitting rooms, stand two old feeding-troughs now filled with soil instead of meal and abundant with geraniums and petunias of many colours – a lone earthenware pot separates them, a dazzling display of impatiens spills over on to the cobbles – these cobbles are fake, by the way, not real at all but created artificially by a process using lots of cement and crafty moulding – looks good enough, but Gregory Price-Masters [the architect, if you remember] should in my view have striven for greater authenticity and made them less even – anyway, they look nice, and as the sun sinks slowly behind the trees the delineation is increased and the effect becomes almost pleasing

good enough for Martin, who takes them as real anyway

– with reluctant feet he walks over them, past the two cars towards the farmhouse, mentally rehearses his request

it's Lance who opens the door, the young Lance who tries to give a smile but succeeds only in looking as though he has an ache in his left ear

sorry to disturb you, but I wonder if you've any matches I could borrow – we're having a candlelight supper and I can't find any

Lance's smile broadens so that he now looks as if he has a terrible ache in both ears – *matches?*

yes, if it's not too much trouble

I think you'll find some in the kitchen – left-hand drawer of the right-hand cabinet, if I remember correctly

in the kitchen?

yes – they're usually kept there

I couldn't find . . .

they'll be in a tin marked 'barbecue' Lance drops his smile and with the pressure off the muscles round his ears appears normal – *was there anything else?*

time for Martin to grovel and look abashed – *no thanks – thank you very much, ta, very good of you, sorry to disturb you* and back across the yard while Lance closes the door on this damn nuisance – Martin's head hangs low, not entirely through a sense of creeping humiliation, in part through an inner anger that he was so compliant with his wife's instructions that he undertook an assignment which ended so ignominiously

the left-hand drawer of the right-hand cupboard does indeed hold a tin marked 'barbecue', and guess what? – within it a large box of cook's matches – nothing else in the

49

tin which might have anything to do with barbecues, no beef-burgers or meths, and there's no sign outside the cottages of anywhere to hold such an exciting occurrence, there was nothing in the brochure about barbecue facilities – and why put a box of cook's matches in a place where no reasonable person can find them! – Martin humphs in the kitchen while Pansy wears an amused smile and gloats instinctively at the downfall of Man

the children are as good as gold, sleeping like babes long before the time for the Waterfords to arrive – with careful programming on Pansy's part the meal cooks steadily in its sequences – more wine is generously poured, partly to get her out of housewifely mode and into a hostess one, and partly to calm Martin's indignation – with the matches handy with which to light those candles, the table laid nicely, the Frascati chilling, the host and hostess dressed as neatly as possible, the scene's set for the quiet celebration of a friendly dinner party – the sun is dimming appropriately, the mood is civilized and . . .

. . . *urban! – we might as well be at home* – Pansy stands by the table, puts her glass down so heavily a few drops of the red wine seize their opportunity to stain the cloth – *this isn't being on holiday, not what I call a holiday – I could do all this at home*

how else would you have it? – we've got to eat

yes, I know – but why this formal? – we do this at home, have meals with candles, social evening with friends

about twice a year, yes – you make it sound as if we do it all the time – what do you suggest, we sit on the floor eating sandwiches?

don't be silly – no, but we're 'entertaining' – we take a farm holiday and we act like we're in the town

so it's no candles then, that what you're saying? – Martin's what you might call a trifle disgruntled – effort and abasement's been his contribution and now here's Pansy wanting to dismiss it as unnecessary – *what are you suggesting?*

oh, I don't know – it just seems we haven't come away – she sits at the table, moves Martin's careful arrangement of cutlery, napkin and glass to make room for her elbows – *we should be more . . . more rustic*

oh aah

it's too formal – we're not going to eat like this every night, are we? – one thing I'm not doing is cooking a meal every evening, I do enough of that at home

it's only tonight – Martin tries to mollify her – *we'll have lunches out mostly, won't we?*

mostly? – we'll have them out every day, we're on holiday – well, I am, on holiday from the kitchen

you can see her point – all right for Martin just to lay a table but Pansy's worried that Beth will return the favour tomorrow evening and then it'll be her turn again and so on – that way she'd be doing four dinners to Beth's three! – well, that's not going to happen, is it? – *where are we going tomorrow anyway?*

well, I expect that what we'll do tonight is get together an itinerary for the week

a programme of events? – can't we just decide every day? – we don't know what the weather's going to be like, do we?

well, we'll be flexible

or have you and Josh already worked it out between you? of course not!

now we see here some sort of underlying dissension, don't we – I suspected there was a difficulty lurking somewhere – it would appear that Pansy's not just fed up with cooking, there's more to it – I think we'll have to exercise my privilege of authorship and go back in time to try to identify why the tension exists – oh yes, I know you're wondering why I can know anything of the characters' history when I pretend to be ignorant of where they live, but that's what I mean by privilege – I can be selective – if I can't be bothered to discover whether they live in an inner city or suburbia it's because I don't much care – but I **am** interested in explaining the reason for Pansy's disaffection, so you're going to learn about that as it may prove to be a crucial element in the story – though maybe it won't, I can't foretell the future, can I?

anyway, this holiday was one that was proposed principally by the men – it came about as a natural extension of Josh and Martin's lunchtime conversations – you know the sort of thing . . . *wouldn't it be a good idea if* . . . – Josh suggested it, Martin thought it a good idea, and it was put to the women to ratify and develop – in a way it was for Pansy a fait accompli – the others were keen to move on the relationship from a sharing of the odd day together to a more generous sharing of a holiday, though she couldn't see why

it'll be fun for all of us – Martin persuaded her, making it seem like a highly desirable objective – *the kids'll love it – and look at it this way, Michael's old enough to babysit while we all go down to the local pub*

Pansy wasn't so sure about this – from what she knew of

Beth's son he had his head in the clouds most of the time and would never be able to cope with PS in one of her more independent moods – but it would be a week in the country, fresh air and a different tempo, so it seemed worth a try – she and Beth, as I've said, were close enough to share hairdressers, go shopping and lunch together, and several good evenings had been passed with happiness all round, so generally it seemed an acceptable idea – there'd still be the week in Fuerteventura later in the year, to make up for last year when because of PS they hadn't been away at all

and yet there remains some niggling anxiety in Pansy's breast, a fragile doubt over whether they'll all get on together – up to now it's been only a few hours at a time, she's not sure she'll be able to enjoy for a week the sort of close companionship evident in a Saturday night get-together or a Sunday outing – there are the children for a start, she's got routines and behaviour-patterns that don't always match the Waterfords' way of child-rearing – she's noticed Beth isn't always strict enough, can't always take the trouble to be consistent, and perhaps because they're older Michael and Abigail have too much freedom of choice when it comes to what they eat – it's little things like that, she won't be in full control over things concerning her own children

*we're not **sharing** a cottage, that would be different* – Martin's tried to explain – *this way we'll be quite separate from them, won't we?*

and so despite her misgivings Pansy's gone along with it – it'll be good for the kids at least, Ellen and Sean have been excited for weeks – nevertheless she still regards it as a bit of an experiment in the kitchen, checking the oven, putting on the green beans – Martin follows her in after straightening his table-setting

Pansy – *we can have another formal dinner on Friday in their place – Beth's turn – otherwise it's ad hoc evening meals, bit of salad or something – all right?* – this is practical Pansy

Martin's not too keen on salad, okay occasionally, but every night? – nevertheless he has to agree at this point – *right you are – salad and chips then* – and to show no hard feelings clutches at her waist, gives her a kiss on the cheek – Pansy kisses him back so as not to be in debt, and peace between them is restored, at least for the time being

it comes to pass then that at eight o'clock on the dot, as if they've been waiting outside stopwatch in hand, Beth and Josh knock on the open door and the Oxfords and Water-fords are joined together

well, we've had a look at Pansy, now let's take a look at Beth – she too is blonde, but if we didn't already know we'd be able to discern from the telltale roots that she's naturally brunette – [why can't women stay as nature intended, that's what I want to know?] – she wears her hair in a fashionable style, the style of the day, one which suggests she's just got out of bed and can't find a comb – the tousled look, which it's said men have a penchant for – [but if you ask Martin what he thinks he'll say he hasn't noticed] – like Pansy she wears little make-up, that's the style too, carefully engineered by Beth where with Pansy it's a natural condition – Beth has larger eyes, not exactly brown but tending that way, they view the world as if amused by its frivolity, its lack of seri-ousness, eyes which look intelligent but careless – a slight

arch to her carefully plucked eyebrows helps to convey a rein-
forcement of this attitude to life – what silly things people get
up to, the eyes seem to say, whatever next – there's a hint of
amusement in the shape of her mouth, a little lift to one
corner so that in repose she appears to be smiling cautiously
– it's an attractive face, one which seems friendly and com-
passionate, in a possibly cynical way

where Pansy's dressed down Beth has dressed up – the
hostess has plumped for simple jeans-and-cotton-top affair
but Beth's given some thought to her appearance – it seems
simple enough [artifice always does] but you can tell she's
spent some time giving thought to it – a denim skirt that
doesn't quite cover her knees and a shirted blouse with the
collar up, cuffs turned back – round her neck a halter of
painted ethnic beads [chick peas?], and on her right hand a
prominent ring with a large jade stone [well, it's green] – as
she enters the room the scent of her perfume precedes her to
the extent that Pansy suppresses a sneeze and Martin feels his
knees go weak – to be fair it's not all Beth's, some of it's Josh's
well-splashed aftershave

I detect here, as you may do also, a distinction between
the two women, one of preference – from the foregoing I
seem to have a warmer feeling for one over the other – Pansy
comes out a favourite with her more straightforward appearance against Beth's more contrived one – is this them or me?
– have I already decided between the goodies and the bad-
dies, if this is to be the case? – or in their own distinctive way
are these two characters establishing themselves, asserting
their right to be in the story, making sure they're in the fore-
front by deliberately, manipulatively making me distinguish

between them? – is there a rivalry, a competition to see who's going to be the most significant character? – the two men aren't so pushy, or perhaps they're just playing it cool, working to the long term, weighing things up before they make their play to be the most important constituent of the story?

yes, you can see how it is – four people who want to insist the story's about **them** – well maybe it is, but maybe it's about Ellen or Michael or even Brewster, who can say at this stage

straight to the kitchen go the women, straight to the bottle go the men – well actually it's the bottle for the ladies, cans for the men, Martin supervising the first and Josh opening the second – conversations take place of a type and content that must be the oldest in history – in mesolithic times they probably said exactly the same things, albeit with different drinks and a slightly more primitive kitchen – but Beth and Pansy talk of food and children, Josh and Martin discuss food and cars – those early cave dwellers would have talked of food and hunting, leaving out the kids – it's a safe bet mesolithic dinner parties, greasier and untidier perhaps, would nevertheless have followed precisely the same pattern as these modern counterparts

Beth's very complimentary, even before tasting it, about Pansy's trout – *I could smell it as we came in, can't wait, delicious – you shouldn't have gone to the trouble of having fish just for me, I could have had an omelette or something – I know Martin likes his steak*

oh, we have fish a lot anyway – I hope Josh is all right with it?

he'll eat anything – well, I say that, but given the chance

56

he'd stick with pizza, I'm sure of it – very unhealthy eater,
my husband, chips with everything and no veg

   just like Martin

   I'm the opposite, I suppose – I'd dearly love to go vegan
but it's very difficult when you've got a family – they won't
take soya milk or tofu, none of them likes nuts or lentils –
but at least I've cut out the meat

   is that for health or on moral grounds?

   moral, of course – I couldn't eat anything with a face!

   now the word to use here is dissembling – the dictionary
has it that to dissemble is to alter or disguise the semblance of
one's character to conceal or deceive as to its real nature –
Beth's insistence on the avoidance of meat-eating is definitely
of the dissembling kind, for the true reason she eats fish
instead of meat is because she believes meat makes you fat
and fish doesn't, but to admit that fact would give room for
argument – by claiming she does it for moral reasons takes
the matter to one of personal religious belief which it's therefore impolite, rude or taboo to question – all Pansy can say
in reply is *really*, and leave it at that, adding *I couldn't do*
without my meat, I'm afraid

   the conversation between the men is less dietary, more
practical but it hovers on the personal, especially when Josh
asks if Pansy's always so domesticated

   Martin, not sure what he means – *she's a good cook*

   Josh – *well, I'm pretty sure she's good at other things*
as well

   like?

   like – well, she's good fun, isn't she?

   no idea what he's talking about, Martin just shakes his

head a little, baffled, prefers to change the subject – yes, Pansy's good fun, but it's a strange thing to say, what's he driving at? – *d'you mean can she change a tyre and make a joke of it?*

oh forget it – what are we doing tomorrow? – a small shortness of temper's noted by Martin, but then he's like this at work, is Josh – some of the men call him touchy, don't make jokes when he's around, keep their heads down, act all serious until the figure of their supervisor's passed from their ken and then revert to that cosy camaraderie that's nowadays mistaken for uncouth ladderie – to a certain extent Martin's learnt to read Josh's moods but he still gets caught out, as now

pick up the pieces, Martin, go on – *tomorrow?* – *well, a lot depends on the weather of course – and what our mistresses decide for us, they're the ones who'll plan it*

a queer little look from Josh – *mistresses?* – *that sounds good*

I couldn't say masters, could I, though perhaps I should have done – our 'masters' will decide our fate

think I prefer mistresses, but that would imply . . .

enter the subjects under discussion, cutting him off in mid-stream, mid-sentence, consigning any of his implications into the void

ten minutes announces Pansy, face flushed from the heat of the stove, two small beads of perspiration, unstringed pearls, poised at the base of her neck – it's when she looks like this Martin fancies her most and the wish crosses his mind that they could be alone and he could take advantage of it *it's delicious* Beth tells her husband, and to be honest she's saying it so he can be equally complimentary when the time comes, not put his foot in it by saying he's not keen on fish, especially salmon which from experience she knows he'll presume it to be – *lovely fillets of trout, mm!* – that's him fixed, let him make a mistake at his peril

small conversation ensues which it would be tiresome of me to relate, tedious for anyone outside the quartet who might overhear, surely tedious for any reader who might be hoping for exciting parley – I work on the basis that if **I'm** bored with their small talk then most other people will be too – of course there are some odd people who thrive on the minutiae of chitting and chatting, persons of curious minds whom I shall sadly have to disappoint – this, you see, is democratic literature, not fine art, so the majority must have their way

the dinner – candles alight, wine flowing, trout borne in triumphantly with its accompaniment of green beans and artfully arranged leeks dozing on mashed sweet potato, fit for a king! – gravy? queries Josh, or failing that ketchup? – but he wisely keeps such provocative sacrileges to himself and makes do without either, the thought having to provide the satisfaction

what of Josh? – enduring a childhood being called Joshua by your parents, your kin, your wider family, aunts, uncles, teachers and the neighbours, a formal address of an old biblical name, well, it's bound to have some effect – your friends will call you Josh, which is okay, but not until you've grown up can you style yourself as such, and that aforementioned crowd of family etc. will continue to use the longer version because that's what they've always done since you were a little babby – even now, fully adult, he can cringe when his parents, determined to establish and sanctify forever their personal choice [which was made willy-nilly because they couldn't agree on the mother's selection of Samuel and the father's preference for Daniel, with Joshua coming out of the blue as a divinely inspired compromise] steadfastly use the proper form

so we can be assured that Josh grew up with an inherent distaste for his parents' authority, having the worm of resentment lurking in his breast, informing his outlook on the world at large – a certain inner anger, induced by the fear of someone making fun of his name by invoking an old rhyme about the walls of Jericho, grew into a condition of suspicious awareness, everyone being seen as a potential ally of his parents – even with Beth he feels she's only being kind by calling him Josh when she'd much rather show her superiority by calling him Joshua, which she does occasionally when she's larking about, setting him off into a sulk which she can't understand – he's consequently jealous of those men who have normal names they can't be embarrassed about, men like Martin for instance, unaffected by either the full version or the friendly abbreviation of Mart – jealousy can be the instigator and the prop of vengeance it's said, so watch out Martin

whether like Beth he dyes his hair it's difficult to say, for it's that tarry sort of black which on sight immediately gives rise to the idea that he does, but of course the roots don't give the game away – nowadays men, some men, vain men, pamper themselves almost to the same degree as women, use nearly as many chemical agents, and from the strength of his aftershave [all that a decent chap will allow himself] Josh could well be one of that persuasion – [incidentally, have you ever considered that the person next to you, if not yourself, may be covered, as intensively farmed fields are covered, by an array of chemicals marvellous in their scope and fiendish in their complexity? – purely as a point of interest do you realize that using just four or five beauty aids you can impregnate your skin with seventy-five different chemicals? – these underpin the efforts made by us to smell nice, look nice, and in terms of self-confidence feel nice – at any one time without the support of these chemicals we should be totally naked and disgustingly ugly] – so Josh has black hair, very shiny black hair that makes you think of piano keys, and he keeps it in a wavy style that can only be maintained by the application of a regular comb – his face is long, with sallow cheeks and the eternal blue-grey shadow of a beard round his chin – if I say he has a sharp nose and noticeable ears you'll think I'm describing a prejudiced character with no redeeming features, casting him in the role of villain before I have any proof of it, but I can remedy this by commenting on his eyes, which are bluey-green and intelligent, a very attractive asset that shows he has humour and sparkle and can when he wants to persuade another person to his side – quite an athletic build, with well-manicured hands [as you'd expect] – he dresses with care, on this occasion in a pale-blue shirt with full long sleeves and steel-grey trousers flat at the front and tight at the back – oh, and a large gold medallion at his throat

back to the dinner table – as something formal it's a success, even to the degree that the candles provoke admiration, thus

61

pleasing Martin with his little contribution, but from Pansy's point of view it's just such an air of formality that makes her want to run screaming from the room – I didn't come here for dinner parties! would be her howl, addressed to the moon and the stars and the free abyss of an informal natural world – she swallows her food, knocks back her wine with a reluctance that nearly chokes her, joins in the conversation tardily with no inner interest in what anyone, including herself, is saying – while deep down her psyche is soaking up the praise for her cooking her superior consciousness is yearning to be sitting on the farm gate in the moonlight eating a cheese and pickle sandwich

the moonlight! – yes there is moonlight now, a pale, wan little sliver of a moon ducking shyly among the clouds but nevertheless giving a faint luminescence to the sky – dusk drifts away, the land becomes undistinguished, landmarks become unrecognizable shapes, the farm gate a mere shadow of its former self – Pansy would stumble if she were out there now minus the aid of a torch, only Sammy would find his way with any surefootedness, padding silently within his territory from one marker to another – [it's said that male cats can travel up to five miles a night while doing their rounds checking on their females, but I think our Sammy's a bit past that now and any females who fancy it will have to come to him] – it's dark now for certain when farmer Broadfield goes without aid of a torch across territory he's known from infancy to let off his shotgun a couple of hundred yards beyond the house – it's a loud report, just one barrel discharged at the slivery moon, flatly echoing on the still air, a hollow crack, a reprimand, an insertion of alien noise into the peaceful descent of night, not near or loud enough to wake the small children but intrusive enough for the dinner party chatter to cease while Beth says *what's that?* beating everyone else to a comment

rabbits, I expect Martin provides confidently – *shooting rabbits, that's what it is*

Josh, the other countryman of many years repute nods sagely – *rabbits yes, or it could be he's shooting at rats*

rats! – Beth's alarmed

how can he see them in the dark? Pansy wants to know – *and why only the one shot?*

no one has an answer to this quite reasonable conundrum but Josh has a suggestion – *he's shot his wife*

or else she's shot him – Pansy

that's more like it, very sensible – Beth prefers it not to be rats – *the police will be all over the place in the morning, we won't be able to move for them*

in the Waterfords' cottage Michael hears the shot, looks up at the ceiling as though expecting a pellet to fall in a corner of the room – he's busy with his father's laptop, and as no other noise follows it's back to the free galleries which provide his evening entertainment – [our architect friend Gregory Price-Masters has done his job well with this conversion, both cottages being fully Internet-wired] – his sister, dutifully in bed but patently not asleep pauses in her critical appreciation of Lily Allen by lifting one earphone for a second, finds herself unable to account for the slight interference and resumes the nodding of the head and twitching of the muscles which are her aids to concentration

Mr Broadfield, duty done, stomps back into the kitchen to lock away his gun, goes through to the living room – here's his wife and son, one relaxed in her armchair with her eyes glued to the television, the other sitting on the edge of the settee waiting to continue a conversation his father broke off by using the excuse of his professional duties – Lance can never seem to have a proper discussion with his father, points always arise with which Mr Broadfield can't agree

that's not true – he just wants to get me into a corner over things, things he gets a bee in his bonnet about

I'm sure you get bees in **your** bonnet

that's different, I'm his father – he wants to talk about the state of the world and saving the planet, that sort of thing, not my cup of tea after a hard day – if it was matters concerning the farm I'd be all ears, but it's not – always airy-fairy stuff, hasn't got his feet on the ground, that lad

perhaps he's not cut out for it

course he is, born to it like I was – the difference is I didn't have the schooling he's had, that's what's done it you know, that and that thing over there

the television?

got a lot to answer for, believe me – they put ideas into people's heads, make them think they can achieve anything they want – well, they can't, people generally stay where they're put

so miners' sons should go down the mines, vicars' sons should become vicars, doctors' sons become doctors, that sort of thing? – and what about the son of a bank robber?

you're as daft as he is

2

Sunday a.m.

dawn comes early for Pansy in the form of a whine from the mouth of PS, not a chorus but a single complaint as she pulls herself up in her travel cot to stand making the noise she hopes will wake her parents – darling little tousle-headed babe that she is Pansy calls out to her to shut up, play with her soft toys, look through the books she's got with her in the cot, stop making a racket! – Ellen fidgets in her sleep, Martin snores, Pansy sighs, it's four thirty-five

they were late getting to bed, the Waterfords hung on until nearly midnight, all right for them with no baby to get up for – leave the clearing-up until morning, said Martin, I'll do it then, first thing – but he always says things like that and he never does, always snores and snuffles soundly until she takes him a cup of tea after doing any clearing-up herself – about as reliable as PS, that's her opinion of his promises – today's going to be no different but she's not going to start it at four-thirty – she rolls out of the bed, goes through to PS

lie down darling, it's very early, we don't want to wake Daddy, do we?

well yes, this is exactly PS's intention, let's wake everyone in the whole wide world and we can all play together, Daddy in particular because he's such good fun and Mummy isn't – she's not placated, definitely not hushed – *get up now* she declares

no, lie down, try to go back to sleep – Mummy's very tired – ssh

for once, and after reiteration PS lies down, closing her eyes in pretence and beginning a small, private conversation with a fluffy lamb while Pansy creeps back into bed – Martin turns over, stops wheezing, a sort of peace returns

but there's no sleep, Pansy's wide awake, lying on her back with open eyes staring at the ceiling – it always happens that when you're woken early like this it's the very devil to get back to sleep again, your mind inevitably begins sifting through a compelling variety of undismissable thoughts – in Pansy's case it's to be expected that her mind goes over the events of the previous evening, re-enacts little portions of them, dwells with unnecessary and pointless concentration on snippets of the conversation – for instance, did Martin **have** to say anything about little Sean's dislike of tenpin bowling? – all it did was get Josh and Beth crowing about **their** children's addiction to it – and why did Pansy herself get on to the subject of line dancing, obviously Beth thinks it a strange pastime – two things that should have been avoided, they should have stuck to mundane topics like the weather and what they were going to do today

just what did Josh mean when, as they were carrying dishes to the kitchen, he dropped his voice to say *this is going to be a good week, isn't it?* – saying it in such a confidential, even intimate tone that it sounded like something meaning-ful – it made her feel rather unsettled, especially as the other two were talking loudly in the sitting room – why did he need to drop his voice? – she hopes he doesn't fancy her in any way, hardly her type – perhaps he always gets like that after a few drinks

PS settles down, despite an active mind Pansy eventually drops off – it's eight o'clock before everyone starts getting up, Sean becomes anxious for his breakfast, even Ellen gets up but only to get a book from the other side of the room, back on the bed to read – quite a heavy tome these days for a nine-year-old, *Wives and Daughters*, you'd think it might be hard going for her but she's following on from *Wuthering Heights*, says in her critical review of the world's literature that this is a lot less turbulent story without the passion but with the love interest – turbulent's her favourite word at the moment – Martin thinks she's a genius because at the same age he was only looking at picture-comics and can't under-stand Ellen's fascination with a book full of nothing but words

where are we going today? asks Sean, adding excitedly so they all know how keen, how desperate he is – *there's that theme park not far, they've got that huge Death-Crasher goes over a big shelf like a cliff and drops you over the edge*

you'll be too young replies Martin – *there'll be a height restriction or something* – but the truth is he'd be forced to accompany the boy and ever since the age of ten when he fell out of a chair-a-plane he's avoided such daring pursuits – no good looking at Pansy, she gets frightened on see-saws

pleeease!

I think we're going on the steam train today, so eat a good breakfast, it'll make you hungry – there's no logic in this statement, Pansy sees that as she says it and hopes young Sean won't pick her up on it, but it's just the sort of thing parents come out with, don't they, as though they can utter any old rubbish so long as it shuts you up – Sean pulls a face and groans loudly in his disappointment while Ellen, having put her Gaskell aside in order to concentrate on her muesli sighs and says *do we have to?* – only PS is pleased at the idea of going on an antiquated railway because she's presently on to Thomas the Tank Engine and expects to see James, her favourite, with whom no doubt she can exchange a word or two

Martin **does** tackle the clearing-up, or at least that part of it he's in time for, wiping the pans that Pansy's washed, putting them away, collecting the cans and bottles, sweeping up some of the crumbs that fell to the floor during Josh's uncontrolled assault on the cheese and biscuits – a good helper but not an instigator, Martin will always wait to do the secondary aspect of domestic routine, being shy of actually initiating a process – if Pansy says *why don't you iron your shirts?* he'll happily go about doing so, but don't expect him to think of it himself – his defence is that she's in charge and he doesn't like to interfere

in the Waterford cottage there's much the same kind of activity but without the conversation – Michael and Abigail are always silent in the mornings, Abigail busily attending to her texting [amazing how many messages pile up overnight] and Michael with that distant aura of otherworldliness appropriate to his age [cynics would call it stupor, others might term it TMW, to use a technical term] – their parents are as usual busy with their own thoughts – Josh comes out with *I suppose it's that steam train* – and Beth merely answers *can't remember if we're doing sandwiches*

they had a late night, the senior Waterfords – after returning to their own domain they sat for a time with a fresh bottle of wine discussing the Oxfords – while Beth thinks Pansy a cheerful enough friend she's reserving her opinion about the extent to which the other woman can let her hair down – too much in control is Pansy, of her family and principally of herself – *did you see the way she orders Martin around?*

he doesn't have to take it if he doesn't like it

well, he's after the quiet life, isn't he? – but she seems very uptight most of the time, there's a lot of repression there

d'you think I ought to try and release it?

I've seen her type before, you tap into that repression and suddenly it's fireworks time – rather you than me

well, it wouldn't be you, would it?

but while there was some discussion along these lines last night [and I consider it indelicate of me to continue following their train of conversation if Josh is going to make such revealing remarks, revealing that is from the direction of his thoughts towards Pansy] it was simply talk for talk's sake, Beth being concerned with thoughts of her own and Josh letting the alcohol organize his tongue – once in bed, despite a feeble stab at a bit of nocturnal activity they quickly fell asleep and let dreams take the place of postprandial analysis

so this morning the silence is somewhat attributable to the recovery of those thoughts which each of them had about the previous night, undergoing a kind of considered review, and if there's anything at all to say about the atmosphere it's that Brewster finds it very satisfying because he gets something of a lie-in

he has his bed in the little passage by the front door from where he can vet the comings and goings of both the family and any possible intruders – it's a floppy bed [they once bought him a hard plastic thing like a toy garden pool but he couldn't get on with it and now it's used in the shed to hold bags of potting compost, a much better use of the thing from Brewster's point of view] – in his present floppy bed he can sprawl about and make people have to step over him, not to mention the fact that with a good tug the whole thing complete with well-chewed artificial bone and rag-wrestler can be dragged to places offensive to the family [like smack in front of the television set] – so he's happy with his bed, doesn't always want to leave it in the morning, age coming to him as it does to all of us, prompting delay in everything – but he's particularly tired today because he was up half the night having to put his nose to the gap beneath the front door, listening for all his might to any sounds from outside – he's quite sure there was a cat somewhere, putting **its** nose to the gap and hanging about out there, on one very unsettling occasion making a very unpleasant smell – he didn't bark despite every nerve in his body telling him to do so because he knew Josh would come down and thump him – besides, it was insulting to his dignity to know there was something out there being impudent and provocative, and there's no point in advertising your inadequacies, is there?

the activities in the two cottages move inexorably towards a common end, so that by nine-thirty doors are opened and children [with Brewster] emerge into the light of day like tired miners at the end of a shift, blinking and with that inner delight at finding the world still as it was when they left it – Sean runs, Ellen stands with hands on hips looking at the farmyard, Abigail walks steadily in circles with her mobile phone in both hands, Michael slouches off to climb on the gate, sitting on its top rail as though waiting for a bus, and little PS, too unreliable to be let loose on her own, holds Pansy's hand as the two of them stand in their doorway taking in the bucolic scene

in the farmhouse Mrs Broadfield harangues a sleepy Tilly over the matter of the cock – it's one of the young girl's duties to switch on the tape before she goes to bed and last night she forgot to do it – she has only two duties in regard to the visitors, make the hens run across the yard on their arrival and supervise the timer which plays a cock-a-doodle-do at six-thirty on the dot – she hasn't done this, the visitors weren't woken to what they expect, were they, and Mrs Broadfield's very annoyed about it

well, she doesn't have much to do, does she – it's only the flick of a switch, is that too much trouble for her? – she thinks of nothing but ponies these days

I've got the Wilton gymkhana coming up, haven't I? – I've got a lot on my mind, what with my GCSEs as well – can't remember everything – I expect you'd like me to fall off a horse and fail my exams, you'd be happy then I suppose

Tilly goes off in a huff, something we've noticed she's good at, but at fifteen huffing is sometimes the only way of getting back at the world – Mrs Broadfield too seems to be a bit huffy at times, something the male members of the household probably steer clear of, a mature huff can be a lot more intimidating than a teenage one – this avoidance of brewing wrath will be about the only thing Lance and his father can really agree on, and their shared subjection in the face of Mrs Broadfield's displeasure will result in their communing together in out of the way places like the old pigsty – here they be this morning, having anticipated the cock business, and here, with a bonhomie not usually in evidence they stand discussing the new arrivals

Lance – *I thought the ones in Wheatsheaf looked a bit surly*

see the dog? – needs a good bit of fieldwork, bet he's never been in a river, looks too much a pampered pet, made to be a kiddie's toy I expect

about the organics

what about it? – got some results?

Lance pulls a face – *not a lot – turned over the two-acre yesterday*

I thought that was carrots! – looked all right to me

no good, not worth salvaging, all deformed, discoloured – never sell them – that's if they'd ever have been worth the trouble of harvesting – no, carrots we'll have to pass on, soil's not right, not without preparation which we can't do

Nicola? – they're all right, aren't they, coming out soon?

oh yes, potatoes are fine, yes we'll make something on them – it's just the carrots – best thing though is onions

ooh, tricky, never had onions – where are they then?

down by the copse, only a corner, about half an acre, but they're doing fine, no disease, nothing, good size too

now this is terribly boring, we don't really want to listen

to agricultural reports, we're on holiday with the others –
I believe the background to all this is Lance's attempts, in
the face of his father's scepticism [contempt, more like] to
develop the organic side of things to the point where they can
go the whole hog, be nothing else – apparently his father lets
him play with a few acres and we're now hearing the result
– *let him get it out of his system, it'll pass once he finds out
how unprofitable it is* – but Lance's motives may not be
influenced by profit, he might genuinely believe we're poi-
soning ourselves and however great the cost the effort must
be made to get away from the constant use of chemicals

    *onions eh? – well, that's interesting – anything's better
than having to accommodate them holidaymakers*

    as I said, the Wheatsheaf look a sour lot to me

I forgot to mention, when they moved in last night, [actu-
ally it's only just occurred to me] that the Oxfords are in
Stook and the Waterfords in Wheatsheaf – these names must
have been dragged out of the Broadfields by Gregory Price-
Masters decrying any other means of designation such as
numbers or pretty words such as Daisy and Dandelion – he
would like the names they eventually came up with but it
would no doubt have been necessary to explain to him what
a stook was – the Broadfields were more than likely self-
conscious about it at first but custom always leads to blind
acceptance and now they trot out the names in a decidedly
matter-of-fact way

    whether sour or not the Waterfords happily load up their
four-by-four as the Oxfords pile into their estate and the two
parties, with Michael doing gate duty, depart the farm for
the first day of their holiday to be taken at the steam train

station, at least to start with – we shall wave them goodbye and bon voyage, Brewster barking at the world as it recedes, the Broadfield father and son unmoved by any hint of excitement, watching the departure from the security of the old pigsty

also watching is Sammy of course, on his wall, screwing up his ears at that awful barking noise – he doesn't know he's going to get a whole day of peace, if he did he'd be turning cartwheels, but **we** know and we can be pleased for the old chap

Tilly goes off to the riding school, walking briskly down the private lane to get the bus and Mrs Broadfield begins her domestic duties – this is the best time of the day, having the whole place to herself and that delightful moment when the world comes to rest while she has a cup of tea – this is when she'll rediscover herself, become aware of the continuity of her progress from girl into woman – though her mind may not dwell on it she's bound to feel an affinity with what she always was when Tilly's age, and seeing her daughter go off can transmute her into being that earlier person once more – memories come more as feelings than as particular scenes, as a mood rather than as a recollection of events

oh, I have the events, they come a lot – these days I seem more and more to be remembering my childhood – I don't think it's anything to do with Tilly, with comparing her to me, I simply keep remembering things – perhaps she prompts the memory, I don't know, but I'm always doing it – five minutes ago I was thinking back to when I was ten, living in the village – used to sit on the wall by the church like the cat there, doing nothing, just waiting for life to pass I suppose –

*children today have got much more to do, haven't they? – we
didn't do much at all really, just waiting to grow up*

waiting to be Mrs Broadfield, farmer's wife?

*waiting for something, yes, but I never had dreams about
being married, having children, that sort of traditional thing
– I wanted to be rich I suppose, live a life of luxury, swan
around in expensive clothes, do whatever I wanted – if I saw
myself as anything it was to become one of the county set [as
if I could!], live in a place like Stanbeck House over the hill
there – d'you know who's got it now? – some American pop-
singer, two hundred and fifty acres, more than we've got and
they use it as a playground, always tearing about in those big-
wheeled things*

but destiny being what it is you've ended up on a farm –
that's doing well for yourself, isn't it, you could be living in
a town, your husband a clerk

*clerk? – do they have such things now, I thought they
were all executives or managers – well yes, I get more fresh
air, but it's hard work, there's lots to do outside – look at my
hands*

Mrs Broadfield has slightly podgy hands with short
fingers, if she doesn't mind me saying so, nothing deroga-
tory's intended

I should hope not!

they're obviously hands that don't get much time to
pamper themselves, like the rest of her really – she has a
homely air that conveys a sense of duty, with the sort of figure
that . . .

*watch it! – if you're about to call me matronly I'll throw
my tea at you – I know I'm well built but I'm not that*

no, I wasn't going to say matronly, merely that you've a figure that reflects a certain contentment – let's face it, if you were anxious or hating your situation you'd be a bit more slender – you've had a happy life, you enjoy your home, your family – your contentment's reflected in your, shall we say, comfortable figure

I like my bread too much, that's what it is – and the butter, ooh – I'm a dreadful warning, Tilly always says, she's terrified of growing into another version of her mother – if she's not careful she'll go anorexic, that girl, never eats anything, bit of a worry sometimes – I keep telling her

she looks all right to me

you should see her with no clothes on, skinny as a rake – when I was her age I wasn't overweight but I wasn't skinny either – mind you, at fifteen I was into athletics, so that kept my weight down

athletics?

yes, athletics! – the Olympics were on, I got the urge to be a champion hurdler, I wasn't always this shape – I was quite good, we used to practise regularly and I won a couple of certificates – nearly won a cup once, at the inter-schools, but just came second – I was very trim then, I could show you the photographs

so Tilly's doing the same thing, only on a horse

we couldn't afford a horse when I was young – but you can jump over anything, can't you, as long as it's the right height – at ten I was sitting on the church wall, at fifteen I was jumping over it

did you do it for long?

gave it up at sixteen when I found an interest in boys –

that's the funny thing, they all fancied me when I was doing the hurdling, not so much when I gave it up

perhaps it was the shorts

probably – she stares absently through the kitchen window into the yard, holds her mug of tea in both hands, memories occupy her – we'll leave her there, ready to start her day, ready to continue [contentedly?] with her life

interesting, that threat of hers to throw her tea at me – how would she manage that, I wonder – would this page have to bear a large brown stain?

Sammy comes in to sniff at his dish – he looks up at Mrs Broadfield's back willing her to turn round, stares at her until she does so – but she turns away again, and ever so reluctantly he bends his head to the dish, licks a fastidious tongue round the edge

3

Sunday p.m.

they're all back by half-past four – well, the Oxfords came on ahead, having to consider PS as she'd had an awful day wetting herself and they'd run out of clean pants – Pansy's cross with her for not speaking up each time she felt the urge, several scenes were enacted where, with much clutching and shifting of foot to foot PS vehemently denied any need for relief, obviously preferring to wait until it became an embarrassing moment – Martin it seems made excuses for her but then he didn't have to deal with it, and Beth would have assumed that superior understanding look of the mother with older children to whom it had never happened – the Oxfords were back twenty minutes early with Pansy desperate to get away from Beth's smugness

from what we can piece together from their comments it hasn't been too good a day for any of them – Abigail and Ellen were bored stiff with the trains and diffident of each other, Michael had the air of someone doing community service and hoping not to be noticed, Sean was disappointed the trains didn't make as much noise as he'd expected, and PS, well James failed to put in a puffing appearance so she wasn't too happy either, which may well have accounted for her toilet difficulties

the menfolk, restored to childhood by the steam and the engineering and the sight of giant toys had a happy enough time discussing mechanics but the constant diversion of their dreams by the requirements of parenthood and consortship wearily interrupted this accord – unfettered by the need to watch her children Beth was bored even by the misfortunes of PS, spending most of her time smiling in his direction each time Martin's gaze swept over her – he failed to notice this overture [or pretended to], but needless to say Pansy didn't

Brewster didn't have much of a good day either, most of the time being forced to inhabit the back of the four-by-four, trapped behind bars and with only parked cars to look at – he was regularly released by Josh or Michael, allowed to walk about on a lead for a short time, cock a leg here and there, drop a packet for Josh to drag him away from, and for not more than forty minutes run around on a grass verge chasing a ball he didn't have a lot of affection for – he's glad to be back sniffing round the door to Wheatsheaf, certain in the knowledge there's a cat somewhere that needs attending to

in each of the cottages it's time for a period of rest at home – it would seem they had a cracking lunch outside a pub where the chips were as large as firewood and the variety of accompaniment to them enormous – steak, sausages, pizza, fish fingers, scampi, faggots – after such a filling lunch it was more or less bread and jam for tea

in Wheatsheaf the evening falls into the sort of pattern

normally prevailing at home, which is to say that each of the children repair to their rooms to do their own thing while the parents sprawl in armchairs and discuss their friends – discussion of a sort, more an analysis of character

I thought [this is Josh] *Pansy was a bit prim today*

prim? – why?

he shrugs – *the way she kept on at Sean about wiping his mouth*

he was covered in ketchup!

he's a kid, what d'you expect? – use your napkin, she said, as though we were at the Savoy – bit pretentious if you ask me

going off her then?

no, she's all right in other ways – but like you said, she needs to let her hair down – are we going there for drinks or are they coming here?

well, it's always going to be there, isn't it, what with PS

right, I'm going to see she has a tankful, she needs relaxing, that one – got to work on her

I'm sure you will, I've not known you fail in that direction – even Pansy can be coaxed round

*I've noticed you're doing quite well with Martin – I think he's a pushover as far as you're concerned – at work he's got a big department but never seems to have any authority over it, they all know how to handle him, how to take advantage – I wonder sometimes if he should **be** a manager, he's such poor material – only got the job because he was next in line – trouble is, you see, it doesn't help me any when his side of the floor's so badly run, I have more trouble with mine*

I thought we weren't going to talk about work – you're here to forget about it

Josh waves a hand in the air – *I covet his wife, so I've got to do him down, haven't I?*

that's an old-fashioned word, covet – you mean you fancy her

I think her primness makes her more appealing, more of a challenge

*you make me laugh, you and your conceit – I think it'll be a matter of making her **notice** you, for a start*

it seems prudent to leave them here, no more eavesdropping on a conversation that's taking an unsavoury turn – not quite what I'd expected, but then I hear you ask aren't the characters merely becoming what I claimed they were, individuals of wilful independence? – can I complain when they go a different way from the one I'd hoped for them? – after all, this is their story, and while I might like it to be all good and sweet with a happy-ever-after ending they're going to do it **their** way – if Josh finds certain of his holiday companions appealing then who am I to contradict him?

let's go off and see what Abigail's doing – listening to the latest charts? – well no, here she is practising with deft application her make-up, looking intently into the mirror to see if her eye-shadow gives her the right amount of mysterious allure – she may be only twelve but in those seduction stakes which she hopes soon to enter you can't start too early with experimentation – finding a style of make-up that harmonizes with the long blonde hair is proving a bit of a poser, most man-eating heroines being dark with black hair and thick mascara, and that disguise is something which doesn't sit at all well with blondies

Michael now, he's got dark hair like his father, but he couldn't care less what it looks like, the tousled look happily being fashionable anyway – he's back on the laptop computer stealing confidential looks at inappropriate web pages, sites that an enquiring, or shall we say prurient, mind will find absorbing and titillating – it would be nice to think that were his father to find Michael looking at these pages he'd be sternly disapproving, but I'm not so sure about Josh now, not after learning of his covetous thoughts towards Pansy – it seems it may be quite possible he'd nudge an elbow and wink

you'd better watch that dog

what?

I said you'd better watch that dog – he's got the cat cornered

who are you?

never mind – it's an old cat, isn't it – call the dog off before he gives it a heart attack – do something about it

all right, all right, if you insist – Brewster, lie down, leave Sammy alone – Sammy, get back up on that wall – there, happy now?

you haven't narrated that, you've got to tell it properly

you're full of orders, aren't you?

Brewster's a funny name for a dog

it's not my dog, I didn't name it

all right, having had my attention drawn to ongoing events the chief concern appears to be the way in which Brewster [a lovable animal with the warm and generous nature I always intended him to have] is standing foursquare, tail swinging companionably, at a point where a corner of the cottages abuts the sheer courtyard face of Sammy's old wall – in this corner, wearing the sort of defiantly contemptuous yet openly aggressive look which only cats can successfully combine in one expression, stands Sammy – not so much standing perhaps as half-crouching, as if on the way up or the way down to or from a comfortable position – he is of course on the wrong side of the wall, palletless so to speak, unable to climb out of harm's way, and what he's doing there is anyone's guess, asserting his rights perhaps, who knows – in his heart of hearts he may know the dog means him no harm, merely wants to play at chase-you-round-the-court-yard, but there are certain rules one has to obey, whether in human life or in the animal kingdom, and one of them is that people and cats and dogs who've not been properly intro-duced must assume a stance that prepares them for either fight or flight – with people we let fear of the unknown cau-tion us, with animals it's fear of upsetting the savage status quo

so how do we quickly resolve this? – one way is for Brewster to get fed up and amble off, sniffing at every odd crevice in the courtyard, but this could be interpreted as backing down and just like Sammy he's got his dignity to think of – we could have someone, some adult, come out and take stock of the situation, order or drag the dog away long enough for the cat to escape – or we could invoke the mar-vellous joys of the creative artist and describe how Sammy, suddenly endowed with a fabulous energy, leaps up to the top of the wall with a felicity that only computer-generated action could actually depict none of these, the reality's more mundane – with an inward sigh and a change in expression from contemptuous aggression to cutting disdain, Sammy settles himself down on his haunches and stares with pretended concentration at a pebble just in front of Brewster's left paw – he doesn't relax, you can see the maintained tension beneath the fur, but the impression he's trying to give is that he's here for the long haul and if Brewster wishes to continue with that tail-wagging, tongue-drooling, stiff front-legged stance which occupies him now, then that's up to him and the cows can come home and go straight to bed

he settles down into the long waiting game, still looking intently at that pebble, and Brewster, just beginning to sense he's being made a bit of a fool of, well, his tail's not swing-ing so much, the impetus has slowed, he's looking at Sammy with his head inclined first one way, then the other like a dog who's forgotten his glasses and can't quite focus – this situa-tion could go on for hours, I could be here forever

Brewster's obviously inclined to play the waiting game too, it would seem dogs have patience as well as cats – how long, he's saying to himself, do I have to wait before it makes a dash for it and I can exercise my canine muscles? – that's it, you see, the difference in muscles between dogs and cats – they each have their own distinctive electrical charge and it's the mental attitude which triggers that charge

their stalemate is interrupted by one of the methods I advocated earlier, when the door to Wheatsheaf opens and Josh strides on to the step with a glass of beer in his hand and a searching look on his face – it takes but a second to locate the animals and he comes across to where the two are locked in their joint communion – things happen quickly then as Brewster's eye is temporarily off the ball – he looks towards his master for approval of his cleverness – enough of a chance for Sammy, old and stiff as he is, to make that dash for freedom – when Brewster looks back there's not even the smile left and Sammy's already halfway across the court-yard

stay commands Josh, a stern, vigorous order which Brewster, a well-trained dog who knows only too well he couldn't catch up with the fleeing Sammy and wouldn't want to show himself up, gives a little twitch and stays as he's told, the thought in his mind [no doubt] that there'll always be a next time

what are you up to, eh? – come on in now, heel! – a snap of the fingers and Brewster obediently suffers up his inde-pendence, saunters into the cottage as if he'd thought of doing so anyway

Beth's urging Abigail into considering getting ready for bed – *we're going next door, darling, I don't want you up all hours*

I'm on holiday

that doesn't mean you stay up all night – you know what you're like, you'll be unliveable with tomorrow if you don't get your ration of sleep

I can lay in

no you can't – we're going off somewhere

oh God, where?

we don't know yet

don't I get a say in it?

you'll be consulted I expect

yes, after you've already decided – this is supposed to be a holiday, I should get to lie in if I want to

then you'll stay here on your own

suits me

and get your own lunch?

I'm not helpless

other ears have been wigging, Michael coming downstairs enters the conversation – *I'll stay too then – I don't want to go off with that lot – we'll be all right on our own and you can go where you like then – get to know your other halves*

a united front from the parents – Josh says *nonsense, we're on holiday together* and Beth responds with *like it or not we're here with the Oxfords, so you can only lie in for so long* – groans from the children, formal in the case of Michael, anguished in the case of Abigail

anyway says Beth – *what do you mean by our other halves?*

you can work that one out replies Michael, scooting back up the stairs

I think he's ahead of us there murmurs Josh, shaking his head as if to say the things children know these days

well, I hope it's not what I think

could be, he's a canny lad – would it matter that much?

I don't want him talking to Abigail – Beth's got a frown on her face – *they grow up far too quickly as it is, I want my little girl to keep her innocence at least until she's thirteen*

Josh says nothing, but there's a trace of a smirk on his face – he bends down to fondle Brewster's ears

now Michael appears as boring as any other fourteen-year-old, boring to us and to other outsiders, but I imagine

86

he has his interesting points – he owns a sharp but elegant turn of wit that tries to impress with its cleverness without appearing to be laboured – I can reveal that throwaway one-liners are his speciality, put-downs, those proto-aphorisms that from an adult intellectual would be carefully collected and made into an anthology – of course, being only fourteen his efforts are seen to be but tiresome wisecracks that people will collect only to throw in the dustbin, but the ambition is there, the aspiration, and one day who knows, he's a television star in the making

he scoots back up the stairs, throws himself heavily on to the bed, rolls on his back to stare at the ceiling, moans to himself the tortured lyrics of a popular song – is all lost? – is there to be no hope for this boy? – are we to write him off unless he has the means at his fingertips of touching into technology? – as he lays looking at the ceiling, and despite the impenetrability of his mindmass, a small but highly significant germ of an idea creeps up on him – the germ develops its theme and becomes a full-blown proposition – *how will the world react if I run away?*

running away's not really what he'd call it – only as he thinks about how his parents might react does he see it from their perspective and the phrase 'running away' looms up – in his own view he'd simply be 'taking off' or 'leaving home' or 'searching for his own ground' – *there's a world out there I'm ready for, a world where I won't be subject to the tiresome whims of these two adults who only tolerate me because I'm their son and they have to – I'd really be doing them a favour by going off, they'd be able to follow their own pursuits – in any case they'd still have Abi to occupy them* fourteen is the age when boys should leave home anyway, having reached the stage of outgrowing their childhood and the biased strictures of parents – *if I was a Masai I'd have been turned out at thirteen to prove myself, that's what I've heard, that's what I've read about – I don't think I'd entirely like that sort of thing, but I do know that at my age I can quite easily shift for myself – what troubles me most is just where can I run away [sorry, take off] to – the big smoke, of course, but London isn't necessarily my ideal, it's a place packed to the kerbstones with disaffected teenagers like me sleeping rough and that appeals to me even less than being a Masai youth – I've a bit of a thing about Dublin, I've heard it's a swinging city and all that, but there again I don't fancy the sleeping rough bit, something which is obviously going to be a feature of my first few days, maybe weeks – if I only knew someone I could stay with for a bit, then I'd be all right – got an auntie in Blackpool, but I don't know anyone else, and aunties aren't exactly my sort of scene*

so these thoughts run through Michael's head with troubling persistence – such an attractive idea, leaving home, but how to do it with a minimum of effort and a maximum of comfort – and he'd need his own laptop computer for a start – of course, what Michael's unaware of is that Josh might be only too pleased to help him on his way, give him some money, set him up, but surely neither party's going to broach the subject with the other – if it were to happen, if pigs might fly, then Michael would quite likely refuse any offer of help as it would compromise the very idea of running away

while he's lying on his bed thinking thoughts of liberty Michael's sister is quietly mulling things over herself – *I hate these holidays where another family's involved – this is the second one this year, at Easter there were those adjacent caravans with a family which included a boy of sixteen who kept saying he fancied me and everyone seemed to think this funny and made crude comments and I had a horrible time and couldn't get back home quick enough – I tried to get out of this one, I wanted to arrange a stay with my friend Leonie, a sort of long sleepover, but it didn't work out – still, at least this time their boy's too young to be interested in me, that's one thing – it's still a drag though, just like it was at Easter, the worst thing then was the way all the parents all got on with each other, they had a wonderful time while we had to put up with it!*

downstairs the parents are eyeing each other up and down, giving mutual signs of approval in the business of dress and appearance – going before the Queen do you think, up for their MBE or whatever? – no, just a case of a shared sense of vanity, what they might refer to as simple presentation but which we, as utterly impartial outsiders, might interpret as obsessive attention to detail – Beth's seemingly simple outfit, as last night's, is the end product of a great deal of careful thought – she tells Josh, whether he's listening or not, that she doesn't want to appear overdressed, that she's chosen the floral skirt because it's full and airy and very casual, the sort of thing you'd go to the supermarket in, and the pink blouse with the trail of linked daisies round the collar and sleeves because it has a kind of rustic charm about it – these aren't her words of course, but her exact sentiments, Beth's vocabulary being of the less flowery kind – it may be something to do with her pretension to veganism, that doing away with the dietary luxuries of life which meat and dairy products represent [where would French cuisine be without butter, cream, veal, pâté and odd bits like guts and snails?] – it may be such a preference which demands her speech is also without equivalent verbal luxuries – say what you mean, get to the point, these would be her instructions were she to face as a teacher a class of English students – flowery concepts are out of the question with Beth, which is why she would describe her skirt and blouse as simply 'nice'

those chemicals I mentioned are heavily employed this evening, both the Waterfords smelling to high heaven of a box of samples I was once given by a representative of a laboratory when I had a job with a manufacturing chemists – I couldn't have made a career of it, not with my allergies, that box of samples had me sneezing for three days – a nice cedarwood box it was, fifty centimetres by thirty-five, full of little compartments each with a tiny blue glass bottle with a screw top containing as many fine distinctions of fragrance as the colours in a book of Pantone swatches – I think I sniffed them all, got high on them, floated home in a dream that evening sneezing repeatedly – this is almost what we have here tonight in Wheatsheaf, and I can feel my nose beginning to twitch purely at the thought of it – I do hope the Oxfords have their windows open

I feel I must mention that I exchanged that job with the manufacturing chemists for one with a food-packing company – I believe it's important to emphasize that my existence isn't simply a literary one, I've had a lifetime of everyday labour of which you should be aware – I wouldn't want anyone to think I was brought into this world with a pen moulded to my hand, put in an ivory tower and spurred on by some fanatical muse who demanded I spend my life writing – no, mate, I've sweated too, I've done my shift at the sharp end – several sharp ends in fact, for the food-packing company was all right while it was peas and lentils and rice, those sort of catering goods packed in 3-kilogram bags – trouble came when the management thought we should instal a flour-packing machine, cornflour at that, horrendous stuff when you've got an allergy and the air-extraction's a primitive fit-up – change of job almost immediately, became a civil servant in Companies House keeping records of businesses – cushy number it was, certainly not one to be sneezed at

anyway, back to the action, such as it is – Josh does look smart tonight, my word, his ribbed cotton shirt, deep maroon and with sewn-in turn-back cuffs is wonderfully offset by the dark-blue moleskin trousers – no medallion tonight, just a couple of buttons undone to display the hairs on his chest – a little more oil on the hair than usual, whether by mistake or design, who knows, but it shines like the M25 after heavy rain – you can tell he feels confident tonight, but confident of what or in what way's hard to say – jaunty, I suppose that's the word, jaunty and with a small smile set on his lips as though nothing in the world's going to upset his plans for an evening of entertainment – does the prospect of a game of bridge make people feel like that?

you look good – Beth knows how to keep him in a good mood – *I'd forgotten you had that shirt*

not too sombre, is it?

you look dashing – who could resist you?

Martin, I hope – and on this little, very little joke, Josh takes Beth's hand, plants a kiss on her mouth – *and you look gorgeous too*

he doesn't mean it, naturally – I mean it's natural for him not to mean it – with someone like Josh, for whom the primary numeral was created, the appreciation of other things can only be tempered by the extent to which those other things will be useful to him – to say nice things to your wife, whether you believe them or not, is prudent if you want to get the best from the domestic situation – telling Beth she looks gorgeous costs nothing, means nothing, and is an easily forgotten sop – Josh will be like this in all his affairs, and in that degree is very much like most men – [I do of course except myself, whose cry of appreciation at the couture of my girlfriend couldn't be more genuine] – but there's a tad more of the egoist in Josh, and the appendage of Number One sits easily on his shoulders – he's a man who considers, in his quaint old-fashioned way, that men are superior to women, and therefore to him all things shall accrue, like barnacles, and in him all things shall begin and end – the family over which he presides is his, their persons are his, their fates are his, disposal of the family income is under his control – all possessions, careers, all ways of thinking, of seeing, of believing are to be within his domain – autocracy shall be his style, a magnanimous autocracy will pour from his very being

Beth, as to be expected, doesn't quite go along with this – in fact if she knew what was in his heart she'd up sticks and leave him – Josh is forced to live by rules that go against his true principles, subsuming his masculine ambitions under the heading of Expediency – it's expediency that prompts him to commend Beth's choice of wardrobe and apply the epithet 'gorgeous' in wanton fashion when he doesn't care less what she wears so long as it doesn't reflect on him and his dignity – I do believe that at work he's known as Dapper Dan, that's publicly of course, a nickname to his face they can get away with – [but there is much rumour that some of the workforce have no love for him and between themselves call him The Smarmy B . . . . d] – very difficult for most of them to tell, as Josh has to wear the white coat and trilby hat which all the non-operatives wear and in this outfit seems indistinguishable from anyone else – it must be something in his posture which they recognize or the angle at which that hat's worn or the style of the shirt beneath the coat – put him and Martin together at the point where their responsibilities meet [there's a painted white line to act as demarcation] and you'd hardly tell the difference, except that Josh is a bit taller and Martin a little less lean

whether dapper or smarmy Josh does have a certain air of the con man about him – you can picture him in a street-market urging you to lose your money in a three-cup swindle, or perhaps more to his taste persuading gullible women to fall for him and give him lots of presents – that he's not guilty of either of these failings doesn't detract from the suspicion that he's capable of them, and once you've formed an opinion in that respect it's very hard to shake it off – but don't be influenced by anything I say, and certainly don't base your view of Josh on the fact that his fellow workers call him a Smarmy B . . . . d – time will tell whether there's any truth in all this

tonight Josh is bounding with confidence and full of the keen anticipation of the theatregoer – after having kissed his wife and run a possessive hand over her bottom [from which she shies away, fearful for the condition of her clothing] he looks at himself in the nearby mirror, adjusts the hairs peeping from his shirt, inspects his hairstyle and runs a finger beneath his watch strap to move it into a visible position on his wrist – after all, no point in having an expensive item if you don't show it off

now here's a digression – I could have said he fingered his 1997 gold-plated Rolex with the sky-blue dial and a facility for telling the time in Japan, but this picky detail is something I abhor – you sometimes get whole novels where the detail is obsessive, like '*she put on her Castelan wire-moulded, rose-coloured, deep-size D bra with the French lace straps and a Wilkins-patented fastener central at the back, stepped out of the crazed-tiled, Hansz-designed, gold-and-jet accessoried bathroom, donned her violet-tinted Marsham-Hoest terry-towelled bathrobe and looked at herself for a long time in the Art Deco-style framed Panache mirror hanging from the covert brass hook Rawlplug-fixed on the east pink-plastered wall of her Buckland Crescent, second-floor, faded-Edwardian, term-rented flat*' – whole novels! – the author spent six years in meticulous research and he's going to make sure nothing's wasted! – you get a lot of it in thrillers, where it's done partly to persuade you of their authenticity [which it doesn't] and partly to pad out a tale without which it would be a mere short story

anyway [as I seem to keep saying] anyway, Josh is pleased with his appearance and apparently confident that this evening he's going to win the approval of Pansy – this is such an obvious objective that we might wonder Beth doesn't resent it, but she seems quite content that he should look his best whatever the reason – after all, she herself wants to have Martin admiring her, not much point in dressing up other-wise, she knows it won't make Pansy jealous or liable to proffer flattering remarks – it's a sure bet that *you look nice* is the nearest Pansy'll come to such appreciation, and that said in an absent way as though she's thinking of something else

Beth's desire to attract Martin's attention may be fuelled by the knowledge that it's in her power to do just that – surely she's already noticed that unlike previous occasions when they've all spent a day together Martin looks at her differ-ently – intimacy of the situation, she could put it down to, a case of familiarity on a lengthened scale – he knows we're together for days and nights, she might think, and he knows I'm only next door

so we might be impudent enough to ask why she should be so keen to attract his interest – Josh's approach is clear cut, he's obviously a natural lecher, but Beth? – could it be it's in response to that, she needs the reaffirmation that to her husband she's as desirable as another woman, in this case Pansy? – by drawing Martin's appreciation she may be hoping to make Josh jealous, look upon her with more favourable, even lusting, eyes – does she feel she's losing his regard?

on the other hand it might be that in Martin she sees a man without the irritating habits of her husband – all women could do a swap in this, exchange one lot of irritating men for another, but it would all end up the same, wouldn't it, irritating habits in men being so universal – you can almost bet on Beth finding Martin's irritating habits worse than those of Josh – better the devil and his habits that you know

or perhaps it's the frisson of a putative holiday romance – away from home, away from the dishwasher and the dryer, a woman such as Beth might have a little dream of stepping for a moment outside the boring run of things – a little dream of running off with another woman's husband, a lover who'll lavish all his fifty per cent of the worldly goods on her, rain praises upon her haloed head – that would be nice, wouldn't it, a profitable holiday romance

but no, is that really in her line? – she's a woman who wants to give up eggs and milk and I can't square that with her taking off with another man – and Martin? – is he really the type to set a woman's heart on fire? – no, we'll have to settle for the mundane reason of Beth flashing her eyes and cosying up to Martin simply because he's there and what else is there to do on holiday, watch television? – it's a worthy little game and Martin should be flattered she's even bothering

back for a moment to Josh and his reasons, there may be something more than just lechery here – could it be he wants to draw Pansy's attention because it would represent a small triumph to counteract the popularity with which Martin's hailed at work? – perhaps he wants to make the point that Martin's full marks in the workplace can be seriously downgraded in the wider market of sexual relations – it comes down to wanting to make Martin jealous – in other words can he pull the birds as well as Josh can?

but who knows what motivates these two in Wheatsheaf – it seems to give them some pleasure to pretend to themselves they're irresistible, that at their time of life something hasn't passed them by, that they retain the youthful charm and personality of their younger years – that's what it is, trying to recapture a lost youth – aren't we all guilty, in some small degree, of that? – Pansy and Martin needn't be on their guard against assaults on their virtue, there's a perfectly normal process going on here

and what about these other two, what about the family in Stook? – is there the same kind of natural behaviour here, do Martin and Pansy feel the need to impress, to lure, the others? – well, it seems not, and we can tell instantly that if anything they're trying to do the opposite – they're not yet dressed, Martin hasn't shaved, Pansy's uptight about the children, the place isn't tidy, toys are everywhere and there's a clothes airer smack in the middle of the lounge with multi-coloured, multi-shaped, multi-various damp items of children's clothing on it – ready? – someone's joking, aren't they?

and who's to blame? – well, that's what children are for, to give parents [who'd otherwise have to face up to their own deficiencies] a very good reason for anything you care to mention – not ready?: it's the children's fault – lost something?: the children will have it – place in a mess?: of course it is, it's the children's mess – short of money?: what do you think – going mad?: wouldn't you? – where would family life be without children?

PS, being the lowest and the slowest as well as the most inherently awkward, is logically the one to get the most blame – well, not blame exactly because it shows how unciv-ilized you must be if you put all the responsibility on a two-year-old – but if it wasn't for PS and her difficult ways . . . – she's decided on two things since returning home full of chagrin at not seeing James the steam engine – the first is to refuse to eat her tea and the second's to whine – now when PS whines you've no idea how a) she can do it so loud and for so long, and b) why you don't grab her and lock her in a cupboard before issuing everyone within two hundred yards a pair of reinforced earplugs – she goes on, and on, and on – it's mainly a Mummy whine, for she's learnt the others are made of sterner stuff, having developed great skill in more or less ignoring her, so it's Mummy this and Mummy that and with PS's vocabulary rather limited to say the least the phrase *altogether now* gets thrown in many times over – there's another feature to all this for PS follows Pansy with every step she takes, clutching at her skirt or trousers or whatever bit of clothing comes to hand, acting as though the umbilical cord's never been cut and causing Pansy to bite back with desperate reluctance a plethora of b . . . . ys and b . . . . rs that she'd happily shout if the children were all somewhere else

having that sort of disruption unsettles the rest – Martin starts getting ratty, Ellen increases her sighs more dramatically than usual, Sean frowns a lot and makes popping noises with his mouth which are supposed to indicate [he's lost in Utah at the moment] the sound of cowboy gunfire but which only adds to the tumult – it's not surprising that the household's unlikely to meet the eight o'clock deadline, which is when the Waterfords are due to knock on the door expecting to be welcomed with gentility, and in fact even eight-thirty seems a trifle optimistic – all should have been in bed ages ago, Ellen expected to read there, but PS [who **was** in her cot until she decided she hadn't done her full quota of whining and had to be taken out again to resume the action] has delayed everyone to a considerable extent

go next door commands Pansy – *tell them to give us another half-hour*

we'll make it in time, it's only twenty to . . . – but Martin stops there because he's seen that look on Pansy's face before and he does so want a quiet evening at some point – *all right, half-past then* – and he's out of the door hoping to find a small patch of peace in the courtyard – needless to say the whine accompanies him and he hardly touches the Wheat-sheaf door before Beth's there saying *having a bit of trouble?*

sort of – *can we make it eight-thirty, we're running a bit late?*

of course, that's all right – we'll make it then, then – don't worry about it – Josh, it's eight-thirty!

Martin creeps back to his pandemonium, Beth closes the door firmly, a tight little set to her mouth – half an hour! – and she's paced herself so well, got herself ready exactly on schedule and now she has to wait another half-hour – if she was a kettle she'd be off the boil and unlikely to be so hot again – Josh is no help, he's happy to be able to watch the end of a darts match – *okay by me* he says, easing his cuffs and settling in the chair – *eight-thirty's fine*

Martin gets back in time to see a staunch Pansy, a wriggling PS under her arm, throw the child in its cot and make the most dire threats about future deprivation of goodies, rights and freedom to which PS responds with greater appeals to Mummy than before – Pansy ignores her, returns to despatch the other two to their beds and instructs Martin to pretend PS isn't here – if you ask me Pansy blames him for the babe's discontent, blames him for not practising his coitus interruptus well enough, it's all his fault for getting carried away on a sunny evening and throwing caution to the winds – she also lays the blame on a certain brand of beer with a stronger alcohol content than he's used to and the liberality with which on that occasion he downed it – there's never been any doubt about the date of conception, it was a little island in a sea of virtual abstention at that time, so she can be precise in her apportioning of blame – their agreed method of birth control having signally failed to be effective, Martin is now expected either to abstain from intercourse altogether or employ the use of rubber, and while this may be the official policy of the house there are many breaches during which fingers are crossed and days subsequently counted – *I'm not taking any pill* is Pansy's avowed stand on the matter, so Martin's in the dangerous position of getting further blame for any future slips and blamed as now for the character and personal traits of any accidental issue

but Pansy doesn't actually come straight out with it – *got her father's temperament* is how she phrases it – *she's so like you* – to which Martin can only ever reply *got her mother's wilfulness* – and the two of them will then engage in a competitive banter that usually ends up with a joint communiqué that agrees on PS [Penny Samantha when she's the subject in this sort of conversation] being entirely her own person and therefore solely to blame for her own tantrums – of course, having arrived at this conclusion, her parents have along the way reminded themselves of her beauty, her winning ways, her intelligence and her lovableness, and the communiqué always ends with a closing statement on how lucky they are to have such a lovely child

Pansy's firmness this time seems to work, for PS gradually subsides and discovers a fresh interest in the soft toys that surround her – restricted to only three small ones at bedtime she always chooses Freddie Frog, because he's got sticky-out arms and legs and she's learnt how to twist them round her fingers, Lazy Daisy, a sort of indeterminate animal with a human face and a big tab on its leg which she can't get off, try as she might, and an unnamed teddy bear which she can cuddle and squeeze and chew when she wants to give vent to her feelings – so now she's quiet, well quieter at any rate, still sniffing a bit, but it means Pansy can now give proper attention to the others

can't I read too? begs Sean, although he doesn't usually have any penchant for doing so at bedtime, preferring to talk to his soldier doll – well, he gives it orders, makes it do what soldiers are supposed to do, obey – *I've got a book*

no, you're too tired, my boy – if you don't sleep you won't enjoy tomorrow

what are we doing?

you wait and see

I want to know now

well, we'll be going somewhere, I expect

don't you know?

it hasn't been decided yet – there are lots of things we can do

such as?

well, you wait and see – now go to sleep, you're tired

wait and see, the parents' answer to everything – you wait

and see, wait for what? – you spend your life waiting and seeing and every time something comes up it's never what you expected – well, it's never as exciting or as comforting or as rewarding as you hoped, indeed as you were led to believe it would be – wait and see, and sometimes it's better not to – what the parent should say is something definite, like 'we're going to Preston tomorrow' and then when tomorrow comes say 'no we're not, we've changed our minds, we're going to Auntie Gladys instead' – at least crushing disappointment would be better than that indecisive mood of possibilities, or sometimes that hopeful state of thinking your parents or whoever have something really exciting up their sleeve they're not letting on about – if Pansy were to say something like 'tomorrow, Sean my little darling, we're going to the fair and having lots of fun' at least the fellow will get to sleep easily and dream of wonderful things – and in the morning, when Mummy says 'no fair today, we've heard it's closed, we're going for a walk in the hills instead' Sean can cope with the disappointment because he's got all the day ahead of him in which to let it dissipate – also, he'll never again believe anything she says

eventually with the children settled [after a fashion] Pansy is able to get herself dressed and Martin can shave and they can have a swift tidy-up before the deadline of eight-thirty arrives along with . . .

are you sure we're not too early? – I know what it's like when the kids are that age, there's always so much to do clearing up after them, they leave their toys everywhere, don't they? – Beth deigns not to notice the railway track peeping from beneath the sofa and the bricks piled by the curtain and the big plastic red and yellow train that plays, if you give it a nudge, 'she'll be coming round the mountain' – when Michael and Abigail were toddlers somebody once gave them a little pushchair with two dolls in it, a boy and a girl who could be induced to turn their heads and speak [in strangled American accents] and on occasion not only did they speak to each other but took it upon themselves to hold a conversation without anyone touching them – they were weird and frightening and were quickly shoved [protesting their innocence] into the further reaches of the garden shed – Josh swore he heard them conspiring to get their own back

Josh stands behind her at the door, looking over her shoulder with the brightest of smiles – like two itinerant tradesmen wishing to fix the tiles on your roof they appear in a state of hopeful but resigned expectancy – his eyes seek out the form of Pansy, neat and trim in her candy-stripe blouse and beige slacks, you'd never guess that until five minutes ago she was looking the most unholy, harassed mess – Josh's eye is approving, a small smile plays round his mouth – over his wife's shoulder he starts to say good evening but her words are out first and so are Pansy's in reply, and Martin's too – a slight feeling of indignation prompts him to give Beth a push to propel her into the room – despite the jolt Beth continues to smile with that obliging 'can I help you?' smile – this is the face shop assistants and receptionists wear, always accompanied by the tilting of the head on one side, a supplicatory, rather fawning posture, perhaps with hands together, 'can I help you?' – in a man, of course, such a pose would be seen as somewhat effeminate and you wouldn't trust him to argue with the manager on your behalf – be that as it may, Beth smiles pleasantly at the Oxfords and Josh leers shyly at Pansy hoping she'll be impressed by his moleskin trousers

Martin: *right – now we haven't got a lot to drink beyond a crate of beer and a case of wine – that enough, you think? – I could send out to the off-licence if it isn't*

such facetiousness doesn't go down well with Pansy, who prefers the more straightforward approach – *what will you have, Beth, red or white?*

as it happens replies Beth *we've brought something to help you out – a bottle of gin? – I don't drink much wine these days, not unless it's organic*

and then it's by the bucket – Josh, trying to get control of the conversation momentarily catches a smile from Pansy – *regular evening drunk, Beth* – an unnecessary addition which of course brings a sharp elbow in the ribs from his wife to accompany the words of rebuttal and a distinct loss of interest by his target

let's skip this introductory chit-chat – most of you could write it yourself if you put a mind to it – I fully appreciate that you want to get to the meat of the story, otherwise what's the point of the whole exercise? – and that's something, isn't it, does it have a point? – where is this story going? – well, as I said at the beginning, I haven't really got much of an idea – as time's gone along I've formed a certain opinion of where it might lead, but then I expect you have as well, and whether our views will coincide, so that we triumphantly conclude together, triumphantly, that is, holding hands and sensing our faces flushed with pleasure, our hearts high with joy, well maybe that'll be the case – we can but hope – what you want me to do now is test that concurrence by seeing what sort of conversation the four might be having after the first hour or so, which means we'd better get back to the action

seating: there are four single chairs, so any ideas Josh may have entertained of cosying up to Pansy on a sofa are out of the question – same goes for Beth if she thought she might be thigh to thigh with Martin – they sit separately like travellers in an airport lounge, a chunky, almost rustic coffee table before them on which the glasses and bottles and packets of crisps reside as subjects under observation – the chairs are occupied with the men side by side and the women facing each other, but such is the way in which the chairs have been moved that the arm of Josh's chair touches Pansy's and Beth's Martin's – thus two pairs, resulting in conversation being lateral rather than oppositional, and a good deal of low murmuring emanating from the Waterfords into the ears of their respective hosts

not reciprocated, I have to say, for both Martin and Pansy, as if by some pre-arrangement, address the assembly foursquare in less than confidential voices – after all, it's a party, is it not? – and even when the words of the suitors might be deemed personal the Oxfords quite cheerfully respond as if the topic or whatever is wide open for communal discussion

Beth might say, intimately to Martin, *I do like your casual look – is that tomato ketchup on your shirt?* – but this is picked up by Pansy – *Martin, really!* – and commented on by Josh – *like your style* – and in no time at all they're busily discussing not only Martin's slapdash ways but the merits and the proper use of tomato ketchup, supposedly only for children up to a certain age – not at all what Josh and Beth want to discuss, so Josh forces the pace a little, using as his cue the introductory topic of clothing

one thing I've always had a yen for is candy-stripe shirts [and he says this to Pansy in a supposed undertone] *– preferably when they're wet – if you know what I mean*

oh, that would be very uncomfortable says Pansy in a loud voice *– wearing a wet shirt, no thanks – better without, surely*

disconcerted is a good word, Josh is disconcerted – the others are amused – Pansy smiles broadly around, relishing her joke *– can't see what you'd find at all interesting about seeing me in a wet shirt – you wouldn't want to, would you, Martin?*

I've seen you in a wet shirt

I was a lot younger then

you were under a shower

so I was – that was before Sean was born, wasn't it? – and the knowing, familiar looks passing between husband and wife serve to exclude the attentions of Josh, as I suspect was intended

he looks downcast, throws a glance at Beth, amused Beth, enjoying the struggle he's having – she throws her hat into the ring

with that tomato ketchup it should be you in the wet shirt – come on, I'll sponge it off for you – and she half rises in her chair, looks expectantly at Martin

it's at such a point that obedient husbands look to their wives for guidance, which is exactly what Martin does, whether an imploring look, a beseeching one, or simply a look which asks if he's allowed to enjoy the prospect of a woman and a wet sponge

Pansy's enjoying herself – the power women have over men! – for a second she just looks straight back at Martin and then, with the magnanimity of the benevolent autocrat says *I think that's a good idea – you'll find something to use in the bathroom, Beth – don't wake the children, they've just gone off – and be gentle with him*

exeunt Martin and Beth, he looking half-pleased, half-embarrassed, and Beth all smiles pulling at his shirt to steer him from the room

Pansy turns in her seat to face Josh, a man also with that half-pleased, half-embarrassed look, but in his case mixed with the surprise of a man who's discovered a turn of fortune

now then she says *what were you saying about a wet shirt?*

well, you were saying you'd prefer not to wear one – I'm all for that

I doubt very much if you'd want to see me in my under-wear

you're right, I don't think you should have the underwear
what, none at all?
definitely not
that wouldn't be very seemly, would it?
I think it would be very seemly – naked as nature intended
oh dear, that sounds frightening – I don't think I could do that

Pansy, what are you up to? – someone so staunch in virtue playing this sort of game, really – Josh, of course, thinks he's well in with a chance here, and such carrying-on isn't something I envisaged, nor of which I approve – Pansy, pull yourself together, the wine's gone to your head

of course you could – Josh oozes intimacy, presses his shoulder against hers, the closest contact he can make, seated as they are in separate chairs

Pansy stands up [good for her, I was getting worried] – *let's see what the others are getting up to – that shirt of Martin's is a fairly new one, I hope the ketchup doesn't ruin it – Beth!*

so disappointment for Josh, triumph for virtue – he flops back in his chair, stunned as all men are by the sudden switch to domestic affairs that women can achieve without any effort

well, in the bathroom there's a wet shirt for sure, as Beth's managed to soak the whole of Martin's chest without making any impression on the stain – when Pansy walks in she's crouching down before him, wet flannel in hand, silkily running it over the open shirt while Martin leans against the basin with a look on his face, if not entirely of rapture, at least of surprised pleasure

Beth – *it's very stubborn*

Martin – *I'll have to take it off now*

Pansy – *bound to be stubborn if it's **his** shirt, goes without saying, doesn't it, darling – I think you'd better change it*

Beth rises, puts the flannel in the basin – as she smiles her tongue peeps out to touch her upper lip – *and I was just beginning to make an impression on it*

over Pansy's shoulder, Josh – *she undressing you, mate?*

it's a small bathroom with a low ceiling, one room

squeezed into what once might have been a horse-stall, and four people congregating here [Josh really only with his head in, taking the opportunity and the liberty of resting his hands on Pansy's shoulders] is a little too much of a press – hard up against the basin Martin inadvertently leans on the faucet, splashes cold water over his back

a loud noise comes from along the passage – *ssh!* – Ellen, not yet asleep, presumably trying to complete *Wives and Daughters* – Pansy wriggles out past Josh to go along to her room, leaving the others to sort themselves out

you'll ruin your eyes, darling, why don't you settle down?

how can I? – it's too noisy – Ellen's suitably indignant

well, we'll try to talk in whispers – Sean's gone off and I see PS is fast asleep, so it only leaves you

well, I don't think you can reasonably expect me, with all the racket you four are making, to lay my head softly on the pillow, close my eyes and fall into a slumberous sleep until the golden dawn, now can you?

it would appear that Ellen's like this, full of long sentences bearing the flavour of the book she happens to be reading – this is quite a short sentence for her, but it's late in the evening – sometimes she'll throw in a few archaic phrases no one understands, to the derisory snorts of her brother who'll accuse her of being stuck-up and the rather aloof reception of her parents who'll look at each other in stifled amusement – Pansy brings on the down-to-earth mother act as she tucks the sheet into the bed [to Ellen's discomfiture, it has to be said] – *if you don't get your sleep you'll not be able to read, your eyes will be too sore – now settle down, we'll try to be as quiet as we can* the book obediently goes on the floor, the light goes out at Pansy's touch, Ellen humours her mother by saying no more and closing her eyes – but she's not laying on her side, she's laying on her back, and we all know in that position she'll daydream for the next hour or so

I've not had enough time to analyse Abigail, but I've already decided that while she may have years on her side she certainly hasn't got what I'd call intelligence – for a start she seems only to be able to think about boys, as if life begins and ends with them – I know all about boys, I've got a brother, and I've watched them at school and elsewhere and honestly, what a waste of time they are! – perhaps when they grow up and become fit for something they might have their uses as fictional characters, but until then they're a waste of space, a waste of space!

and another thing about Abigail, she's so materialistic – in the short time we've spent together I've had to endure long lists of what she's got at home in her bedroom, really it's surprising there's room for a bed – and what about this mobile of hers, you can practically communicate with the people on the space station, and watch them eating their breakfast! – I'm almost alone among my friends in having no phone because, what for? – why spend time, let alone your parents' money, fiddling about talking to people for the sake of it when you could be curled up somewhere reading a good book? – Abigail told me she was the fastest in her class at sending a text message to the girl sitting next to her, as if that was something to be proud of – I'm thinking of asking her if she's come across Jane Eyre *yet, but I expect she'll answer that she must go to another school*

Ellen snuggles her head into the pillow, listens to the whispers and the shuffles of the adults as they go back into the sitting room and close the passage door – she's tired, physically at least, but her mind will still be full of Molly Gibson and Roger Hamley and whether or not they ever married – it was surely a tragedy their story wasn't finished – what a good idea it would be for someone one day to write the ending!

back in the sitting room the quartet of grown-ups settles down again, this time with Martin wearing a clean shirt – the arrangement of figures has changed as an accompaniment to his discarding the tomato ketchup shirt, for Josh now has his wife nearest to him, while Pansy perches herself on the arm of Martin's chair – they talk in low voices for the remainder of the evening, subdued by the reminder of Ellen with her stated wish for quiet – the spark of enjoyment has gone out now, no more flirting is done by anyone, least of all by Josh, who's beginning to feel he needn't have left his shirt under-buttoned and regrets the lavish use of his expensive after-shave – Beth still gives coy looks at Martin, but he fails to notice them, being uncomfortably aware of his wife's staid assessment of all the goings-on

by ten-thirty the evening's staggered to a damp end and all four readily agree that it's time for an early night – whispered farewells are exchanged and Martin thankfully closes the door on the visitors, as equally thankfully they leave

when Beth and Josh step over Brewster as they enter their front door the dog gives a huge sigh, troubled as he is by the inconsideration of these humans – he likes to get a full night's sleep and he's hoping Josh won't remember there's been no evening walkies – he doesn't care if there is a cat out there, the thought of having to be paraded round a dark yard with whispered admonitions to do something and quick just doesn't appeal to him at this moment

at two-twenty-three precisely PS calls from her cot – *Mummy, Mummy – bed's all wet*

at four-seventeen Brewster barks loudly, twice, having been awoken by a sniffing sound outside the front door

at six-thirty-two both barrels are discharged from Mr Broadfield's shotgun, presumably at rabbits, but one can't be sure

4

Monday morning

did that have to be done, was it necessary at such an hour?
– babies waking are one thing, dogs barking another, but
shooting off your gun at such an unearthly hour, that's a bit
much, isn't it? – these people are on holiday, remember

that's the time you go after rabbits

but you're only pretending – you didn't shoot any rabbits,
did you?

*not the point – if I had been after them I'd have been out
earlier still – early evening and early morning, that's the time,
that's when they come out and socialize – they sit there staring into space, best time to get them – if you're quick you can
get two before they bolt – done it often enough, so I should
know*

then why don't you do it for real now?

*rabbit? – peasant's food, pot-food, and you've got to skin
it, haven't you? – why go to all that trouble when you can
have a nice bit of steak from the supermarket?*

rabbits are free

steak's nicer

those chickens of yours, do you eat them?

what? – go to all that trouble? – I can get chicken where I get steak – have you ever plucked a chicken? – my father used to get me at it when I was a boy, one of the worst jobs imaginable, feathers everywhere – we ate off the farm in those days, everyone did then, but that was long ago

Mr Broadfield rubs his chin – the rasping sound reminds him he hasn't yet shaved – he's got a large chin, one of those rough kinds that always look as if the owner hasn't shaved, whatever time of day it may be, he's got leather-tanned cheeks and a slight reddish tint to his somewhat bulbous nose, so all-in-all he looks a bit of a colourful fellow – oddly enough, despite the fertility of the chin and cheeks, his eyebrows are hard to distinguish, just a few wispy hairs that curl in all directions, one of them probing upwards like an antenna – his grey eyes lurk in deep sockets, an evolutionary design feature no doubt due to having to peer over the landscape in all weathers, bred into him like it's bred into certain breeds of dogs – I must say that Lance hasn't inherited this characteristic, but then he's not the farming type, by all accounts

I'll say he isn't – bit of a worry, that lad

he'll find his way

don't know about that – couldn't have got him plucking chickens, that's for sure, not him – vegetarian now, or supposed to be – still eats fish

piscivorous?

that what it's called? – well, if you say so, he eats fish – don't know where he gets it all from – not from me or his mother, she likes a nice bit of bacon and eggs and sausage for

114

breakfast – which is where I'm off to now, if you'll excuse
me – I've got a lot to do today

market day?

course not, don't be silly – we don't have market days any
more, not round here – well, if we do it's not a farming
market like you probably mean, where you take your geese
and haggle over hogs, fairy-take stuff that – no, we're off to
the big stores this afternoon, she wants to get some clothes,
you know what women are like

Mr Broadfield strides off, wellington boots, wax jacket,
woollen cap, gun under arm, looking the part at least – the
lights are on in the farmhouse kitchen and the tempting
aroma of that bacon's beginning to pervade the courtyard –
there's Sammy, slinking along the cottage wall, taunting
Brewster – it seems even old cats have evil intentions

it's a glorious day! – across to the east there are golden
strands of wispy cloud clothing the sun, but everywhere else
the sky's a watercolour blue – the air that the breakfast aroma
floats on is of a slight crispness, like the bacon should be –
fragrant hints of straw mingle with other hints of animal
hide, the raw smell of silage lurks beneath them . . .

that's dreadful, isn't it? – perhaps it's best to leave out any
attempt to describe the air, the atmosphere, I've never been
very good at it – when my wife left me, oh, nine years ago
now it was, one of her complaints was that I was forever
trying to impress people with my descriptive powers, of which
she was convinced I had none – well, that was one of the
reasons she left, there was this other bloke, of course – no, I
mustn't get on to that, this is no place for my sad story, I'm
supposed to be telling other people's stories

well, they're not about yet, of course – in the Waterford household there are snores all round, Mr Broadfield's broadside hasn't had much effect – even Abigail's snoring gracefully, but then I believe she's always been a restless sleeper, throwing herself about the bed, wheezing and breathing loudly even as a small child – Michael's more refined, only an occasional *phew!* as if something in his dreams surprises him – the parents are reasonably quiet, just a snort now and then from Josh, a deep sigh from Beth

the Oxfords? – let's not go too close, PS is asleep but at this time of day she can create havoc if she wakes up – Sean is as quiet as a mouse, an angel on a pillow, golden hair and pink cheek – Ellen lies on her back, in repose, hands clasped on her stomach, posing like some church effigy – Martin's a bit like Josh, a gentle snort now and then, but Pansy . . . Pansy's wide awake – her mind is full of things, she can't sleep – the gun woke her and now she finds all the previous day's events crowding her, chief among them that dialogue with Josh

mixed with my feeling of embarrassment is fear – primarily I'm afraid of having given Josh, in making those flirtatious comments, the totally wrong idea of my character – not that I can't be flirtatious when I want to be, but it all depends on whom I'm being flirtatious with – it was only when I noticed a certain gleam in his eye that I realized Josh wasn't like Martin say, like other men – where the flow of the conversation's some kind of game, where it's recognized by both parties as such, then flirtatious banter remains just that – what I saw in Josh was the deadly earnest desire to take it as a serious overture to other things, and that's what frightens me

that Beth was doing something similar with Martin doesn't bother me, I know it was no more than the sort of frivolous exchange I thought I was having with Josh – Beth can't possibly have designs on someone like Martin, not in the way Josh has on me

she lies awake worrying over Josh's intentions for quite some time until it isn't worth staying in bed – creeping into the kitchen she quietly makes herself some camomile tea, takes it into the sitting room – *if Josh does have evil intentions he knows what he can do with them – I'm not so unworldly that I don't realize this kind of thing goes on, this 'let's go on holiday together and swap partners' routine – yes, but only if you're the type that would do it when you weren't on holiday, only if you're the immoral, promiscuous type to begin with, which neither Martin or me are*

Pansy sighs, just a little one, the matter's not as important as all that, there are much bigger things to think about – PS will be awake in a moment and she's not the kind of child to spend long in her cot of a morning, she wants to be up and about, rattling her bars and all but calling *get me out of here!* – Pansy gets up, goes through into the kitchen to start warming some milk – *I'll just have to be firm with Josh, try to avoid situations where he thinks he can try it on again – the best way is to treat him as a little boy having a fancy for a big girl, keep reminding him that his mother in the shape of Beth has got her eye on him, won't let him do anything naughty*

true to form it's PS who first awakes, doing just what she always does, crying *altogether now* in an attempt to wake the household, and then a litany of all the names she can say from Mummy down to Sean and adding in for good measure all her grandparents and the boy next door who's three and a half and thinks she's funny – Sean wakes easily but Ellen turns over with a frown, buries herself beneath the duvet – Martin, trained as are all men to awake only to the sound of a dripping tap, continues his gentle wheezing

eager to help, Sean accosts his mother in the kitchen, offers to let PS out of her cot

are you going to change her as well?

no! – that's your job – boys don't do that

Daddy does – sometimes

ugh, no! – I'm not doing it

Sean goes off to play with his trucks in the middle of the sitting-room floor, Pansy lifts PS from her cot with a cuddle and a squeeze or two, words of endearment in her ear, a quick glance at Ellen frowning away, pretending to be fast asleep, a look in at Martin still experiencing the beauty sleep which she knows she needs more than he does, and the day begins with the joys of a soiled night nappy and an uncooperative toddler

Sean has great imagination, he's one of those blessed boys who can create a vast world of excitement from two small toys and the use of all the furniture in the room – he makes noises, he talks to himself in various accents, sometimes out of the side of his mouth, and providing you're not in the line of fire will ignore any other human – of course, it's a well-known fact that babies like PS aren't human, well, not yet anyway, and so Sean finds she's a bit of a nuisance when placed on the floor to run [waddle is a better description] across his plan of battle – unable to ignore her he endows her with the status of the enemy, instructing her how to avoid having one of his toys run over her toes, suggesting instead that she become a large piece of terrain over which he can deploy his armies – PS has her own ideas on warfare, wants to have the two trucks to herself, so intervention in the shape of Marshal Pansy is inevitable and, to Sean's mind, desirable, but equitable dispensation of justice means he comes off as badly as PS, so he sits on the floor and sulks, a forlorn general with no hope ever again of overall command

when Martin gets out of bed the world has to know it, for is it not true that men are masters in their own household and must be respected, if not worshipped? – excessive stretching of the arms accompanied by wide uncovered yawns is the first sight the world, well Pansy and the children, has of its master, and it's not, as she has often said, a pretty one, especially as the stretching reveals his navel, one of man's least attractive bits

can you wake Ellen? – she's gone back to sleep

this is a guess, but Pansy has to find something for her master to start his day with and it's best that it takes the form of an instruction, something he understands – *we want to get breakfast out of the way before getting ready*

oh yes, it's the beach today, isn't it?

if the weather holds – it's fine at the moment but we want to get there early in case it changes, as it has a habit of doing – I expect the others will have to be chivvied, I don't get the feeling of them being early risers

no yawns Martin – *not like us* – and he goes to wake Ellen

Pansy sits PS on the booster and gives her a yoghurt – the

child's quite good at feeding herself but she's got a clumsy spoon which today has a will of its own, takes itself out of her hands and on to the floor with a large dollop of peach yoghurt going splat on the only bit of good carpet – *never mind, dear* soothes Pansy – *not your fault* – which is said to avoid any possible ructions on the part of PS who thinks she always gets the blame for everything and is quick to state her innocence loudly – she stares down at the deposit with a look that transfers any culpability directly to the yoghurt, which as the world knows has as much a mind of its own as any other inanimate thing

that's naughty she says in admonition as Pansy bends with a piece of kitchen roll – *all gone now*

what would you like now? – do you want some toast?

PS thinks about this, mouth open and eyes to heaven, her over-acted pose of a child giving great consideration to a matter of serious concern – *toast!* she finally decides, spitting out the word with a sharp nod of the head, an action of positive affirmation – *toast!* she repeats in case her mother's about to ignore her

toast what?

toast and butter! – good game for PS

toast, please

toast and butter! – too good a game to give up easily

Pansy's the one to give up, it's too early in the day to make a stand and risk upsetting the child – she makes the toast while PS plays with her empty yoghurt cup and sticky spoon

Sean, sit up, please – you want some toast as well?

I'm having cereal

yes, but toast after that?

okay

pardon?

yes, please

so, one little success there at least – Martin comes to
report that Ellen's refusing to get out of bed

*says she'll get up at nine today – **rise**, she said, I'll rise
at nine*

did she – I trust you made her see otherwise

well . . .

Pansy sighs – *I'll sort her out – Ellen! – come for breakfast, you've got two minutes* – which elicits only silence from
along the passage – *do you hear me, two minutes* – a groan
floats along in answer, neither assent nor refusal

sorry about last night says Martin

why?

the shirt, the ketchup

oh, one of those things – but with a thoughtful air Pansy
adds – *you'll have to watch her*

watch who?

Beth, of course – she rather fancies you

*very sensible of her, in that case – but I noticed Josh was
all over you*

*a dose of cold-water treatment will sort him out – I think
Beth has a more subtle approach*

*I can't imagine there'll be any holiday romance – don't
worry, she was just larking about*

think so? – Pansy gives him a straight look – *yes, you're
right, she's not the type to lead you on until you find
you've gone too far*

he smiles, gives a little laugh – *I'm hardly likely to go for my mate's wife, even on holiday*

Pansy butters the toast, looks down at what she's doing – *all the same . . .* she breaks off to give PS a half-slice before going up to Martin and continuing by whispering in his ear, being conscious of Sean's own flapping ones – *I think we both need to dampen their ardour*

Martin looks at her quizzically – the idea that another woman could take a fancy to him, while a suggestion gratifying in itself, seems to be something he's never considered – *it's a bit unlikely, isn't it? – all the kids everywhere? – I think they're just being silly*

well, you've been warned – and that's the last thing Pansy's able to say on the subject, for to everyone's surprise a sour-looking Ellen stands in the doorway in a pose of abject displeasure

not much of a holiday when we have to get up early every morning

we're going to the beach

in the breasts of millions of children these words would produce a surge of excitement, they'd cry yippee and hug their parents, rush off for their buckets and spades and swimming costumes and be so excited they'd want to skip breakfast – Ellen, we must remember, is a mature woman with a view of life drawn from a cursory study of classic novels, and that's more than enough to sober her up to the point of restraining her childish emotions – *the beach? – so?*

do I have to? – it was trains yesterday, and now the beach today – it's going to rain, I know it is

no, it's not – Martin's the only person in the family who

dares to provoke argument with his eldest daughter, but that's simply because he's unable to learn from experience – *it'll be fine and sunny and you'll enjoy yourself, you know you will*

Ellen gives him a look which, if you didn't know it was something she practised in a mirror, would be regarded as one of contempt – *I'm not a beach person, you should know that, Daddy – I hate beaches – where is it anyway?*

just ten miles – lots of sand, plenty of rocks to climb about on – you'll love it

I don't want to go

come and sit down, have some breakfast intervenes Pansy – *we'll be having only a picnic lunch so you need to have something now*

Ellen slouches to a chair, sits leaning away from the active elbows of her brother

all together now chants PS – *all together now – toast, Ellen?* – and gives the bigger girl the tilted head and expectant look which she's tried to copy from her mother

during breakfast Martin's obviously thinking hard and once it's over and he's momentarily alone with Pansy he returns to the subject of the ardent Waterfords – *so you think Beth's a flirt?*

Pansy gives him a warm smile – *and what are you hoping for?*

don't be silly – no, do you think she's like that?

I think if you respond to her playing around she'll be quite ready to carry on with it

Martin's face registers every one of his emotions, passing across his face so rapidly that Pansy laughs and cuddles him *don't worry* she says with authority – *I'll protect you*

what about Josh? he asks as the impact of the subject reaches him – *is he like that with you?*

probably – but don't worry, I can handle him

what is it with these two then? – middle-aged fantasy?

Pansy draws back, looks thoughtful – *I think you're right, it must be that – they think hey, it's a holiday, let's swap partners*

Martin appears horrified – *we hardly know them, they're not exactly our best friends – anyway, being on holiday doesn't mean you lose your sense of judgement – as far as Beth's concerned I couldn't fancy her less – where do you pick up this stuff, some women's magazine, I suppose – holiday swapping! – terrible thought – you don't fancy Josh, do you?*

good God no! – far too greasy for me

well, this is going to be a fine holiday if we have to keep fighting them off

Pansy adopts a philosophical mien – *it won't be like that – I don't suppose they sit there of a night and plan it out, it's just what you said, little fantasies, each of them getting fed up with the other and grasping at straws – how long have they been together?*

with a less anxious appearance now, Martin frowns as he thinks – if you merely ask the time of him he'll frown before he answers you, as though the effort of producing an answer is as taxing as if you'd asked him to calculate the square root of seventeen – he owns slightly unruly eyebrows which come together at the deep line of his frown giving him the appearance of a tawny owl looking down from a tree – his round brown eyes increase this fancy to the point where you almost anticipate a hoot

much longer than us, about twenty years, I suppose – is that what it is, twenty-year itch?

could be, but it'll pass if we don't make any response – play a straight bat, isn't that what you'd say?

Martin, delighted at his wife's grasp of male terminology, produces a wide smile before kissing her forehead – *no more ketchup* he says – *yes, a straight bat*

let's withdraw from this cosy scene of a family having breakfast, a family, shall we say, of impeccable moral characteristics – the rapport between the parents could, to a jaded outsider, appear as something rather cloying, almost to the point where you wish one of the Waterfords **would** advance their suit with determination, just to test the security of the Oxfords' drawbridge but who knows, maybe that will happen before the week's out, I certainly couldn't guess what might turn up, despite me being technically the author of their fates – ha, that's a laugh

the Waterfords are beginning to stir – Josh lets Brewster out into the yard and goes into the kitchen to join Beth as she makes the coffee – dressed in a loose dressing gown he stands watching her, staring vaguely, rubbing a hand across his chest as though the medallion's absence is bothering him – Beth, still in a little world of her own, prepares the drink mechanically, nothing to say to her husband any more than he has to say to her – when the business is done he follows her with the tray into the sitting room, where they still say nothing, almost as if they've fallen out over something left to himself in the empty yard Brewster prowls all the corners, marks out some territory and has a good, satisfying scratch – at the closed gate he stands for a while, staring across the fields, sniffing the cool morning air with all its perfumed perplexities – this is the place for a dog, not the cramped fences of a suburban garden and the soft carpets of a centrally heated home – this is the life, he must be thinking, space, air, the smells of nature – could he induce Josh to make him a kennel in the yard? – that would be a **real** holiday, sleeping outside of a night

instinct makes him turn his head – on the far side of the yard, up against another gate, the one that leads to the back of the farmhouse, sits the cat, no movement on its part, Brewster hesitates – he's not a stupid dog, he can work things out and he can see that with any hint of a charge from him, any bark even, the cat can easily slip between the palings of the gate he sits beside – no, Brewster's not silly, and he's not one to make a laughing-stock of himself – he too sits down, prepares to give as good as he's getting and wait for the cat's next move

like all cats Sammy's highly conscious of his dignity – when you get to be as old and as wise as he then you don't put yourself in positions that might undermine or possibly assault that dignity – so both animals, like commanders of opposing forces, use intelligence to dictate their strategy

the stand-off, or sit-off, lasts some good few minutes before Brewster, adopting a more leisured approach, lies down with his paws stretched out before him – this incurs some activating momentum in Sammy, who stands up and very slowly, silkily, begins to walk along the wall of the farmhouse away from his protective gate – it's obvious to both of them that a point of no return will come, a point where Brewster can charge, a point where flight on the part of Sammy will be the only option – but so slowly is he moving, so carefully, that Brewster can do nothing but watch raptly with bated breath

Sammy continues gliding [no other word for it] along the wall, head low and held stiffly forward as though stalking some unaware mouse – Brewster, tensely attentive, mesmerized by the moment, keeps **his** head up, chin in the air, eyes unblinking – then, with a slow turn of the head, Sammy looks across with large calculating eyes, looks directly at Brewster, freezes in position – Brewster begins to quiver with excitement, but disappointment strikes again for him as, less slowly now, possibly because he's just remembered his breakfast's waiting, Sammy turns back to the gate, slips between the palings and disappears from view – Brewster can't help a short, crisp bark escaping as he stands up – a quick trot across to the gate, snout poked through, fails to satisfy any of his expectations – no sign of Sammy, nothing – cowards, that's what they are, these cats, no moral fibre, always taking the easy way out at the first sight of a challenge

the short brisk bark of the dog, staccato, crisping the morning air, cuts into the dreams and sleepful escapism of one person, Michael, who wakes with a start and turns towards the window to look at the day beyond the windowpane – *my heart sinks, I'm waking with a sinking heart and why's that? – because I remember now, this is the day they've planned to go to the beach, they, the adults, them in charge – I suppose I can say that even recently, right up to this year,*

I've nearly always in the past enjoyed going to the beach – and I did enjoy it this Easter when we caravanned in Cornwall – well, not really enjoyed it so much as tolerated it – but now with a sense of doom I feel no excitement at the prospect of going to a beach, none whatever – I've grown out of it, that's the trouble, I'm too old now to be going off with my mummy and my daddy and my little sister like some ideal happy family, and then we've got to go with those others, that other ideal family, it'll be dreadful, it'll be sickening – the only one of the Oxfords I can possibly give any time for is that little Ellen, but she's too young to pay attention to, people would think I was funny if I did that, think I was a paedo or something, though I wouldn't mind looking her up in a few years' time when she'll be old enough to have fun with, she's got a certain something about her – but overall it's a dismal prospect of a day on a beach with a lot of people I'd rather not be with, people who'll only annoy me, people who'll keep on talking at me, ranting at me, telling me I should be enjoying myself

would you call life exciting when you have to spend it with your family? – going to school's better, not when you're actually in the classroom, in my school that's a complete waste of time, no, it's being with your mates, especially at hometime, out on the street, that's the only reason school's better – half the trouble with the idea of going off to Dublin or Manchester is it's not where your mates are – well, you call them your mates but to be honest I've no close attachment to any particular ones, they're really just the kids I hang around with – there are plenty of others in other towns, aren't there, easy to find another crowd of mates – it's being with *like-minded people, that's the main thing, people who under-stand about life and think like you do, instead of 'Mummy' and 'Daddy' who only think about themselves and how many 'friends' they can make – there's no way in which me and Dad will ever see eye to eye on anything, no chance whatever of him trying to see my point of view, that's a dead dog – and my mum's given up on me, she only ever considers her dar-ling Abigail and what she might like – to be truthful, and I'm being bold in this, when I say I don't like any of them, and God, I feel a sense of relief at being able to say that now, to come down firmly with that opinion – no, I don't like them, I don't like them, and I know for a fact they don't much like me, that's obvious*

Michael rolls on to his back, puts his hands behind his head and stares at the Artexed ceiling in a manner not too far removed from contemplation – he'll be fifteen in a couple of months, fifteen, and here he is with no girlfriend, no real mates, no lifestyle, nothing – *there are boys my age who have it all and more besides **and** they don't get aggro from their parents – what they've done is to say so what! and put up two fingers – I should do just that, shouldn't I? – I should put up two fingers to the world and say so what – look at it now, look at me, stuck miles from anywhere, nothing here of any interest whatsoever and having to be carted from here to there with my family doing things I absolutely hate – it's no go, there's got to be more to it – look, what I need to do is get back on my own patch – or find a new one where my parents won't bother me, that's a better idea – right now I should plan things*

mind you, unless I've got some money where do I go?

*– and if I do have some money what do I do? – I know about B&Bs but that's not exactly my style, is it, not really independence-street – **lots** of money, that's what I'll need, and I've always known how I can get it, out of a cash machine, that's how – all I've got to do is get hold of a card – with lots of money I can get myself set up in a studio flat, that'd be good, that'd be very good*

these are thoughts of revolution, aren't they, revolution with knobs on, revolution that looks as though it's pretty certain to encompass blatant theft as well as deceit – where does he think he's going to get the card? – that's the trouble with doing away with real money, real cash that jingles in your pocket when you play with it, what they once called the grand spondulix – now all you have is a microchip popped in a slot and you can get everything from fish and chips to condoms, and what's more, if you're greedy like Michael, you can still get cash, wads of notes spilling out of the wall at the press of a button and all you need is the card – and of course a PIN-number – that might stall him a bit, the PIN-number, some folks are real cagey about letting on what theirs is, they don't go round with it tattooed on their forehead [but if they do, don't forget it'll be back-to-front] – he lies here now, hands behind his head, sorting out one little peak of the Artex from all the others as an aid to concentration, focuses hard on it, must have lots of things to consider, must Michael, not least the acquisition of that PIN-number

Abigail, now what of her? – she's now awake too, not quite as wide as Michael but still with her eyes open

all the girls in my class are going for brunette now, it's all the thing – definitely not an addiction to fashion, no, those girls that come in next morning having changed overnight claim to be merely experimenting, as you do – well, you have to, you're almost expected to at my age – I've thought about being a redhead, not quite going all the way to brown because long, flowing copper tints can be almost as exciting as proper brunette, and in any case you don't say brunette, you say auburn, that's the colour today – what about my friend and close associate, my closest mate, Nula? – what a colour she's got! – that's the auburn shade they're all trying to get, if only I was brave enough to try it, but what would Mum say? – still, she's not the colour she was born with, anyone can see that and it's not very well done – growing it out, she says, oh yes? – I wouldn't tell her what I planned, that way would be certain prohibition, all right for Mummy, not at all suitable for a girl my age, I can hear her saying it now, so the best way is to follow Nula's example, she just went ahead one Saturday morning and got it done, faced the music afterwards – fait accompli, that's what it was

well, not so revolutionary as her brother, that's a relief, though for her I suppose it's a massive step towards independence, perhaps in its way as big as Michael's – fly on the wall, that's the expression to use when they each do their deeds, pity we'll not be there to witness it, but they'll all have gone their different ways by then, the Oxfords and the Waterfords, gone back to their everyday lives well out of our sight – but while they're still here we can enjoy their company

Beth talks to Josh – now I'm privileged to be able to inform you that there's never much to be said at this time of a weekday morning, it's the same when they're at home, each of them getting ready to go to work, caught up in their individual lives – Beth has to shout a lot but that's at the children, urging them to get off to school, Josh just slips out sometimes without a goodbye – weekends are different, I believe, they actually talk to one another, but not much before eleven o'clock, or in Michael's case twelve and then he's more of a grunter until after lunch when he wakes up and talks nineteen to the dozen – but today Beth breaks the mould, she talks to Josh and it's not even nine o'clock

Pansy wasn't impressed when I told her of my pyjamas, she just shrugged and said she always wears a nightie

well, so do you

but she hasn't even seen them, I only told her about them, I expect her to show some interest – anyway, I know I wear a nightie but that's not the point, these are designer pyjamas

can't they be worn?

I don't wear pyjamas, as you just said, I wear a nightie – these are designer label

so you've got a pair of pyjamas you're not going to wear?

oh, why is it so hard to make men understand things?

I may not know a lot about Beth, but one thing's certain, she's a woman of fashion – when it comes to up-to-the-minute styles, whether of clothing or household articles, Beth knows her onions, knows what's in and what's out, knows what she should be wearing, what she should be owning – if she says designer pyjamas are an essential constituent of every woman's wardrobe, then so be it, Pansy's obviously got no sense of style and no hope of ever being an example to her daughters – it's Abigail who's the inheritor of her mother's awareness of style, and this is one of the reasons why Beth is so eager to employ her talents in sniffing out the good and true from the junk to be found in all the chainstores – she wouldn't want little Abigail growing up at a disadvantage, so she's duty-bound to set a good example – *I can see that little Ellen looking a frump when she's fifteen*

wanting designer labels and affording them are two widely differing positions, and the only way any reconciliation can be made is by Beth having a full-time job in the perfume section of a department store – Josh will often complain that his dinner, which once used to be waiting for him when he got home, now has to be hastily constructed from ready-meals and slammed in the microwave, a lot of difference to the home-made steak and kidney pudding or braised lamb chops with new potatoes that used to be the style before she went out to work full-time – *it's not your fault* Beth'll say to him *but your salary doesn't cover all the essentials like it used to – we don't want to be scrimping and scraping, do we?* – and if he makes any mention of extravagance [not that he does now, having had his fingers scorched several times in the early days of her employment] she'll counter it with reference to his 'boy's toys' as though there was some equitable yardstick of comparison

but when it comes to matters of dress and matters of style Josh is not one to be left behind, as we've seen – if any of his money goes on boy's toys then they're more likely than not to be items of jewellery, for which he has something of a penchant – most of us have one watch, for instance, or if we have two the other's an old one someone once bought us a few years ago and we hate it or it's bust, but Josh, believe it or not, has nine! – I'm forced to put an exclamation mark there because it represents a raised eyebrow – nine? – nine watches? – oh yes, one for each day of the week and two for special occasions and if you tell him you're surprised by this news he'll put on his rather offended look and say *doesn't everyone?* – so between the two of them there's quite a lot of competition in respect of wardrobe space and vacancies in the small wall-safe hidden behind a picture of Beth's grandad dressed in full military regalia, a traditional place and the first spot burglars will look at – their wardrobes have strayed, or rather they've taken on a life of their own and like some wooden organism spread themselves round the upper floor of the house to occupy any available room or landing space that will accommodate them – Josh knows a carpenter who within a few days will competently fill any spare corner with a wardrobe, though it has to be said the upper floor is now full and plans are having to be made for an extension to the dining room which will give space not only for more wall-safes for jewellery but plenty of shelves for further designer pyjamas

tell me honestly, Josh – do I embarrass you?

what?

do I embarrass you? – do you find me dowdy, don't I dress right? – I always try to look my best, I make sure my hair's well styled and always presentable, you don't see me in the sort of casual clothes other women wear, women like Pansy for instance – I always try to look my best

what are you talking about? – you dress fine, you always do

you're proud of me?

of course I'm proud of you! – what's brought this on? – with the cautious movement of one who's not sure where the conversation's leading and is it going to mean trouble for him, Josh picks up his coffee and takes it into the bathroom

Beth's unable, of course, to say what brought it on, she doesn't know what made her say anything in the first place, it came out spontaneously – *what was I thinking of, has it anything to do with Pansy not being interested in my pyjamas? – it wasn't so much the way she said 'that must be nice' as the look in her eyes, as if she was thinking I was being too critical in making a comparison between us over the quality of clothing – was she thinking 'well, pyjamas are one thing, but look at you now'? – and who was she to talk anyway, looking like a woman with no idea at all of how to dress for the occasion? – I found myself asking Josh for his view out of a panicky moment of self-doubt – fancy asking him, what does he know about it? – I'm better off getting Abi's opinion, at least she's interested in how I look and what I buy*

thinking of Abi, I wonder if she's ready yet for a new hair style, she's had that dreadful let-it-all-hang style for six months now, I really ought to persuade her to visit the salon again – she didn't like what they did last time, but she was a lot younger then, now she's almost grown up, I can hardly believe it, nearly thirteen – when I was that age my mother would have had a fit if I'd said I wanted it styled, you wait until you're sixteen, she would have said, and I had to as well – Abi's lucky, she's got a mother who understands what a young girl wants

re-enter Josh, this time without the mug of coffee or the dressing gown – *what time are we off, did we agree anything?*

go and get something on! – Abi might come down any minute!

oh, she'll be fast asleep, you know what the kids are like

don't bank on it – go and get dressed!

you're so prudish – what time are we off, do you know?

no, I don't, but just go back to the bathroom

a slight smile on his face, Josh does as he's told, goes back to the bathroom – Beth shakes her head in disbelief – *how can he be so thoughtless, wandering about naked as if it didn't matter! – not just Abi, is it, how would I feel if Michael walked in?*

as it happens there's no chance of that, both the children are heavily occupied with their thoughts of rebellion, each of them plotting and planning their respective moves – my experience of children of any age is limited as Theresa never wanted any – a childless, loveless marriage it was, otherwise I could now have teenage rebels quietly brooding in their bedrooms – my girlfriend's adamant she doesn't want any more, so the chance of my being a natural father's rather gone by the board, I have to make do with being a surrogate literary one

enough of that – the Waterfords, as we've seen, are up and about, at least the older ones, so perhaps it won't be long before both families decide what time they're leaving for the beach – Brewster's still out in the yard, lying against the Wheatsheaf door, making sure no one leaves without disturbing him – that's what dogs do, don't they, lie across your feet, make you aware you're going nowhere unless they go as well – in Brewster's case he's also got an eye out for that cat and the cottage door gives a well-placed view of the whole yard – additionally it catches the early sun just right to warm his bones, which unfortunately makes him drowsy against his will – he wants to be on guard just like dogs are supposed to be but it's so nice to close one's eyes, isn't it?

5

Still Monday morning

back to Stook, back to the Oxfords, back in fact to Martin
– we haven't got much of a picture of him, have we, he's been
a bit faceless and nondescript so far – we've seen he's a good
soldier where Pansy's concerned, does what he's told, tries
to help where he can, pulls his weight with the children etc.,
etc. – I can't help but think that perhaps facelessness is his
essence, he doesn't come over as dynamic, does he, well not
to me at any rate – and beyond having hazel eyes he could
well be the invisible man for all we've been able to describe
of him – one fairly distinctive feature is the slight angle of the
head which he exhibits, a sort of quizzical tilt, not unlike that
used by Brewster in one of his nonplussed moments, a tilt
which suggests he's waiting for an answer to a question, making you feel you ought to be thinking up such an answer

he's a couple of inches taller than his wife, of heavy build,
with thin dark hair – his upper lip looks as if it should be
wearing a moustache, not a big one, something trim and neat,
but moustaches are out as far as Pansy is concerned, she can't
abide them, says men always look sinister and up to no good,

never trust a moustache, she says – many moons earlier Martin tried to grow a beard but that was a no-go as well, and only his eyebrows are allowed to develop the sort of idiosyncrasies more appropriate as accompaniments to a naval full set of beard and moustache – his upper lip, bare and broad, does however have its own ideas about growth and he has to shave twice a day to satisfy the criteria for being called cleanshaven – unlike Josh he's not a man to advertise his presence and moves about modestly and somewhat diffidently, earning him the nickname at work of 'lurker', which is obviously a great deal more polite and inoffensive than the 'smarmy b . . . . d' attributed to Josh – but then Martin would be liked among his workforce, not a bad word to be heard against him other than a vague complaint of ineffectiveness, usually relating to his inability to persuade the management to increase its salaries

he's bustling about now, helping to get the children ready, collecting up all the bits and pieces they'll need for the beach, their towels and drinks and sun hats – while Pansy attends to the sandwiches and Penny Samantha's infant diet, Martin in a general sweep becomes responsible for everything else, and of course if he omits anything or forgets something or includes more than he should then he'll be in trouble with the lady of the house – but his shoulders are broad, he can take it – there's an air of insouciance about him today, as if he's just realized he's on holiday and can let everyday routines go to hell – he's reckless in his approach to the organizational requirements of the business in hand, almost playful, somewhat relaxed as he chivvies the children and jauntily answers Pansy when she enquires how things are coming on – this could be a dangerous condition, it's to be hoped he doesn't slip up in some way

relaxed – but is he? – something about the look in those hazel eyes suggests his mood doesn't extend all the way to his soul, it's almost as if his carefreeness is a cloak to mask his true feelings – I'm on holiday, he tells himself, so put those troubles behind me [whatever they are, if any] and just get on with enjoying the moment – that's how it seems to me, at any rate – but an immediate cloud appears on his face, a shadow of a nimbus, when Pansy calls out to him

when we were leaving home, didn't we have post? – I thought there were a couple of things – I meant to ask you

Martin's quick to reply – *oh yes, just bills, my card and the electric – do you want Sean to take his haversack, he's attached to it*

Mummy, yes, I want it, I need it – I might get shells and stones and things

oh, all right – as long as you carry it, and carry it back if it's full

and the nimbus lifts as Pansy concerns herself with cling film and plastic boxes while Martin continues sorting the children and their accoutrements – Ellen intervenes between Pansy's memory and Martin's response by asking if she'll be allowed to take a couple of books, just in case she doesn't want to swim or anything and Abigail's otherwise engaged with her phone – *I won't get them wet or anything, promise*

you'd better not, they're library books – put them in a plastic bag

altogether now – PS feels she's entitled to her say and having noticed her food being packed can't think of anything else to ask for

so what was it with Martin? – those bills, credit card, electricity? – has he got some problem with paying them, something Pansy doesn't know about, some dire shortage of money he's hiding from her? – it could be, a lot of provident husbands, as Martin surely is, don't like their wives to have to worry over finance, one person worrying is enough – and some of them don't like their wives knowing just how bad they are at managing things, men are supposed to be cap-able, responsible and reliable in that area – that's probably it, the bank balance is low and he's having to juggle

the Waterfords call, they're ready, waiting outside the door with Josh already in the seat of his vehicle and raring to go – they're ready in respect of him and her and Abigail, for Michael's made his excuses, wriggled out, skived off, opted out of going to the beach with his family and how he's managed to do that without attracting the wrath of Josh [who does like the family to do things together, chiefly on the basis that if he's got to do it, then everyone else should too] is one of those wonderful conundrums of which we know little – we heard no arguments, no raised voices or slammed doors, no forbidding voice from a stern father, not even a whimper from Brewster who would be denied his young master's guiding hand, and nothing, not a peep, from Beth, whose main concern seems to be for the well-being of her clothes, are they suitable for a beach? – we can rest assured that young Michael will make the most of his day alone, per-haps put in hand a scheme to acquire that oh-so-necessary PIN number – let us leave him to his machinations and not intrude upon him, at least not yet, not until this lot, both lots, have left the premises

the Oxfords mount up, PS being securely strapped into her seat, Sean into his more senior version, and Ellen, a young woman of nine remember, being allowed, perhaps illegally [and the law would have to argue their case with **her**], to strap on a seat belt just like a grown-up – and the little convoy with Josh leading the way [grr] goes through the gate with Pansy, a capable volunteer, closing the gate behind them – no seaside songs accompany them, no tuneful airs escape, they travel silently, each with their individual thoughts

a pair of almond eyes, golden in the morning light, watch them go – from his eyrie on the wall Sammy would, if he could, smile broadly, and would, if he could, leap up and cry yippee – everything's back to normal, the yard below him rests in peace, no sound, certainly not that of a barking dog, disturbs this rural haven – he lets his eyelids droop, gazes through the lashes, enjoys a wide, wide yawn

ah, Mr Broadfield, good morning – how are you today?

you don't really want to know, it's one thing after another – my foot's playing up again – years ago I broke my ankle when a tractor turned over and every so often it reminds me of it – bit of a nuisance because I have to rely on Lance, and you know my opinion of him

I should think he's of great assistance, isn't he? – young and fit?

he's young, I don't know about fit – when I was his age I could throw great bundles of hay on to a wagon, no trouble, but it's just as well we've got machines to do it now, he'd never be able to lift the fork – I can't rely on him, you know, how he's going to manage the place when I'm gone I don't know – we've got Bert down the road, but he's forty-something now, not so young himself, he'll want to retire in twenty years' time, and Lance'll be on his own

Bert? – [you see, here's another character sneaked up on me]

he's got a farmhouse down the lane, he's worked all his life for the farm, like his father before him – you didn't think we managed all this on our own, did you?

I suppose I did – but from what's been said, are you sure Lance wants to follow in your footsteps when you're . . . when you're gone?

oh, you don't want to pay any attention to what he says – got fancy ideas but he's a farmer's son, and he'll stay with the farm – it'll be all his, won't it? – mind you, God knows how he'll handle it, he's got no head for the business side – very little on the farming side too, if you ask me

what if he wants to opt out altogether, do something else entirely?

something else? – he's a farmer, he can diversify, I suppose, like I have with the cottages, he could come up with something – so long as he keeps things together, keeps it basically as a working farm – this land's been farmed since Doomsday or before, the Saxons cleared it, I expect – got a history, this place

well, it's very nice having a chat, Mr Broadfield, but I don't want to keep you from your work – I do hope your foot gets better, are you taking anything for it?

best bitter, three pints after dinner, that's the recommended cure, recommended by me – and he goes off chuckling to himself, goes off with a little limp to demonstrate the extent of his infirmity

so now it's just Sammy in the yard, and he's up on his wall, eyes now closed, dozing – somewhere in Wheatsheaf Michael must be lurking, probably playing hard with the computer – perhaps he's trying to find Josh's password, hoping to access his father's bank account – Tilly's left for her riding school, Lance has gone off to look at his onions, and Mrs Broadfield's probably in her kitchen

no, I'm not, I'm changing the beds

oh yes, it's Monday, you keep the old traditional washday, do you? – always remember my mother . . .

no, I don't do the washing on a Monday, nor any other day, I use a laundry – I don't believe in slaving away unnecessarily – the washing machine's only for the underwear, and that's usually on a Saturday

I do apologize – I just thought . . .

I know what you thought – that I was the farmer's wife, doing farmer's wife things – don't be fooled like the visitors are with a bit of flummery – given the chance I'd have a cleaner and a cook and a bottle washer, and given the chance I wouldn't be living in a draughty old farmhouse

you'd modernize it?

no fear – it might need modernizing but I don't care what the next people do with it, I won't be here to see it

what do you mean? – you're leaving?

well, not yet, but I'm working on it – look, I'm forty-five next birthday, I've had quite enough of this farm over the years, came here when I was twenty-one – he's ten years older

144

*than me and plans to die here, die with his boots on like he
says his father did, but not if I can help it*

what are you planning then?

*scheming, that's what I like to call it, scheming – don't
you say anything to him, or anyone else, but within the next
couple of years we'll be living in a nice modern house in that
development next to the village I was born in – there, full
circle, but you should see those houses, everything up-to-
date, even got solar panels built in*

you're going to get him to sell his farm?

no, no, of course not – but there are plans afoot

which are?

*I don't know if I should tell you – he doesn't know yet,
you see, he doesn't know about Lance – guess what he's going
to do, go to London to work in the media*

Lance? – not going to be a farmer?

*of course not! – he's never wanted to do it – it's his father,
he's got this bee in his bonnet about the continuity of farming families, handing it all down the line – as if you can force
children to do what they don't want to do, especially these
days – no, Lance is plucking up the courage to tell him,
wanted me to break the ice, but I told him, you've got to do
this yourself, you've got to stand up to him, tell him what
you intend to do and not be browbeaten – he was going to
tackle him Saturday, but he said the time wasn't right, what
with the Chelsea match and all that*

and what will happen when he goes? – is Bert able to help
Mr Broadfield, just the two of them?

*ah, that's the scheming, you see – you remember the
architect?*

Gregory Price-Masters?

that's him – well, you know what his plan was, don't you? – he wants to make it a complex, turn this house into more holiday accommodation, convert that other barn, put in a swimming pool, and bingo! – a nice little development – we get to move out to that house I mentioned and get a fat income from renting out all the fields to other farmers, plus the income from the development – don't you think that's a good plan? – I can't wait to get it all moving – Bert's all right, he'll stay in the house down the lane and be a manager and caretaker – so you see, it'll work perfectly

I can't help thinking there might be some objection to this in the shape of Mr Broadfield – I mean, his plan is to die here

then he'll do it on his own – once Lance goes off, he'll have no option

surely . . .

*because if he doesn't I'll be taking Tilly away and he **will** be on his own, so there*

that's a bit of a bombshell, isn't it?

look, I've had twenty years of this place, of being his skivvy – do you know what farmers are like? – every time there's something domestic to do it's a case of 'oh, I've got to see how the pigs are' or 'can't go on holiday, got the plough- ing to do' – he doesn't even know how to make a cup of tea, he doesn't have a clue about cooking – I moved in when his mother moved out, God rest her soul, and he's never done a thing about the house, ever – when the children were born he didn't want to know, he went and stayed with Bert, said he needed his sleep, not babies crying, both times he was there for the first month – I'm getting out now whether he wants the development or not, but he'll come, oh yes, he can't manage without me telling him where his socks are, cooking his meals, doing his cleaning

what if he persuades Lance to stay on?

well, I'm still going, I've had enough of being a farmer's wife – they won't be happy together, not a bit

I must say I didn't quite expect this course of action – I got the impression, as one does, of a happy home, but it seems to be seething with discontent, to put it mildly

it just shows you, doesn't it – nothing's ever what it seems – it's like him and dogs

you won't let him keep one, apparently

is that what he's told you? – that's the impression he gives, isn't it, that I've told him he can't have one – well, I'll tell you the truth, and it was his last dog, Ben, lovely little collie but a bit independent – I had no problem with it, slept in the barn, didn't come in the house – well, one day it ran off over the fields, and when it came back about an hour later he lammed into it with a stick – what did it do? – it turned and bit him, and serve him right – anyway, he comes straight in the house, gets his shotgun, goes out and shoots it – Tilly was only six then, she heard about it, and I'm sure it put her off him for the rest of her life – might have affected Lance too, I don't know – but it opened **my** *eyes, I've never seen him in the same way ever since – he hasn't had a dog after Ben because of what it did to his family – now you know*

there's a poignant look in Mrs Broadfield's eyes as she turns away to carry on with her bedmaking, a look which indicates she could be close to tears – but it's more than sadness, there's a wistfulness that prompts me to ask if she perhaps considers she made a wrong choice all those years ago, does she feel she's wasted her life?

she straightens up, looks out of the window, the view straight across the fields towards a low wooded hill, gives a little sigh before answering, as though it's a question she often asks of herself – *wasted? – Lance and Tilly? – well, I could have had someone else, but at the time you make your choice . . . – no, not wasted – perhaps not as well directed as it could have been, that's it, not as well arranged – what are you at forty that you weren't at twenty? – more mature, but chiefly you don't expect so much of people – when you're young you think people have the same attitudes that you have, or at least the attitudes they show you – later you find out you interpreted things wrongly*

let's leave Mrs Broadfield staring at the view, leave her with her philosophical opinions – I must say these characters are beginning to show some surprising traits – perhaps it's turning out as I said it might, they're all like those in television soaps – or perhaps it's simply turning into real life, where first impressions of strangers aren't always substantiated and you constantly revise your view of them – it seems we've got a bit of a crisis on our hands here, if Lance is going to declare independence at any minute and Mrs Broadfield's going to walk out, then it won't be a very cheery time for the holidaymakers – they might well be affected

one thing's for sure, Sammy's either staying with a man who doesn't like him and probably won't feed him, or he's going to have to adapt to a new life in a modern environment

6

Monday evening

they're back – today they've all returned together, the convoy in the same order, with Josh in front – there's a pause at the gate before Abigail emerges from the vehicle to undo the nylon rope – she's not happy, you can see that, she's not one to leap out and do things that should be strictly within the province of her brother, but she's obviously lost the battle with her parents, neither of them prepared to effect the chore – with fumbling difficulty she manages to free the gate and push it back, looking about as familiar with the process as a turnip would be – once it's fully back she walks on grumpily to the cottage without a backward glance

the cars pass through, and it's Pansy again who has to be dropped off to close and secure the gate – she waggles her fingers at the children as they pass before her, apparently quite happy to be pedestrian and showing a near-delight in the procedure of fastening the gate, pausing to lean on it for a few seconds so that she can soak up the view – this is the same aspect which prompted deep thoughts in Mrs Broad-field, a long perspective across fields to the low wooded hill a couple of miles away – the field to be seen first, running from the rutted, dusty, potholed track has had broad beans in it, some remain, standing awkwardly like intruding visitors at a garden party, their flowered heads browning and dismayed, their leaves despondent, pondering their inevitable decline into compost – the field runs on, bumpy, part soil, part mangled vegetation until it comes up against a weak hedge, one patchy and inconsistent where parts of it have died and never regrown – and then another field, indistinct but with a pale green shade to it that goes on a long way until the low part of the hill is reached, a skirt of bushes and rising small trees introducing it – the hill itself is dark green, low trees here are in the mass except for one or two grand specimens of ash and oak – Pansy lets her eyes wander this scene as she wishes her feet could, a gentle longing to be on that hill fills her

I have to go in – I have to go and get their tea – God, why is that? – can't I just take off, begin walking, walk across to that hill, stand there, look on the other side, see what there is, what vistas? – when will I be able to do that? – is there to be a time when without restraint I shall be able to do such a thing, when I can walk across fields without seeking permission of anyone, without telling anyone, without owing duty to anyone? – when my children grow up, when they go off to lead their own lives, I shall have Martin to consider before any impulse I might have, always that consideration – we shall go together perhaps, we'll cross fields, mount hills, follow paths, seek beautiful vistas, but together, I shall want that – yet I shall also want the solitude, the isolation, the spiritual freedom of going alone along those pathways without

restriction of time or duty or obligation – will that ever be?
– can that come without a heaviness of heart through the loss
of a companion? – I doubt it, it's a desire of the mind that
can never be satisfied – it was there once, when I was a girl
and could do such a thing, when I could be free and impul-
sive – no longer, that will never come again – I shall have
Martin or I shall have his shade, or some other attendant, or
I shall have the memory – such memories bring no satisfac-
tion, no peaceful solitude, they accompany you to the grave

the gate's closed, the moment of introspection over –
Pansy turns towards the cottages, joins Martin in helping to
release the younger children from their car seats – when she
closes the door after Sean the boy goes to the edge of the yard
to stand and look across the same fields and at the same view
as his mother seconds before – she watches him, ignores PS
pulling at her trousers and saying things she doesn't hear,
gives all her attention to her son as he remains motionless –
Sean seems in a world of his own, his slight body makes no
movement while he takes in the panorama before him, wider
and more mysterious than the adult panorama seen by his
mother

PS is insistent – *Mummy!* – *Mummy!* – there can be no
ignoring her, so Pansy turns away to leave Sean to his view-
ing, picks up the girl and with affectionately chiding words
carries her into the cottage – Ellen is already inside, carefully
taking her books from the plastic bag in which she was made
to preserve them, Martin wanders in and out with the bag-
gage, sand dropping from everything – Sean is forgotten, left
to continue his communion with the countryside

apart from Brewster the Waterfords are nowhere to be

seen, having scooted into their cottage the moment the vehicle came to a halt, Abigail closing the door behind her with a petulant push – it's almost as if there's been some sort of an argument between the families, but I'm sure that can't be so, there didn't seem to be any tension in the air and that's something we'd have all noticed – the Waterford ma and pa are probably concerned to know what their independent son's been up to, out of whom, we might say, we haven't had a peep all day – one presumes the day at the beach went reasonably well, Brewster seems worked out, he lies on his side in front of Wheatsheaf's door, not even anxious for his evening meal, perhaps he's been given some goodies during the day – all is quiet in that direction so for the moment we'd best not disturb it

which brings us back to the Oxfords – while Pansy deals contentedly with PS and Martin deals with the buckets and spades and picnic remnants, it leaves Ellen to throw herself on her bed to finish the final chapter of *Cranford*, one of the books she took to the beach, and of course it leaves Sean, forgotten Sean, still standing at the yard edge taking in the view – for his age he's quite slenderly built, a sweet-faced boy of seven who must find his burlier contemporaries a bit rough when it comes to playground games and unless he puts on some weight before he gets to secondary school there's the possibility of his being bullied, such a rampant tendency these days – maybe Pansy can feed Sean a few chips and burgers, even if it does go against her principles

what's in his mind as he stands here, this lovely boy with the golden hair? – thoughts of drama, of action, of exciting times in distant lands? – is the field before him peopled with cowboys or soldiers or knights in armour, do strange beings from outer space tumble from their spacecraft on to the fading beans? – he's been to the beach, is he thinking of boats, of mariners, of shipwrecks and coral islands, does he daydream of travel and Robinson Crusoe?

if that hedge runs across to the edge of the field there could be a footpath there, all nettles and weeds and bushes, a hidden path, a secret path – when it's dark the badgers will use it, foxes, they'd go about all through the night looking for food – and it goes up there, to the hill, a long way to walk, up to the trees – will there be deer there, they like trees, they hide all the time but sometimes they'll come out into that big field – if we went there and hid by the hedge we might see some, we could watch them – but we'd have to know which way the wind was blowing, that's important, they could smell us or hear us and they'd run back to the trees – and look at that cloud, that white one, just over the edge of the hill, perhaps it's going to rain, I wouldn't mind that, I like the rain, I like getting wet, feeling it on my face – Daddy will come with me, tomorrow we'll go and look for the path, we'll go to the top of the hill, go through the trees, but we'll have to be very quiet so's not to frighten the animals

in his lonely position before the field Sean joins his hands beneath his chin to stare hard at the hill – will he see what he wants to see, some animal moving there? – without him noticing a figure approaches, no wild animal, a human one, it comes up slightly behind him to stand a metre or so away

do you like the country? – Lance, hands in pockets, not looking at the boy but at the same scene, eyes taking in the hill, the sky it makes Sean jump – he turns and looks up and smiles politely – *yes, I wish I could live here*

are you from a town?

yes – we're on holiday

enjoying it?

well, we only came on Saturday, but we've been to the seaside today, it was all right, the tide was out and we played on the beach

which do you like best, seaside or country?

oh, the country – the seaside's all right but it's not very interesting – it hasn't got any animals, has it, and there are no trees like those over on that hill – do you know what they're called?

the trees? – well, the bigger ones are oak trees, and the smaller ones are rowan and hazel and alder – the hill's called Broomhill because once upon a time there was a lot of broom growing there

brooms?

no, not brushes – broom's a bush with red and yellow flowers on it, there's one over there, just to the left of the hedge, do you see – there – probably the last one left, can you see it? – it's a long way away

I can see it, I can see it – I'll go there tomorrow – can we walk there?

of course, as long as you don't walk on any growing crops – do you know what they look like?

they're all in long lines, aren't they?

that's right – in long lines

Lance has crouched down beside Sean to point out the bush and he now straightens up, stands level with the boy while together they survey the fields – *you get your daddy to take you there and then you'll know what broom is – you'll be able to tell him what it's called, won't you?*

that golden head nods vigorously, the hair flies in all directions – *I will, and I'll tell him it's called Broom Hill, he won't know that*

no, he won't – my daddy doesn't know it either and he's lived here for ages and ages – he always calls it Price's hill, that's because a Mr Price owns it, he doesn't know it's really called Broomhill

Mr Price owns a hill? – does he own the trees?

yes, of course, it's his land

and the deer and the badgers and the foxes?

well, I don't think he owns them, but I suppose he has to look after them

does he own this field and that one, and the hedge and the broom?

no, my daddy does

Sean stops asking questions – the answers seem to puzzle him, he frowns away as if trying to work out some huge sum in mental arithmetic – Lance taps him on the shoulder

I think your mummy wants you

and Pansy does, standing in the doorway of Stook, smiling across at Lance in greeting – closing the door behind her she walks across the yard – *is he asking questions? – he always wants to know something – not being a nuisance, I hope*

no, he's very keen to learn things, isn't he?

Sean spins round to look up at his mother, speaks

excitedly – *Mr Price owns that hill, and the trees and . . . and this man's daddy owns the fields*

well, I never – come on, Sean my love, it's time for your tea – Ellen's having hers – say goodbye to . . .

Lance – goodbye, Sean, see you again

thanks for keeping him occupied – to be honest I'd forgotten he was out here

no trouble – if he'd like a conducted tour of the farm tomorrow I'd be happy to show him around – we haven't got many animals, I'm afraid

that's very kind of you – we'll see if there's time, only we tend to go out a lot, but thank you all the same

Sean finds his voice and his manners both at the same time – *goodbye, Lance* he says – *thank you very much* – and waves gaily as he goes back with Pansy to the cottage

nice little lad, don't you think?

Lance nods in agreement – *bit like me at that age, I was full of the wonders of nature – you get to the point where you think that's all very well, but you yearn for something less restful, something more of a pace*

your mother tells me you're thinking of going to London, that should be pacy enough – what are you going to do there?

Lance looks round nervously – *my father doesn't know about that yet – can you keep it quiet? – he's not going to be happy about it – I plan to enrol on a journalist's course – I can get a grant, you see, and I've got a friend I can stay with – but don't let him know, whatever you do, he's convinced I have to follow him into farming*

rest assured, nothing will be said – I can see you have to pick the right time

I don't think there'll ever be a right time – and with the sort of gait that suggests to the observer he's carrying some invisible load, Lance goes off to the barn which houses the machinery

when Pansy tells Martin about the offer of a conducted tour he pulls a critical face – *is he all right, this lad?*

what, Lance? – I expect so, why not? – he's the farmer's son

well, you never know

know what?

Martin becomes uncomfortable and shrugs his shoulders – *well, young man, young boy*

oh, don't be so silly – he's just kind, that's all – you always want to think the worst of people

Martin lets it pass, the business of getting the children bathed and ready for bed taking away any incentive to prolong the discussion – but ever since Lance gave him that lop-sided grin when he asked for matches Martin's had his doubts about him, at first thinking him slow-witted but now considering the possibility of something worse – however, the thought doesn't linger long with him, there's obviously a greater subject on his mind, one which, once the bedtime stories are concluded and things have settled down a bit, with Pansy busy in the kitchen washing things through, he sits down to contemplate

I have to tell her – it's no good hoping it will go away, it won't – the moment we get back he could be sitting on the doorstep, waiting, just sitting there – or there could be a note, a message on the answerphone, something like that – one

thing I don't want is to have it forced out, it'll come as a shock to her as it is, I've got to prepare her before we get back – why did he have to do it now? – why does he have to do it at all? – couldn't he have just gone on with things as they were, let sleeping dogs lie? – no, he's got to do this, he says, he owes it to himself – well, I owe it to Pansy to put her in the picture before we get back, and I've got four or five days in which to do that – it won't be easy, probably it's best to leave it until Friday otherwise it's going to ruin her holiday like it's ruined mine – but if Friday's busy, if we're packing and getting the kids organized, having drinks with the others in the evening, then it's leaving it a bit late – better be Thursday then, perhaps we'll have the evening to ourselves, it would be hopeless during the day

Martin takes a crumpled letter from his pocket, folds it more carefully and puts it back, a deep sigh accompanies the final action – whatever it is that's worrying him, the letter holds the key, that's for sure

Pansy comes through from the kitchen – in contrast to his sombre mood she's bright and cheerful, smiles happily at him – *we'll get that Shiraz out once they're asleep and we've eaten – thank God for a night in*

what about the others?

Beth and Josh? – where were you? – we're on our own tonight, didn't you hear? – when we were leaving, it was decided we'd each do our own thing – to be honest I think Beth wants to sort her hair out, she got sand in it when PS threw her bucket over our heads – can't say I'm sorry, I could do with a bit of relaxing, not something I'm able to do with Josh about – he's getting to be a bit of a nuisance, always giving me looks and making innuendos – why, did you want an evening with Beth?

don't be silly

I'm only joking – we've got those chocolates, remember, the ones we've hidden from the kids – they're all ours, we'll make pigs of ourselves and we'll finish a bottle of wine, the Shiraz, as I said – cheer up, it might never happen

Martin smiles, trying to make it as broad as possible – *yes, we could do with some time to ourselves – we can relax and have a nice chat* – he says this with some deliberation, not enough to raise any suspicion in Pansy that there's something serious afoot, but with an inner deliberation which reflects the direction of his thoughts – he watches her leave the room to go and check on Ellen, still ruining her eyesight by trying to finish a chapter or whatever – taking the book from Ellen's hands is always a nightly ritual, usually accomplished with difficulty though occasionally, when she's fallen asleep over it, with comparative ease, when the only danger is that she'll awake and snatch the book back – Martin leans back in the easy chair

well, I could tell her tonight, might be a good opportunity, perhaps the only one – get it out of the way early on, I suppose – half a bottle of wine each? – she'll be more receptive, that's a fact – we'll see how it goes, play it by ear – I still, for the life of me, can't see why he should do this, and in any case how on earth did he find me? – am I making too much of it, building it up into something it doesn't merit? – but it's going to be such a shock to Pansy, such a shock – and she'll want to know what's going to happen in the future, and I don't know, do I? – what's it going to mean for us, what'll it mean for the kids? – and is it just going to be only him that turns up, or her as well? – he takes the letter from his pocket again, opens it up secretively, his eye on the door and his ears attuned to Pansy's whereabouts – with the letter open he quickly scans the words, shakes his head slightly – *no help there, just him, he doesn't mention her at all – you'd think he would* – the letter is quickly refolded and returned to his pocket just before Pansy re-enters

I think she must be tired out, they all are, thank God – what do you want to eat? – still the happy Pansy, relaxed and bright as a button, in observing which Martin looks even more miserable – *cheer up* she tells him *we'll have something to eat – what do you want, cheese and pickle sandwich? – after that huge porkpie you had for lunch I don't think you could manage much more – or you shouldn't – sandwich then?*

yes, sure, I'll give you a hand

no, it's all right, doesn't take two of us – you sit there and relax, you look as though you need to

once more, as Pansy goes out to the kitchen, he fingers the letter, not removing it from his pocket this time, as though merely assuring himself that it and the threat it contains are still there – he sighs again – *she's going to think I've deceived her, not telling her in all this time, and she'll wonder what else I might be concealing – not a very good husband then, am I, don't suppose I ever have been*

now this is Martin being self-pitiful, he'll have to buck himself up – whatever it is that he's got to tell her I'm sure Pansy will be understanding – there are times when we all feel like failures, I know I do constantly – I'm a failure with women, as my ex-wife will tell you anyway, let's not get morbid, let's take ourselves off to the farmhouse, see if Lance has plucked up his courage yet – in the far corner of the yard he's busily cleaning an old car, polishing vigorously

I told you, there's never a right time with Dad – I've only got to sound uninterested in what's going on, like caring how much we get for our milk, and he jumps down my throat – I suspect he's got an inkling that I don't want to follow him into the family tradition

er, what do you think your mother will do after you've gone off to London?

oh, she'll carry on being the good helpmeet, I expect – she'll probably start trying to persuade him to retire early or something

he did mention early on, and he may have been joking of course, that he saw no reason why Tilly couldn't become a farmer

Tilly? – that's the last thing she'd want to do, run a farm! – no she's tied up with her riding, but that's the nearest she'd want to get to anything to do with animals – I doubt if she'd ever want to marry a farmer, she's more choked off with it than I am – yes, he must have been joking – but it means he may have been thinking along the lines of me not taking up the reins, so I suppose that's encouraging

what are you two gossiping about?

ah, Mrs Broadfield, yes gossiping is the word, I suppose – Lance was just telling me about his difficulty in letting Mr Broadfield know what he wants to do

well, he's aware of my opinion, he's got to take the bull by the horns that's exactly it – I don't want to put him in one of his bullish moods

well, perhaps he won't be – he must have an inkling – you've got to do it, Lance, and soon

I know, I know – and with a face as long as a fiddle Lance takes himself off, hands deep in pockets, shoulders hunched – Mrs Broadfield watches him go and once he's out of earshot asks if I mentioned anything to him of her own plans – I assure her I was the soul of discretion

I hope so – not that Lance would normally tell him of anything, but I think it safer if he's ignorant of my plans – it's the sort of thing he might blurt out if they get into an argument, and it would ruin everything

I appreciate that

I do feel for him though, it won't be easy – as I said, he asked me to make it easier by preparing the ground, but you can see why I don't want to, it will put my own plans in jeopardy – my husband's an unknown quantity when it comes to telling him things, you never know how he'll react – well, I must be off and get something edible on the go – still have to be the farmer's wife, don't I, got to keep it up

as she leaves, Brewster takes his head out of his bowl and looks across at her – while we were talking he was chasing the bowl round his bit of yard, trying to lick the insides off it – satisfied that Mrs Broadfield's got nothing to offer him he tries again, pushes the bowl into a corner by the trough of flowers and buries his head inside it – after a few seconds he comes to the conclusion that there's no more to be got, turns away to stand facing the world and with a large pink tongue smacks his chops when Mrs Broadfield returns to the house she finds Tilly in the kitchen mixing herself a smoothie drink – the girl's dressed down after being in her riding clothes for most of the day and wears a small white T-shirt that doesn't cover her navel, with a pair of pale-blue shorts that also fail in that respect – you can see what her mother means when she calls her skinny, there doesn't seem to be a lot of her – long-legged with prominent knees and her shoulders somewhat bony, she's nonetheless not remarkably lean of body, having a sturdy enough waist, towards which her blonde hair descends, resting some of its tresses on those shoulders as it does so – she wears a sad expression, her face naturally long which adds to the impression of great tragedy, and while her mouth is formed into a smile to greet her mother the round blue eyes remain sober and serious

do you want some, there's enough for two?

Mrs Broadfield declines – *not for me, lovey, I've just had a cup of tea – are you all right?*

Tilly takes a sip or two of the drink, moves towards the door but hesitates, bites her lip before saying *I've given up the riding for a bit*

what? – given it up, what do you mean?

under the force of her mother's swift interrogation Tilly blanches a little, takes another anxious sip at her drink – it's almost Lance's problem repeated, this time between mother and daughter, although with less underlying antagonism – I wonder how long the girl's been trying to pluck up the courage to give out the apparently bad news

I think I want to give it a rest just for a time while I

concentrate on my exams – I'm finding it a bit much at the moment

but you love it! – what about the Wilton gymkhana, you've been training for that? – it's not far off, is it?

Tilly shrugs – *it's a question of balancing things – I don't want to miss it but I find it real hard to study at the same time – I want to get good marks in my exams*

Mrs Broadfield's baffled – *I must say I've never had you down as the studious sort, lovey – Lance, yes, but you've always had your head full of horses*

Tilly stares at the kitchen floor, those granite slabs that somebody's great-great-grandfather laid long ago and which now show the ruts and declensions of constant usage – *I know – it'll only be for a time, but I've seen the importance of having a good record academically – Lance has got ideas of studying journalism somewhere, I want to be able to do something like that – it's not as if I've got my own pony*

this last comment strikes home – Mrs Broadfield instantly feels its barb and becomes mollifying – *well, you know the reason for that, don't you, your father doesn't want to have a stable – I know it's been difficult for you, your friends have theirs, but I've tried to get round him, I have*

oh, I know, it's not your fault – it makes it easier for me to have a break, doesn't it?

well, I suppose I ought to be pleased you've chosen education, but it won't be for long, will it?

no, not long – the girl cuddles her drink close to her bosom, looks pensively at the top of the glass – *no, just a few months*

a big sigh from Mrs Broadfield almost coincides with a

small one from Tilly as she turns and leaves the room – her mother follows her with her eyes, shakes her head sadly

bit of a turn-up, Mrs B? – what was that about not wanting a stable?

oh, that's him again – he's always been against anything he might have to dip into his pocket for – and it costs more in the long run, all these school fees, it's not cheap – I made it up long ago about him not wanting a stable, the truth is he just won't pay out for anything – Lance had to work in the village pub for months to get himself a car, and it's only an old banger – no, when it's come to paying for his children he's always done the minimum – and, of course, Tilly's had to fend off her friends' questions, they find it strange that a farm can't house a pony – poor girl

yes, very sad – we're not getting a very good picture of your husband, I'm afraid, we've been learning a lot about him

oh, I've only scratched the surface, believe me – so saying, Mrs Broadfield follows Tilly from the kitchen, leaving us to scoot up to Tilly's bedroom, that pink and purple delight with its wallpaper of rosettes, where she lies on her bed in the manner of the other young people, in this case staring at a rather attractive beamed ceiling

your mother was surprised, Tilly, came as a shock to her

yes, well so I've done it now, told her – he can find out for himself, he'll be pleased to save the money, that's all he ever thinks of – I suppose I'll have to spend all my time in here now, swotting up

it's probably a good decision – I suppose the riding did take up a lot of your spare time

it's all I've ever wanted to do – can't remember not riding

then you've shown great determination, the right choice at this stage in your life

oh, go away!

well, yes, perhaps we should – she's obviously upset by having to make such a choice, though it should be possible merely to cut it down rather than exclude it altogether, just go riding once or twice a week – but it's best not to make any suggestions, she's looking rather tearful – it's her choice, and a tough one for her

in Stook now the Oxfords have finished their sandwiches and are well into the box of chocolates which Martin originally said would last the whole family a whole week – the wine has flowed, the bottle's nearly empty, and in view of Pansy's continuing sobriety Martin's made the suggestion of opening another

I didn't know we had any more

saved it from last night – I don't see why the others should drink it all

no, perhaps we'd better not – I don't want to have a headache in the morning

well, there's no good reason why you should – but he can't persuade her and the bottle remains undisturbed in its hiding place – bit of a choker this for he was hoping to have his darling wife in a bit of a dreamy state before he hit her with his news, and Pansy is as wide awake as a spring lamb on a hillock – but he knows he's got to do it tonight, there might not be another opportunity, and from what we learnt earlier some fellow will be sitting on his doorstep the moment they get back he offers another chocolate, which she declines, pointing to her mouth, full with the hard caramel – with a moral effort that you can almost see described on his face he pulls the by now crumpled letter from his pocket and begins to open it up

what's that? Pansy asks, though it's a bit mumbled in view of the toffee

but it gives Martin his lead-in – *this is what came as we left – the other one was a bill, but this was a personal letter*

sounds mysterious

not really, but I've got to explain something

Pansy doesn't stop her chewing but the rate slows down, a guarded expression comes into her face – *money?*

no, no – nothing like that – it's from someone I . . . someone in Yorkshire – his name's William and er . . . and he's my son

all of us at one time or another has had this sort of revelation thrust at us, and if you haven't yet had one, just wait, something like it will come at some point in your life – one's jaw doesn't actually drop but it feels as though it does, you stare hard at the person who might have made the announcement and your mind goes all fuzzy with a thousand milling thoughts – Pansy's expression hardens but her jaw's unable to drop anyway because of the toffee, though she does stare hard at Martin, waiting for him to explain himself

his name's William and he's . . . well, I suppose he must be about twenty, twenty-one – it's not a very nice story, I'm afraid, and I know I should always have told you, years ago I should have told you – I saw him when he was a month or so old and that's all – and now he's written this letter saying he'd like to meet me, and he's in town and will turn up God knows when – I don't know how he got my address, his mother disappeared from my life twenty years ago – I was nineteen when I met her, she got pregnant, I wanted to marry her or at least be with her – but she went off to her parents in the north, refused to see me, it wasn't a very good time – anyway, she had the baby and stayed up there, told me she wanted nothing from me – I went up and saw her and the baby but she was adamant in having nothing to do with me, said she didn't want the baby to know me – her parents weren't particularly happy, put all the blame on me, said I ruined her life, all heavy Victorian drama – that was it, all over – she never answered any of my letters, made it plain she wanted nothing to do with me – years and years ago

and you forgot about it?

no, never forgotten it, how could anyone? – suppressed it, I suppose – I should have told you all about it when we met, but the boy would have been nine then and I thought it was all in the past, that I'd never see him, I presumed she must have met someone else in that time – it seemed point-less to bring it up

I told you all my secrets

yes, I know – Martin sighs heavily – *but I didn't want to spoil things then*

a silence, Pansy swallows her last mouthful, looks into Martin's eyes with a careful intensity while he shakes his head as if not believing himself – it's a long silence, there's a still-ness between them that lasts until Pansy takes a deep breath

so – the children have a half-brother she says quietly

he nods – *I'm afraid they have – I'm so sorry*

they're sitting in the easy chairs facing each other – after a moment's pause she rises and goes to kneel beside him, places a hand on his knee and looks up into his face with a gentle smile – *well, we'd better make him feel at home when we see him, hadn't we?*

7

Tuesday morning

now I think we ought to have a little roll-call before we begin
the day, to satisfy ourselves that no one's left out – we can,
of course, and perhaps it's only meet that we should, start
with Sammy and Brewster – after all, these are the two most
lowly [he's lowlier than me, Sammy would say] and deserve
our attention because of the natural antipathy between them
– Brewster we can see in his usual position in front of Wheatsheaf, lying in the early morning sun with his back to the
door, legs straight out, dozy eyes flickering open intermittently in case the world passes him by without telling him
– no sign of Sammy, he must be having a lie-in, the moss on
top of the wall not warm enough for him yet, no need for
Brewster to be too alert

there was no early morning shotgun today, and still no
recorded rooster from Tilly – [perhaps we can understand
why she's remiss in her duties, there's obviously a great deal
on her mind] – the farmyard witnessed an early parade as
Lance took out the tractor and Mr Broadfield took the old
Land Rover to distant parts – a brief smell of fried bacon

preceded their appearance and the clattering sound of washed dishes followed it, but now no sound nor smell, and certainly no sight, of the working farm prevails – to all intents and purposes it's closed for the day

which is bad news for little Sean who hoped for a guided tour, or at the very least when looking into the yard through a window expected to see some activity – he complains to his mother and father in disappointed tones, telling them the nice man called Lance promised him the tour, and he's so disappointed he leaves half his breakfast in demonstration – his big sister Ellen, she of the literary inclinations, manages to dispose of it, claiming to have worked up an appetite from the previous day's visit to the beach which, despite herself, she thoroughly enjoyed, and also because she's just read a description of a six-course breakfast in a history book

Penny Samantha is her usual self, getting called that in full because of her lack of cooperation and her presumption, which is what Pansy calls it when she can't get the better of the babe – with non-stop chatting and a complete disregard for the requirements of communal living, not to mention her tendency to make a mess with her food, PS draws censure from all her family one by one and all together [as she might, and continually does, say] – Martin's in a very good mood, having confessed his wild oats and been comforted nocturnally by a loving wife [it'll be your fault, she said, if there are any repercussions] and he hums and whistles which alarms the children no end

so much for Stook, what of the Brewster-guarded Wheatsheaf – well, as usual they're late getting up, Abigail and Michael are still abed, Josh and Beth are sipping their coffee in their normal state of diurnal daze which, it should be noted, doesn't apply to working days, when smart alertness becomes imperative and is in consequence adopted – Beth lounges on the sofa in a silk negligee, the rose-tinted white one she always takes on holidays, while Josh sits inelegantly in an easy chair wearing his towelling bathrobe, absently fingering his left ear – they don't speak of course, there's nothing to say beyond 'nice coffee' and Josh has already said that once, automatically, whatever it's like, just to ensure he gets one the next day – Beth really would like to talk, she's eager for conversation, but not with Josh – her preference is for another woman with whom she could exchange opinions, views, criticisms, character assassination and scandal, in other words gossip, but beyond Pansy, who in any case isn't here and if she were would no doubt prefer not to be, there is no woman for this purpose – she watches Josh fiddling with his ear and longs for the time when Abi will have grown up enough to fill the necessary bill

and the Broadfields, what are they up to? – well, on his tractor Lance is halted in a field corner, eyes closed listening to a radio programme, while his father sits down with Bert and a large pint mug of tea – Tilly's in her room doing some yoga on the floor, deep breathing and all, Mrs Broadfield, having temporarily finished in the kitchen, has her head deep in the summer catalogue of a mail-order clothing company

and Bert, I imagine you asking, why do we know nothing about him? – to be honest he's not someone I considered, in fact I'd forgotten he existed until talking to Broadfield about how Lance would manage when he's gone – Bert lives in a small cottage owned by the farm, pays no rent and works [for a pittance just like me, I hear Debbie say] at Broadfield's disposal – never married, got the house to himself and seems quite content with his life – he's not simple but likes the simple life, has a wonderful vegetable garden to which he dedicates the love and time which Martin, for instance, dedicates to his family – the cottage was where he was born, when his parents died he just carried on, and to Broadfield he's indispensable in his knowledge and in his total loyalty to Upside Farm – and what's more he never has anything bad or difficult or contradictory to say and is thus the ideal conversationalist for Broadfield to take his morning tea with – of medium build, a doubtful rounding of the shoulders which will have him at sixty looking older, slightly balding already, ruddy cheeks and a look in his eye which says nice day today, ain't it?

that's the roll-call, anyone missing? – [I'll refrain from mentioning the architect by name just in case he comes out of the woodwork again] – fourteen people, fifteen if we anticipate Martin's new son, and two animals – I think they're all accounted for so now what are they going to do with themselves on this rather cloudy, south-east windery, not-very-fine-weather-for-the-beach sort of day?

for a start it's been decided that the families will each go their separate ways today – this was a mutual agreement reached before they arrived back yesterday, but who actually initiated it is not clear – it was generally felt that two days at a time was sufficient fraternizing and each of the men wanted to do something particularly different anyway, the women relieved but not publicly so – it seems it may have been due to the absence of Michael, that he was left out of things and the Waterfords want to make amends by doing something in which he can be included, but that's only a guess – however it is, with nothing planned Sean makes demands on his father to take him to that hill, being careful not to step on the crops, and with a happy heart Pansy despatches them off in that direction – Ellen's pleased because she can read, PS is pleased because she gets her mother's full attention

in Wheatsheaf Josh, now dressed in a careless fashion, jeans and loose shirt of no distinction, tries to quiz Michael on how he spent his day

what did you get yourself for lunch? – always a safe start, to talk of food

oh, there was a pie there, that and some bread – end of conversation

he knows he's wasting his time but Josh perseveres – *not bad on the beach, quite empty, you might have liked it* – no response beyond a grunt – *we got talking to some girls, about your age* – a raised chin, as if to say so what do I care – *Brewster missed you throwing the frisbee, your arm's stronger than mine* – another grunt

Josh sighs, gets up to go into the kitchen, and at this move Michael proffers some information

played some games on the laptop

oh yes, did you win 'em all?

some

right

communication, as we can see, and as we might have guessed, is sparse and extremely difficult between father and son – is it something we should always expect, boys get to a certain age and rebellion sets in? – perhaps not rebellion, just an awareness of their masculine status which makes them resent their fathers – does Oedipus really raise his head? – let's get back to the action, and I mean real action, the sort that has you on the edge of your seat, sweat on your brow, nails being bitten, heart in your mouth stuff

for Sammy's come into the yard! – Brewster's dozing, hasn't seen him – Sammy sizes up his chances of doing a bit of a prowl – this is his territory, this is where every day he does a circuit or two, checking on the security of the farm, establishing his presence – he uses his head – if the dog's over there, go round the other way, take the drive side, cut across to the main gate and use that as an escape route if necessary – if all goes well then swing round towards Stook before that animal wakes up and make a dignified dash back home, back to base – Sammy follows the route with his eyes, calculates the movements – yes, it should be possible

now cats may have their guile, but dogs aren't all out in the open – from beneath half-closed lids Brewster watches, aware that any slight movement will be detected, and that will be the end of that

with a dignified glance across the yard at Brewster, suffi-cient to persuade himself that the dog's still asleep [typical of dogs, either fast asleep or going round being a nuisance] Sammy pads slowly past the gate, ducks beneath the Oxford's car – good vantage point this, unassailable beneath a car, a cat's favourite resort – no movement from Brewster, playing the waiting game, not tempted into barking at a car

in due course Sammy emerges – his plan is to make such a gallop of it that by the time the stupid dog wakes up and realizes what's happening Sammy will have reached the cover of his home sanctuary

but there's a danger the cat hasn't foreseen – the door of Stook opens and Pansy stands there, a smile on her face as PS wanders into the yard – Sammy freezes against the wall – this will wake that dog up for sure

PS spots him – *pussycat!* – *Mummy, pussycat here*

it was wrong of Sammy to freeze, he should have run back to the gate

pussycat!

he's indecisive – years ago he'd have legged it, but here at this advanced age he hesitates, acts like a senile old moggy! – what to do!

PS has the answer – with clumsy but vicelike fingers she makes a grab for the pussycat, her hands slip down so that she holds only his tail – a shriek comes from Sammy, his feet strain to take him out of her grip, he tries to get his head round to bite her but she's pulling him backwards, his claws make grooves in the gravel

two things happen simultaneously – Pansy leaps forward with loud admonitions and Brewster admits to being awake – springing to his feet he barks and barks, loud and continuous, the raw sound echoing round the farmyard – he's awake all right!

and yet he remains where he is, makes no attempt to cross the yard, just barks

Sammy escapes as Pansy pulls the child's hands away, some random fur goes with them – across the yard, right across Brewster's line of fire, within range of a chicken, let alone a dog, Sammy belts it to the safety of his small gate and disappears

Brewster continues to bark, but it's winding down – when Sammy ran across the yard he didn't watch, he just kept his eyes fixed on Pansy and PS – he watches them take themselves hastily indoors before he turns his head to see where Sammy went, presumes it was through the gate – quiet now, he slowly walks across to it, stands for a while looking through the rails – he gives one gruff noise, not quite a bark, then goes to sniff at various parts of the yard – excitement over, except that rather belatedly Josh comes to the door of Wheatsheaf and asks Brewster what all the fuss was about, looks round at the empty yard, goes back inside

what was all that about? – Beth asks

oh, something got him going, I expect

Josh resumes his seat, Beth goes back up the stairs to Abigail's room, seats herself on the only chair in the room, which she vacated to enquire about Brewster – Abigail sits on the side of the bed and continues brushing her hair

I was thinking, darling – you should really do something with it – you want to go to the hairdresser's again?

this must startle the young girl, does she suspect her mother of reading her mind? – she's got to wonder what made her come up with that idea? – last night she possibly arranged with Nula to fix the appointment for her, was she overheard? – Abigail looks worried – *what for?*

well, to get some style into it – at the moment, well . . . – wouldn't it be nice to have a new style, something shorter perhaps?

I like it long

I know, darling, but isn't that long enough? – just a trim, maybe, and possibly a little highlighter?

Abigail sees a bit of a chance here, risky, but worth trying – *I wouldn't mind darker*

darker? – oh no, darling, dark wouldn't suit you at all – you've got lovely natural colour, lots of girls are desperate for that, it's the shade they're all trying to obtain out of a bottle

I like auburn

you can't possibly, no one likes auburn, you'd just be mousey and you wouldn't look right – no, the shade of blonde you've got is all you'll ever need – perhaps with a little lightening in places, that's all

boys are going for auburn this year

ah, now on the subject of boys Beth's not sure quite how she should handle Abigail – the girl is patently concerned that boys should notice her hair, all the more reason for staying blonde – but she's twelve and three quarters, and Beth knows for a fact that some of Abi's contemporaries are regularly having sex with boys a couple of years older – it's now time to have a serious talk with Abi about the matter

darling, is there any boy in particular you like?

why?

I just wondered if there was someone you might be fond of

why?

I thought that if there was some boy you liked you might be thinking of . . . of . . . going with him

going where?

oh, you know what I mean

having sex

yes

of course, that's always likely, isn't it?

is that why you want auburn hair?

perhaps – not particularly – Nula's got auburn hair

she's like you, fair!

not any more – she's had it dyed

Beth realizes she's been led astray by this consideration of hair, tries to get the conversation back on track – *if you were to . . . have sex with someone, you'd be very careful, wouldn't you?*

take precautions, you mean?

well, I've been wondering if it wasn't time we went along to see the doctor

I'm fine – what do I want to see a doctor for?

Beth pauses – the words have to be carefully processed – *the doctor can give you a prescription – you'd be able to get tablets – you know, contraceptive ones*

go on the pill?

well, yes

oh, I do that already – the school's arranged it – you're a bit late, Mummy

Josh's conversation with his son is far from the wordy exchanges of mother and daughter – intermittent comments, usually in the form of questions from Josh and monosyllabic one-word answers from Michael are all that the sitting room witnesses – long before Beth comes downstairs again a lengthy silence has reigned, with Michael deep in a magazine and his father wondering whether this holiday was a good idea *we could have gone to Malaga – weather's more reli-able – we could have gone without the kids, like we did last year – they enjoyed it with their gran, well, I think they did – hard to tell with **him** – this whole thing would be better if that woman wasn't so prim – we haven't got started yet, of course, it's only Tuesday, three more days yet – three more nights, but I haven't been too successful up to now – what am I doing wrong? – should I have a better approach? – it's always delicate when they have to be coaxed, maybe I've been too obvious – what was it Beth said to me once? – gentle wooing, that was it, women like wooing – well, I haven't got long for that, only three days, and one thing I'm certain of, I'm not going home empty-handed – Martin's the problem, just like he is at work, always getting in the way – if Beth dis-tracted him a bit more than she did the other night then I could move in on Pansy properly – I know she'll be up for it, I can tell, but I've got to wean her away from her conscience, that's where the difficulty lies, as it always does – if she thinks Martin's taken by Beth then we'll be halfway there – I don't like to think this has all been a total disaster, a waste of money – a whole week when we could be in Malaga – I wouldn't have suggested it if I thought she was as coy as she's pretending to be*

Beth enters the room, a look on her face of affront, that's really all you can say it is, affront – with Michael immersed in his magazine [and when Michael reads anything his whole body absorbs the book or whatever it is, his back's a grace-ful curve and his hair hangs down over the pages to shield them from prying eyes – it's as if he's trying to persuade the book to enter his soul through his stomach rather than

through his mind] Beth makes signs to her husband that he's
needed urgently in the kitchen, goes there to await him

what?

Abi – she's on the pill

on the pill? – since when?

God knows, the school's put her on it

they didn't tell us – they can't do that!

*well, they have apparently – they could at least let us have
some control over our children – we should be the ones to
decide*

she'll start now, won't she?

I've a feeling she already has

this is a rare moment of unity for Beth and Josh – usually
they're like two icebergs floating separately in a cold sea,
both going with the same current but nature ensuring they
don't collide – for the moment there's silence between them
as they contemplate the import of what they've learned, but
this is broken by the voice of Michael as he passes the kitchen
on his way upstairs

isn't she the lucky one

it's a well-known fact [one of those many and distin-
guished well-known unattributable facts] that all children
have big ears until they're fifteen, and then they're deaf to
anything anyone says – Michael's right on the edge of that
particular facility, to the dismay of the parents huddled con-
spiratorially in the kitchen who are made to realize that their
offspring are way ahead of them – where will the world end
if kids keep getting more and more worldly-wise earlier
and earlier?

over in the farmhouse, having finished her cup of tea and

decided against ordering anything from the catalogue, Mrs Broadfield puts both to one side and sits by the window looking through the bushes into the yard

I was reflecting [not unlike the parents in Wheatsheaf, as it happens] *on the difficulties posed by having brought children into the world – I'm thinking primarily of Lance, my eldest, my boy, my lively little chap who gave me such happiness when he was growing up, and who still does of course, still does, don't get me wrong, he's an angel – but what a pickle he's got himself into*

I suppose it's difficult when they grow up into a tradition like this, all their lives feeling they've got to continue with the family business – not so bad if you had another son who might be interested . . .

well, you're near the truth in that – Lance would be the younger boy if Brett had lived

oh dear, I'm sorry – didn't mean to . . .

no, I can deal with it easily now – a long time ago I learned what the word irony means, learned it the hard way – Brett died when he was two, sweet little fellow, died of pneumonia – this was a terribly damp and cold place then, the man I married lived here with his mother, and she was a witch, she really was, tighter than he was, wouldn't spend a penny on anything, certainly not on heating – I've always blamed her for Brett going like that, I didn't weep any tears when she went a year or two after – then I had Lance and he lived, and then Tilly, of course – I've been blessed with those two

and the irony you mentioned?

oh that – you have to understand what it was like round

here back then, well, it still is – the country life might appear to have kept pace with that of the cities, but I can tell you, old ways die hard – I was pregnant with Brett before I was married, and I had no option then but to marry Broadfield – didn't want to, I wanted to either have an abortion or go off somewhere else to have the child, which is what I should have done, regardless – it was a fling with him, little else, I was young – my parents and his mother put on the pressure and I came here as his wife – and then Brett died – that's the irony, I married him for nothing – when the baby went I stayed with my parents for a bit and they had no hesitation in sending me back to him when I was better – he's your husband, they said, you're married now and that's that – no choice – do you know, I thought of the two options open to me, suicide or running off – but I was in no state to argue, I came back – and life continued

never been a happy marriage then?

that's one way of putting it – you adapt, you learn to live with things – I suppose you could say you pay for your sins – there's a double irony really, because my parents in their old age now say they wonder why I stayed with him

I can understand why you're making your plans – but if it works out as you say and the farm becomes a holiday centre, you're talking of having a house in the village, and he'll still be living with you

no, I know him inside out, believe me – that will be the choice on offer, but the last thing he'd want to do is live in a modern house in a little close in the village – he'll move in with Bert, he did it before and he's always down there at any time of the day – I'll have the new house to myself and the

183

children – that's what'll happen, you see, he'll dump himself on Bert

lucky Bert

I don't think he'd notice, to be honest – he's a nice enough fellow but so easygoing – he works for a pittance, you know – [now where have I heard that before?] – as long as he's got his garden he's happy

will he wait on your old man, do what you do for him?

he might, quite likely would, I don't much care – I'm sure they'll both be very happy together

Tilly now, is she getting down to her studies, do you think?

Mrs Broadfield shakes her head, gives a sigh before answering – *I don't understand her, honest I don't – she's been mad about horses ever since she was five, now she's suddenly gone all studious*

it could be she's looked at Lance, worked out that riding in gymkhanas is all very well, but if she wants to escape to London, say, then she'll need to have an academic record – it's her age, I expect, she decided to get serious

she doesn't have to go to London, she'll be with me in the new house, not stuck here like Lance has been

but she doesn't know that, does she, she doesn't know your plans – in any case, did you want to stay in the village when you were young? – if you hadn't dallied with Mr Broadfield you would have gone to the big city, wouldn't you?

she chuckles – *I like that, 'dallied with Mr Broadfield' – I'd call it more than dallied – perhaps you're right, I ought to encourage her, I expect – young people today need all the qualifications they can get* – she nods her head several times, in confirmation of her right conclusion – *I can't help her edu-cationally, I never sat any exams at all, too busy with my athletics, my hurdling – that was the trouble, too eager for sex instead – sorry if that offends you – I suppose it was all that jumping, I took the first fellow who came along – my tough luck it was him – I suppose we pay for our sins, don't we? – I certainly have*

on this sad note we'll leave her – she's right, isn't she, we all pay for our sins in the end

the morning's moving on now, none of the holidaymak-ers has gone out apart from Martin and Sean to walk across the fields, but Abigail's emerged into the light of day – come to that so has Ellen, both girls now ambling across the yard to the main gate locked, well engaged, in a conversation of sorts – the difference in age precludes any great confraternity [that should be sorority, shouldn't it? – but I like the word confraternity, so I'll leave it in – we'll use it in the sense of 'gang', a gang of two] – well, they haven't a great deal in common agewise, and come to that nothing much culturally, intellectually or recreationally, so the talk is limited to obser-vations on the things around them – Ellen leans against the gate while Abigail climbs to sit atop it

don't you hate farms? asks Abigail – *they smell awful*

I like the country – it's nice to see it all open

suppose so, but farms are always mucky, as well as smelly

Ellen looks dreamily towards the hill – *we went to Exmoor last year, it was wonderful, so open*

we've been across Dartmoor, didn't like it, too wild for me, all those rocks – I like Hampshire

oh, Jane Austen lived in Hampshire

did she? – I don't know anyone there, we've just passed through it, but I like the look of it, I like the red-brick houses – I might live there when I'm older

when you're on Exmoor you can just imagine Lorna Doone running across it, all wild

Abigail climbs down from the gate, looks towards the cottages – Brewster pads across to the girls, inviting both of them to reach down to pat him

isn't he lovely? remarks Ellen – *I wish we had a dog, only we can't because of PS – Mummy says you shouldn't have babies and animals together*

she's not a baby

well, she is in lots of ways, she's only a toddler – but Daddy says we can have a cat when she's three

we've got two cats as well, they're in a cattery

I like cats – Ellen looks down at Brewster, and in case he can hear her adds *dogs are all right too*

there's a bit of a silence – if it wasn't for Brewster patiently allowing himself to be petted, his tail moving slowly in appreciation, neither girl would know where to look or what to do – after a pause Abigail starts to head back for Wheatsheaf – *come on, Brew, come on*

Ellen follows at a slower pace – by the family car she stops and turns, looks back at the hill – *Sean and Daddy have gone there* she says wistfully – *I should've gone with them, but I wasn't ready*

you'd have got all muddy observes Abigail – *that's the sort of thing boys do, anyway*

the sorority never got off the ground, did it, and it's really not likely to – Abigail goes inside, Brewster comes to Ellen for one last pat before she too goes inside – it falls quiet again, the dog once more alone

when Sean returns from his field trip he runs excitedly to his mother – *we went miles, right to the top, you can see for miles, you can see the sea! – there's lots of trees, and lots of fields, no houses – and we saw some sheep, they ran away from us, and there were some horses in a garden!*

in a garden?

in a paddock says Martin authoritatively

and some cows, only they were a long way off, we couldn't see them properly, lots of them all in the corner of a field

that's jolly good says Pansy, smiling at Martin – *come on, wash your hands now, we're going to have lunch*

and what have you three been up to while we were out? – Martin asks

oh, this and that – not a lot – Ellen talked to Abigail, PS nearly got herself scratched by the cat, I've done some washing

sounds exciting

oh, it was, it was

Martin steers Sean into the bathroom while Pansy remains alone in the kitchen – she glances at the pots on the stove and then out of the window – not much to see from here, only the roof of the car and the few bushes at the edge of the farmhouse – there's the sky of course, a cloudy, grey sort of sky with no trace of joy in it – *you can see for miles* – she sighs – *from the top of the hill you can see for miles – who'd be a woman, and a mother at that?*

and I'm forgetting, there's going to be this boy, isn't there,

William – for all we know he wants to stay with us, like a lodger maybe, not want to go back to his mother in the north – I might have him to look after as well, do his washing and include him in the meals – oh, stupid, stupid man, why didn't he tell me years ago, why didn't he give it a thought – forgot all about him? – how can you forget something like that? – how can you not have it on your mind that one day your long-lost son might turn up? – oh, Martin!

Pansy sighs, a great big sigh that could be heard in the sitting room were anybody there – she attends to the pans, stirs and prods with a fork, looks in the grill, puts plates to warm and sighs again at the completion of this routine, a smaller sigh this time, inaudible, repressed – she calls to her family to come and sit up for lunch, have they washed their hands, take your places please for this grand repast from the lady of the house, that slavey in the kitchen, the one you all take for granted

in Wheatsheaf there's no talk of lunch – with the children being the age they are it's a case of scrambling in the kitchen to see what can be made, what can be concocted, what can be thrown together in sandwich form or jacket-potato form or simply potato-crisp and soft-drink form – it's a case of everyone for himself, elbows and barging not excepted, a free-for-all regulated only by custom and tradition, the custom being that Josh does his food-gathering first and the tradition being that Abigail claims not to be hungry but still manages to tag on the end and fill a plate with more than any of the others have – Beth is dainty about it, as befits a woman of fashion, sensibly watches her figure by having only three crispbread and a sensible portion of low-fat cream cheese, accompanied by three seedless red grapes and a glass of elderflower cordial, and she's not going to fight for it, not her, she waits until they've all done and then with decorum prepares her meal and with dignity carries it to the table, where she sits like Lady Maud at an afternoon soirée

8

Tuesday evening

what of the situation then? – the families did go out eventually, separately to places of interest and came back at teatime, a bit of fractiousness on the part of PS and a heavy moodiness in Michael being apparent as they dismounted from their cars and went inside the cottages – the Waterfords were the first back, having gone, from what they said, not much farther than the nearest town – the others seem to have gone to the beach again, but not with enough time to swim or do very much more than stroll along the strand – a bit of a listless day for them, but that's often the way, isn't it, when you're self-catering, on the third day you feel ready for a rest – of course, the weather's not been too grand, overcast and a little fresh, not much sign of the sun, so I can't say I blame them

and now in the Oxford household all the children are abed, while in the Waterfords the two youngsters are doing what they do best, lying on their beds listening to music – in the Oxfords the adults are tidying themselves up for their evening reception, while in the Waterfords the adults are prettying themselves up – to be neat and clean and tidy, to be presentable in fact, that's the face of self-respect, and in tidying themselves up that's what the Oxfords are doing – what does one say of the Waterfords prettying themselves up, for though such a process also means neat and clean and tidy, does it mean presentable or extra-presentable, is it due solely to a sense of self-respect? – or does prettying-up, as opposed to tidying up, suggest as I suspect it does a touch of promotion, of advertisement, of saying yes, I am neat and clean and tidy but I want you to notice that I am, so I want you to make a point of appreciating it

so while Martin slips on a shirt and does up the buttons without thinking about it very much, Josh will slip on a shirt [**don** a shirt maybe?] and wonder how many buttons to leave undone, whether the cuffs should be turned back and by how much, and whether the shirt will clash with anything else he's wearing, always assuming the colour is appropriate both for him and for the occasion – where Martin simply dresses, Josh will pursue calculations – trousers, socks and any other items will, for Martin, be no more than adjuncts, where for Josh they'll be considered accessories – you could be forgiven for thinking that Martin's a sloppy dresser, but then his answer to this will be that Pansy will put him right if he's failing in colour coordination or suitability

with Beth it's simple, unadulterated vanity – there's a faintly, no, totally, patronizing air in her view of Pansy, someone she sees as having the misfortune to lack the flair, the sensibilities, the fine appreciation of genteel grooming which it's Beth's good fortune to enjoy – not Pansy's fault of course, the poor woman's probably inherited it from her mother, some women are like that, plain and simple in their customs,

191

and they pass it on to their daughters without a second's thought for the poor girl's chances in life

it's an agonizing time for Beth – she knows exactly how she wants to look for this evening, knows precisely what would be the best thing to wear, and she goes so far as to lay out the clothes on the bed prior to her bath – but surrounded by foam and luxuriating in the heavenly bouquets of the expensive oil which was highly recommended by that American actress on television, Beth has second thoughts – she has a charitable nature, she's not one to be oblivious to the humiliation she might cause Pansy should she wear the clothes she's selected – she can be sure that Pansy will be simply dressed in her practical manner, and to swan in there gorgeously attired [albeit in a modest unflaunting sort of way] might provoke envy and hurt in the other woman's breast – let it not be said that Beth doesn't have feelings

it can be taken as certain that no such difficult moments are encountered in the Oxford household, where the ablutions and dressing of the hosts occupy no more time than is necessary for good order and appearance, and in no time at all both of them are trim and tidy, with just a hint of the aftershave on Martin and a faint aroma of his Christmas-present perfume on Pansy – it may be that they're practical people because for them this sort of evening is nothing at all special to sing about, and if truth be known it's to be the kind of evening they've already found out isn't particularly to their liking – in the short time of this holiday they've come to realize that while previous social fraternization has been acceptable and not entirely unpleasant, somehow this week's fratting has thrown up a different chiaroscuro which makes the prevailing anticipation fairly sour

I'm getting drunk says Pansy with a firmness of decision quite unusual for her

so am I announces Martin in close accord with his wife – *I bet I get drunker than you*

bet you don't

such harmony of purpose, such unity of view! – in actual fact neither of them really has such an aim, they'll get no more than tiddly, or if carried away on a surge of hospitality then perhaps extra merry, with a fragile sensation of instability in Pansy's knees and a tendency in Martin to talk too loud – being responsible parents the idea of getting drunk to the point of forgetting your duties wouldn't enter their heads – obviously we can see in these two the antithesis of Beth and Josh, and maybe that's how these things work out, in story-writing terms, I mean – quite without authorial direction the bones of the tale put on flesh and clothes, and we've seen what their attitudes to dress are like – I won't regale you with the difficulties of my own life, there's quite enough happening here as it is, what with bolshie kids, unhappy farming families, oppositional animals

when the time gets to ten past eight Josh says to Beth *ought we not to be going now?*

in a minute – she's not too happy with her simple look, it looks too simple, the result of careful selection and shrewd arrangement hasn't quite given her the effect she desires and something extra's called for, some small decoration to bring the ensemble to life – *I'll add that craft necklace Abigail gave me, thoroughly useless for anything else but just fine for this occasion – we're on a farm, so the wooden beads will be appropriate – what do you think?*

fine

well, seriously – do you think it looks all right? – not too chunky for the blouse? – not too rustic?

it's fine

yes, well, so much for a man's opinion, no use at all

we'd better be going – Josh is impatient – he doesn't want his cosmetic aura to diminish nor his clothes to lose their freshness, he's out to impress tonight – he stands by the door, a well-manicured hand on the knob, trying not to move his head too much in case his hairstyle misbehaves itself – *we did say eight o'clock*

I don't suppose it matters if we're a few minutes late, it'll give them time to settle the children – we don't want to go in there to the sound of babies crying

the difference here, of course, is that while Josh is trying to impress Pansy in a male/female way, Beth is trying to impress her in a female/female way, the difference being not so much in the element of impact [Josh's aim] as in the aspect of competition – [or would it be better to say rivalry, something I touched on way back near the beginning] – Josh doesn't in the least care what Martin might think of him, not tonight anyway, so long as Pansy approves – with Beth it's a case of impressing Pansy first and only then catching the eye and the approval of Martin – what a palaver! – and does it really matter? – no it doesn't, so let's get them to the Oxfords' front door as swiftly as possible

while PS and Sean have both dropped off, fast asleep and looking so peaceful, such good little children, so adorable when they've got their eyes closed, Ellen's insisting on her seniority being respected – it's holiday time, and she's always been told that when there's no school the next day she can be a little bit later settling down, so she's interpreted this little bit later as an unambiguous nine o'clock – no amount of pleading by her mother, specifying once more the strain on little eyes, will alter Ellen's determination to stand on her rights, so Pansy's reduced to bidding her be a good girl and making her promise to settle down promptly at the stated hour

which means that the guests have to be greeted in a low voice and an admonition to keep their early remarks in suitable key – no trouble for Beth to whisper away, and as it happens no trouble for Josh either, for it allows him to introduce a little sexiness into the way he asks Pansy how she is and isn't she looking lovely – in no time at all the four are sitting in the easy chairs like players at a card table, except that only a low coffee table, very unsuitable for card games other than snap, is between them supporting a goodly supply of drinks – oh, and some crisps and nuts and a little dish of green stuffed olives which Pansy assured Martin would go like hot cakes

the conversation hinges not on the nature of the day they've separately had but on the character of the Broadfields – *don't you think* asks Beth *their son's a little drippy – I mean, he's not like a farmer's son, is he? – I'd expect him to be a bit beefier, more of the country look about him* – and a small sigh of disappointment escapes her lips, whether at disillusion with a failed stereotype or at the absence of a genuine one – *I mean, put a suit on him and he'd look like a store manager*

it's not what it used to be, farming – this from Martin, as if he knows anything of the matter

I envy the girl says Pansy, and a faraway look comes into her eyes – *to be able to grow up surrounded by all this – she goes riding, you know, I've seen her in her gear – I'd love to have been born on a farm, really would*

you say that, but I bet you wouldn't – Martin's shaking his head sagely – *the smells, the noise – you hate chicken manure, and the word silage turns your stomach, not to mention pigswill – and there'd be lost nights helping with the lambing, pulling calves out of their mothers, all that sort of thing*

oh, I can see her on a farm says Josh – *she'd be like this girl here, riding gear, jodhpurs, being masterful with ponies – I bet you're masterful with Martin, aren't you?*

so I'm a pony now, am I?

Pansy lifts her chin – *I can be masterful when I want to be*

feeling somewhat left out of the conversation, seeing as how she initiated the subject of farms and farming, Beth re-enters with *I couldn't live on a farm – that shotgun did it for me*

Josh's reluctance to let go of a good theme impels him to ask Pansy on what occasions she's inclined to feel masterful – *after all, it would help me to know how to handle you – I'd know when to submit*

it's patently on the tip of Pansy's tongue to ask *submit to what?* but this is something she stifles, being aware that this sort of banter, which so concerned her the other evening, will readily be taken as encouragement by Josh – she instead deliberately ignores the inference and asks him about Michael – *what did he do with himself yesterday?*

it annoys Josh that the seating arrangements in Stook are different to those in Wheatsheaf, where a sofa and two deep upholstered armchairs are provided – here he finds himself remote from Pansy in one of the four rather upright, only-part-upholstered easy chairs that denote independence and abstention from intimacy – were he in their own place he might get on the sofa next to her, or at the very least be able to perch with familiarity on the arm of Pansy's chair, from where contact would be feasible – he leans towards her as much as possible, but she leans in the other direction, and from this he deduces she's deliberately playing hard to get

it's when Martin goes into the kitchen to open another bottle of wine and Beth follows him there that Josh boldly seizes his chance – he reaches out and before she can move it grasps Pansy's hand firmly in his own

it would be very exciting if we could run away together he says in a low voice

oh, don't be so silly she replies, snatching her hand away – *I've given up running*

you know what I mean – I'd love us to be alone together

and what would Beth think? – I don't think it would be a good idea

just you and me? – a very good idea, I think, you're extremely fanciable

that's nice to know, I hope Martin thinks so too

no, seriously – can't we work it so that we can get to bed?

– we don't have a lot of time – you're ready for it, I know you are – I certainly am

in the world in which he operates, and in the inner reaches of his being, Josh has little available space for the exercise of subtlety – with a direct approach, strong aftershave and an unwavering regard for the strength of his personality, not to mention his conviction that all women are 'up for it' as he might say, Josh finds subtlety an unnecessary form of delay – be honest, he'd aver, come straight out with it, don't dilly-dally, always gets you what you want

except, of course, there are women of Pansy's ilk in the world, open neither to the straight, brutal approach, nor to subtlety – she stands up quickly, looks down at Josh as one might look down on something the cat's left on the carpet, and gives him her straight opinion

I think you're rather nasty

this is the exact moment when, as if on some proper cue, Beth and Martin re-enter the sitting room – they hear the words, they see the tableau, they draw conclusions – Beth looks at Josh, Martin looks at Pansy, the dissenting couple look at their partners, she with an appeal for support, he with an appeal for understanding – a frozen moment, usually described as pregnant, though I can't say why, prevails – the scene breaks up as Pansy, brushing past Beth, leaves the room and takes herself upstairs

Beth has a weary tone to her voice when she asks Josh what's happened, almost as if she's asked the question on many other occasions

she took offence at something I said

and what was that? – Martin wants to know before he

goes after Pansy – his tone has a sharp edge to it, an unusually sharp edge

I was making a joke – she took it the wrong way, that's all

as Martin leaves the room Beth gives a sigh and sits down – *you and your big mouth!*

in enforced whispers [because that naughty little Ellen's still awake, though not reading, thank God] behind the closed door of their bedroom Martin and Pansy enter into a discussion of the issue

a proposition?

it's not funny – he's revolting, he's lecherous

what exactly did he say?

he said let's go to bed together, and that he knew I was ready for it!

Martin goes to the door – *right – I'm going to have a few words*

oh no, don't make a fuss now, not with the children asleep – leave it till the morning, and then it'll probably be best not to say anything at all

I've got plenty to say!

yes, I know – but let's leave it for now – he knows what I think, and we'll just do our own thing tomorrow

we can be assured that the remainder of the evening, fractured as it has been by this little contretemps, doesn't pass as joyfully as it was intended to – Pansy and Martin are in the bedroom for such a long time that the others quietly leave and return to Wheatsheaf, where Beth proceeds to admonish her husband and Josh practises his indignation – when the incumbents tentatively venture downstairs they find an empty sitting room and gratitude pours from them freely, God is thanked wholeheartedly

don't know what we'd have done if they'd still been here

chucked them out says Pansy with feeling – *I don't know how Beth sticks him – and you've got to work with him, haven't you, that won't be easy*

it's not easy as it is – we've had one or two differences of opinion – on management issues, not personal

well now it's personal for sure – let's finish that wine, I need to get the image of him leering at me out of my head

I didn't know he was like that – well, I'd heard he was a bit loose, there's always talk about him, but I didn't think he'd try anything on with you – has he been like that before?

thank God no, or we wouldn't be on holiday with them – the other night it was a bit of a joke, but it wasn't tonight

with wine and green olives they console themselves and we'd do best to leave them with their melancholy view of the coming days – how will it be tomorrow, and the day after, how will they face one another in the morning? – we shall have to wait and see – perhaps in the meantime we can skip over to the farmhouse, to Lance with his problem, maybe that's all sorted now, maybe he and his father are the best of pals, maybe they're having a drink together, laughing over something Bert said – let's drop in on them and see for ourselves

here they are, well, not together, the old man's in front of the television and Lance is dithering in the hallway outside the living room – done the deed yet, Lance?

I don't see the funny side of it like you seem to do – it's going to cause ructions however I put it to him well, you can't delay forever – haven't you got a date when you have to start your course?

yes, I have, two weeks' time, but I've got to sort a lot out before then – I can't just go off and leave him in the lurch, I'll have to leave things in order – and he's got to come to some arrangement with Bert and possibly another hand

is it going to cost him money?

of course, he gets me cheap, I live in and I'm always available – yes, it's going to cost him the going rate for farm labourers, which'll be a lot more than he's ever paid me – I sometimes wonder if his stance on the perpetuation of the species is really no more than a matter of economic consideration – sons who follow their fathers into the family trade always save the business money, most of the time they're working for nothing – well, I aim to be independent and get rewarded for my labours, I've done with trying to live life on a pittance

that word again, very popular in these parts! – so, Lance, here you are poised outside the room, about to burst in with the news?

I'm waiting until this programme's finished – after it he always just reads the paper, so I'll go in then – another minute or so

take a deep breath

well, I know what I'm going to say, but whether or not I get the chance will be a different matter

I wish you the best of luck, and I'm sure all the readers do too

thanks – of course, it's not the best night tonight, but then it never is – tomorrow would be better, but I think I should try now

yes, of course

you wouldn't like to disappear, would you? – only I'm better on my own – you don't mind, do you?

oh, certainly, I understand, these things are much better done without an audience – best of luck then – we'll go and see how Tilly's doing, get out of your way – let's just pop in here to this pink and purple room and ask . . .

oh, do you have to? – why can't you stay downstairs with Lance?

he's otherwise engaged – besides we haven't seen what you're up to for a while – what **are** you up to, by the way – why are you lying on the floor with your legs up the wall? – some sort of Buddhist exercise?

no, don't be silly – it's just a stretching exercise

to flatten the tummy?

to strengthen the abdominal muscles – it's good for the digestion as well – it's not the only exercise I do, you've just caught me at this one

how's the studying going?

how does it look? – am I holding a book? – I can't very well write precis in this position, can I? – it's not term time, anyway

well, no, I meant how's it going generally?

it's coming on, I suppose, I'll start next month in earnest – I'm doing nine subjects

that sounds a lot to take on

it is – some are easy, some are too difficult for me to do

at home, like the science, I'll have to do that at school – but
we'll see, after Christmas it'll be different

it'll get harder, will it?

it certainly will, in more ways than one – oh, here comes
someone else to check up on me

what are you doing that for?

she's firming up her abdominal muscles, Mrs Broadfield,
exercises

why don't you go for a run, do some jogging?

can you see me doing that? – really?

well, that doesn't look very good for you

well, don't watch me then!

I think we ought to withdraw, Mrs B – a word in your ear
out on the landing

you haven't been telling her about my plans, have you?

of course not – but I just wondered if you know that
Lance is about to tell his father about **his** plans – he was waiting for a television programme to finish and then he was
going to go in and break the news

I haven't heard anything – I'm sure if he had there'd be a
bit of a rumpus going on, and it's all quiet down there – he'll
be reading the paper, I expect

perhaps Lance is still hovering outside the door, plucking
up the courage

he wasn't there when I came up – I expect it's like always,
he keeps saying he's going to do it and he never does – I've
seen him outside that door before, and he just gets cold feet
and goes to his room – but he'll have to tell him soon or give
up the idea altogether – that's what I fear, you know, that
Lance will never have the guts to leave, and then he'll be

stuck once I've gone – just the two of them, sniping at each other all the time – what a life for the boy! – well, whether he makes the break or not I'm still going – if he does stay on then we'll never get the holiday complex off the ground, that's for sure, so it'll have to be a case of a straight divorce

and that means he'll have to settle something on you?

what's he got? – only the farm – he'd have to sell it, wouldn't he, to give me my half-share – I suppose that way Lance will be free, I've never thought of that – that might be the best thing, blow the complex

except that the complex would be a source of income

well, what do you reckon this farm's worth? – I'm sure I could live on half of its value, couldn't you? – buy a house and have some investments, that'll see me nicely

have you consulted a solicitor about this yet? – I mean, are you sure you'll get half of everything?

well, you do, don't you?

I don't know for sure – there are all sorts of different settlements, and in the case of land there might be other factors involved

now don't you worry me – one way or another he's got to give me some money, and as far as I know I'm entitled to half of everything – now thinking about Lance, as I said, it might be good for him if I forgot about the complex and just sued for divorce – if the farm's sold then Lance will be free anyway, he won't need to face the question of following in his father's footsteps – I think I'd better tell him that, put his mind at rest

tell him your plans?

he's got to know sometime or other – off goes Mrs

Broadfield, whether to tell him straight away or whether to mull it over further, who knows?

her saying that about the wife getting a half-share doesn't always work out, which is why I cautioned her – it doesn't always go like that, certainly not the fifty–fifty Mrs Broadfield expects – still, she'll find out when she goes to a solicitor

9

Wednesday morning

with Brewster in his accustomed place, sunning himself before Wheatsheaf's door, Sammy places himself behind the gate and looks through the rails – the two adversaries stare at each other without blinking or moving – Brewster's not going to make the first move, a decision seemingly motivated partly by indolence and partly by diplomacy, he remains supine but alert – Sammy too is in no hurry to begin the process of provocation, sitting primly with his tail curled round over his feet – then he unfurls his tail and stands up – he yawns – he reaches up with both front paws and opens his claws on to the still-painted wood, then with slow delibera-tion begins the scratching, digging those claws in deeply to score new channels beside the old

Brewster's not impressed – exchanging this warm, easeful condition for one where he has to gallop across a dusty yard holds no appeal – he remains with his head on his paws, just that one eye watching – when no response is forthcoming Sammy leaves off, stands for a moment indecisively behind the gate – what is he to do? – eventually, and with a fair amount of trepidation, he steps through the gate, begins walking across the yard – Brewster is a-quiver with excitement, for Sammy's not taking the usual course of slinking round the edge but coming almost straight towards him – when he's only three metres away he stops, sits on his haunches and with an elegant paw begins to wash his face – Brewster watches this display of bravado, tries to comprehend it, tilts his head this way and that

Sammy gives one look at Brewster then turns to the side to walk to a spot by the wall within two metres of Brewster, whose head is turned sideways to watch but who otherwise makes no movement – Sammy lets himself flop down with his back against the wall, makes small attempts to continue his washing before closing his eyes and allowing the sun to play upon his stomach

Brewster lays down again, paws stretched before him – he places his head on his paws and he too closes his eyes, well, one of them – close together, the two animals take their ease in the morning warmth

no one witnesses this exceptional camaraderie, for no one has yet ventured outside their door – but you can rely on at least one human being coming round early, that little terror in the cot

I'm not going to wake up Mummy – I'm not going to wake up anyone – I'm not going to wake up Ellen – I'm going to stand here and talk to Timmy – hello, Timmy, what's your name? – is your name Timmy? – all together now – we're going to the seaside, I'm going in the water and the sand-castle – you can come, Timmy – what's your name? – is it Timmy? – I want to get out of the cot, you go first, Timmy,

*you go first – all together now – I can see you on the floor,
Timmy, can you see me? – I'm getting out now, I want to get
out – MUMMY! – MUMMY! – WANT TO GET OUT
NOW, WANT TO GET OUT – MUMMY! – MUMMY!*

Ellen turns over, pulls the duvet over her ears – *shut up,
Penny! – you wait till Mummy comes*

MUMMY! – MUMMY!

shut up!

but it's not Mummy who comes in all bleary and tousled,
it's Daddy, rubbing his eyes and yawning, plucking PS from
the cot and taking her from the room – Ellen throws herself
on to her back, slaps the duvet with her arms and gives out
a great humph of a sigh

*if I'd been born into a different family I wouldn't have to
put up with her – I'd have a room to myself, I'd have a nice
window looking out on to a lovely garden, a big lawn with
a tremendous oak tree . . . no, a monkey-puzzle tree, yes that
would be nice, a monkey-puzzle tree with a seat all round its
trunk – and the branches would dip down, there'd be a lovely
hammock to lie in – in my room I'd have a kidney-shaped
dressing table with lots of pretty things on it, and a writing
desk near the window – there might be peacocks there, walking about the lawns, calling, making that loud noise – oh,
why can't it be like that!*

it never is, dearie, never is – but it's so nice to dream, isn't
it? – Ellen reaches out for her book, opens the page at her
linen bookmark to bury her head and her mind in fiction

meanwhile we ought to visit Michael, someone we've not
seen or heard of for some time – he too is awake, unusually
for him, awake to the teeming thoughts running through his

head and awake also to the sound of his father's snores – he stares at the Artex ceiling without seeing it, his eyes blankly roaming the rough surface

3726, 3726 – better not write it down, I might lose it and someone'll find it – 3726, got it fixed in my head now, just like it was my own number – well, it is, isn't it? – shows how stupid he is, doesn't it, leaving it on the computer, so easy to find, only took me ten minutes – 3726 – the card's no problem, always in his wallet, all his cards, I could have the lot – I need the wallet, it's got a wad of money in it, saw it last night, I'll need that to get away and start off – 3726 – still got the problem of where to go, I don't really fancy Liverpool, or Manchester come to that – I think it's got to be London, that's the only place, and there's lots of others there – it's a big place, easy to get lost there, so I shouldn't worry about them finding me – got to go home first though, that's where everything is, everything I'll want to take with me – 3726 – I wish I'd done it last week, wouldn't have had to come to this crummy place – I'll have to act up a bit though until I go, got to pretend I'm enjoying myself, I suppose – what great excitement's on the agenda today, I wonder?

and in the next room, Abigail, what are her thoughts? – only just waking up, roused by the snoring of Josh, she lies on her side with eyes open staring at the window with its pink Roman blind – thoughts? – has she had time for any yet, or is she still coming to?

that pink is awful, don't like pink – it should be dark red, maroon or something – whatever makes people put pink everywhere? – and I wouldn't have a blind anyway, I'd have curtains, nice long ones to the floor, maybe red, but with a pattern of some sort – that would clash with this carpet though – ugh, blue! – pink blind and blue carpet! – it's a wonder they haven't painted the walls yellow, they might just as well have done – they should get the carpet up, work on the boards, they'd come up nice, and a wooden floor looks marvellous – Nula's got wooden floors all over her house, amazing what a difference they make

the only one who doesn't wake up to the snoring of Josh is Beth, but then she's got this ear-muff arrangement [in pink, I'm afraid, Abi] and she lies on her back in some sort of regal repose with her nose in the air and mouth open to match her husband's – no snores from her though, she just wheezes in a ladylike fashion – have you noticed that when talking to a woman about such things she'll insist that men snore and women merely wheeze, just as they don't sweat like men, merely perspire? – [I imagine there's a scale for these things somewhere where you pass gradually from wheezing to snoring, or from perspiring to sweating, a scale which could be used quite handily to judge the depth of a man's virility or the height of a woman's grace – a queen must wheeze most tenderly, an out-and-out villain snore horrendously]

another person who's just woken up, not only because of PS shouting Mummy but also by Martin making a lot of noise carrying her back to a sighing Pansy, is little Sean – he's got his favourite soldier doll in his hands almost before he opens his eyes, holding it up and by the look of his actions pretending it can fly like an aeroplane

I can see over the hill, I can see where they are down there, all across the fields, all right to that tall chimney –

quick, back to the trees – this accompanied by the action of stuffing the doll beneath the duvet – *can't see me here – right, hide, wait, we'll jump out – lots of trees here, I can lie on the ground – if I look up there's all the branches, they're moving about touching each other, the leaves are falling down sometimes – I can make a bed, get all the leaves to cover me, I'd be like an animal, a hedgehog – I could be a badger, going down a hole – when we climbed over that stile I didn't sit on it, but I could have – I will today, we'll go there again – I could go on my own! – I know the way now – mustn't tread on the crops though*

if we leave young Sean with his daydreaming we can take ourselves into the yard to watch the continuing interplay between Brewster and Sammy – we left them sunning themselves, a cautious détente in existence, a couple of metres separating them – so far, so good – Sammy still lies on his side against the wall, eyes closed [apparently], with only an occasional twitch from his tail but otherwise looking the very picture of relaxation

then he moves, stands up, stretches and yawns – hard to tell whether he does this naturally, as he might in the privacy of his own spot by the pallets, or whether it's done for effect, to demonstrate to the watching dog that he isn't particularly bothered by Brewster's presence – Brewster lifts his head, fixes his gaze on Sammy, both eyes wide and curious

then Sammy begins to walk – he stares at Brewster and makes directly for him with a steady, unhurried pace – Brewster looks at him with quizzical eyes but remains in his sphinx-like position – Sammy doesn't falter in his steady walk, keeps going until he reaches a spot immediately by

Brewster's head, and then with unconscious care steps over Brewster's front paws to pass beneath the dog's snout, lifting his tail vertically as he does so – Brewster's chin comes up as the tail sweeps beneath it, his eyes show their whites as he follows the cat in its continuing walk across the yard – Sammy doesn't look back, Brewster doesn't move – within another minute the cat has gone, the dog remains alone in his position – after a few seconds more he lowers his head on to his paws again, this time closing both eyes firmly

this harmony, this goodwill between the two animal creatures is not matched, I regret to say, by the human creatures who currently inhabit the cottages known as Stook and Wheatsheaf – within the confines of each cottage there may be harmony, but between the front doors a cold demarcation has sprung up – whirling round the old stones on the prevailing breeze there is rampant indignation, an indignation taking the form of righteousness in one residence and resentment in the other – Wheatsheaf witnesses the resentment, that the other lot should be so stuffy and easily offended – Stook houses the righteousness, that anyone should be so grossly improper – this air of hostility, at the moment unexpressed but as potent as methane gas, might well explain why there are no signs of activity – behind the front doors preparations are no doubt being made to service the day, to gather the troops for an expedition, but there's a sense of waiting for the others to make the first move

eventually, seemingly hours after Sammy left the scene, Brewster is awoken and looks up as the door to Stook is opened – Martin emerges with bags and clothing, unlocks the car and begins loading – a minute later Ellen and Sean follow, go quietly to their seats – following them comes Pansy with PS in her arms, deposits the child with accompanying whispers in her seat, leans in to fasten the straps – Martin brings more goods from the cottage before closing the door and stowing them in the boot – having secured PS Pansy goes briskly to the gate and opens it, stands there until Martin's started the car and driven it out of the yard – the gate is shut, tied and left behind as the Oxfords disappear for the day – it's safe now for the others to emerge

I've said disappear for the day, but it could be that they've gone altogether – it didn't seem as if enough loading was done, but who knows what's in their minds, we can only wait to see if they return at a later time – in the case of the Waterfords this family seems to have been waiting for the first move to be made by the others, for no sooner has the Oxfords' car passed from view than first Josh and then Michael step into the yard – Brewster, for so long on his own with but a cat for company, leaps up, wags his tail, dances round them as they open the doors of the car – fond words are spoken to the animal, pats and taps are its rewards, and once the tailgate is opened Brewster happily leaps in to take up what must be his accustomed place – Abigail, pale-looking in the light of day, precedes her mother carrying a couple of plastic bags, while Beth, firmly closing the Wheatsheaf door as if it was her own home and security was paramount for the sake of the wardrobes, brings with her a small basket out of which peep several bottles of soft drink – all but Michael are mounted up, the vehicle goes towards the gate where the boy does the honours before joining his family on what must be **their** day's outing well, everyone's gone now and I think we need a little diversion, just for the hell of it – let me talk of the tricks of the trade – read this: 'she experienced the sequacity of the pellucid gossamer satinate chemise as it descended gravitationally' – this trips you up, doesn't it, slows you down, makes reading tiring, and this is done intentionally [sometimes] to prolong or delay the forthcoming action – what that really means, and let's face it the raciness is all to the good, is 'she took off her slip' – that makes easier reading, but that's too quick and (a) the action when it comes is less dramatic, and (b) the book's too short – trick of the trade, you see – another trick is to put in something totally irrelevant, such as this little diversion, to change the tone and pad things out a bit

having done that, let's get on with real life – not much going on once the families have left on their outings – no good scouting round the farm, there's only Sammy, comfortable on the Broadfield bed, happily sleeping off his adventure – Mrs B and Tilly have gone shopping, left just after the Waterfords, walked down the lane [their private lane, the decent one behind the hedge] to get the bus – perhaps she's going to have a look at the new estate, select her house – Mr B's gone off in his Land Rover again, probably to spend some time with Bert over a cup of tea, and Lance is back on his tractor – the cows, that little herd we've seen nothing of, which makes us begin to doubt their existence, are presumably in some distant field, and the chickens which we last saw on Saturday, seem to have left home altogether – very quiet, this farm, eerie almost, gives you the creeps – a couple of crows, big and black, reminiscent of vultures, sit silent and menacing on the farmhouse roof – across the rough shingle of the yard only tiny insects scamper, flies congregate near the empty pigsty – the sun becomes hotter as the day progresses, hoverflies appear, and one lone cabbage butterfly passes quickly across the yard into the farmhouse garden – this isn't really a garden, it's simply those bushes I mentioned, chaenomeles, hydrangea, lilac, clustering round one wall with a fence to keep them in order, relics of an attempt at softening the look of things – straggling up the corner of the wall is a Boston ivy, clinging for dear life to the crumbling pointing – time indeed for all this to be brought into a different era, to be given that makeover Gregory Price-Masters recommends – *they won't regret it* he's bound to say, getting out his drawing board

Mrs Broadfield returns alone – *Tilly's stayed with a friend, they're going to bring her back later – well, that's what she says, but I've got my suspicions, I think there's a boy involved somewhere, if you ask me – she's so secretive, that girl*

well, she's bound to have her own life, she's fifteen now, isn't she?

oh yes, of course, but up to now it's been all horses, horses – never had time for any boyfriends, she always told me

then it might be the reason for her change of heart – perhaps she's in love

nonsense, she can't be in love – I'd know about it, wouldn't I? – mothers can always tell

still, you never know

no, you don't – from one day to the other you just don't know what's going to happen – I always say there's only one thing you can be sure of in this world, and it's that you can't be sure of anything – but I'd be very surprised if she'd suddenly got herself a boyfriend, that I would – never shown any inclination up till now

has Lance got a girlfriend?

well, sort of – there's a girl called Rosemary he sees, but I don't think there's much in it – nice girl, bit old-fashioned, lives with her mother and an auntie, funny couple they are – don't know what happened to her father – yes, he goes out with her now and then, but I don't think it's much more than a friendship – they were at school together – to be honest, I don't think he has much luck with girls

into the farmhouse she goes, a small bag of shopping in hand, not much to show for nearly a day out – perhaps she too has a boyfriend!

so it's quiet again, nothing happens until Tilly returns, not brought back by anyone but walking slowly up the lane into the yard – she has an expression of weariness on her face, as if the effort of the walk's been too much for her

buck up, Tilly! – had a good day? – might there have been a boyfriend?

a sour look from her, she's definitely fed up about something – *none of your business – I've been shopping – and it's a long walk up from the bus stop*

you didn't get a lift? – your mother said someone was bringing you back

well, they obviously didn't, did they? – I walk for the good of my health, like I do yoga – anyway, she doesn't know everything about me, she wouldn't want to, either – I'm entitled to a private life, private friends of course you are – it's just that I was wondering if you'd swapped your pony for a boyfriend

she stops walking, pauses near the small gate – a swift glance towards the farmhouse door seems to indicate a measure of confidentiality – *perhaps I have, perhaps I haven't – I don't have a regular boyfriend, not any more*

I'm sorry – has something happened, is it all over?

yes – very much over – not today though – I had to go . . . – well, never mind, you wouldn't want to be burdened with my troubles

it's sometimes good to talk about it, I wouldn't find it a burden – you can't always talk to your family, can you?

you're right there – you can't talk to Dad, Lance can't even talk to him

what about your mother? – she seems an understanding sort of woman, and she's concerned for you

there's a long pause followed by a deep sigh – *yes, I know – I'll have to talk to her sometime, won't I?*

and with that enigmatic statement Tilly goes inside, the door closes behind her

by five o'clock Lance is back at the farm, rattling into the yard on his tractor, tucking it away in a shed round behind the farmhouse – he comes across stiffly, rubbing his hands together as if to signify satisfaction with a good day's work

well, Lance, the opportunity fizzled out yesterday, did it?

you could say that – it just wasn't the most appropriate time

trying again tonight?

no – I'm going out, and I want to enjoy myself – the time will come, don't you worry about it

and he too goes into the happy household, leaving only the villain himself to come back from his day's industry – I'm not going to wait that long, I'm off to chapter ten

10

Wednesday evening

by now we're quite used to seeing them come back, usually after an exhausting day – last out, first in, and it's the Waterfords, Michael quite cheerfully doing duty at the gate and then almost sprinting across the yard to the cottage – Brewster's happy to be back, immediately goes to the pigsty to cock a leg and then across to the little gate where he pokes his nose through the rails for a minute

having noticed the Oxfords are not yet returned there's no apparent hurry to disappear inside – the females hover at the door finishing a conversation while Michael stands with hands on hips [a most unusual pose for him, as there's generally a bit of the slouch about him] surveying the yard and the fields beyond it like a commander planning his field of battle – whether or not he's enjoyed himself today is hard to tell, it seems unlikely though – but he doesn't look so miserable, so downhearted and preoccupied as he has of late – could he have changed his mind about leaving when he gets home? – have he and Josh reached some plateau of understanding? – it doesn't seem so when we look at Josh, walking slowly round his vehicle, touching it here and there, bending to look closely at a wheel or a particularly dirty mark which might be concealing a scratch – they all seem very relaxed, in fact they look just the picture of a family on holiday

they go inside, one by one with Michael last – Brewster settles himself against the door, scans the yard to make sure he doesn't miss anything – the yard returns to that air of timeless desuetude which prevailed before Mrs Broadfield broke the spell

I'd better do that, then, what I said, go and see her – this is Beth, continuing an earlier conversation once the children have gone to their rooms – *later on, once they've settled the kids*

I can't see why you should bother – if they want to take that attitude then that's their lookout – we don't have to put ourselves out – just write them off, that's all

that's easy to say, but we've got to get through the rest of the week, and if we're at odds with them it'll make it hard for us, not them

please yourself then – as far as I'm concerned I've lost interest – if she doesn't want to know, that's it

Beth sighs – *we've got two more full days, I don't want to have to spend my time avoiding them – I don't mind going to apologize, tell her it was all a mistake*

this whole week's a mistake

oh, we'll recover from it

Beth concerns herself with things in the kitchen, while Josh gets himself a can of beer from the refrigerator and takes it into the sitting room, to throw himself heavily into the armchair – ***you might*** he calls he stares at the empty fireplace, taking long swigs from the can, letting things drift through his mind – *no, I'm amazed at how quickly I've lost interest in her, but it's to be expected, I suppose – my advances have been so rudely spurned that I've rapidly crossed the line between desire and cold disinterest – in my case [which may well be the case with everybody, for all I know] cold disinterest quickly becomes dislike – I've gone from seeing in Pansy everything wonderful to a view of her as some sort of disagreeable old hag – I'll find it hard now to be civil to her if we come face to face again – I've no remorse in my breast for this state of antipathy, no sense of guilt, why should I have, the guilt's all hers, turning suddenly from someone covetable to someone distasteful – she's the one to bear all the blame, not me – she isn't what she gave herself out to be – it wasn't me misreading the signs, it was her fabricating them – she was playing with me, and that's something I can't easily overlook*

so a difficult time then for Josh – surely at some point he's got to act normally, treat Pansy naturally – it seems Beth will apologize for him, but I think it should come from him, don't you? – as I said, it was really rather trivial and a quick apology might calm the waters sufficiently for the remainder of the holiday to continue in some kind of pacific way – if he persists in his condemnation of her then it **will** be difficult

Brewster barks to let his family know that the Oxfords have returned [didn't decamp after all then] and settles down again at the door to watch them – it's once more Pansy at the gate, swinging it wide for Martin to drive through, then with practised ease closing it and tying up the string – she's getting very good at it now, not like the first time, when she had to be helped – she walks across the yard while Martin opens the door for Ellen and Sean to climb out – there are no signs of haste, no trying to get inside quickly before they're spotted by the Waterfords, not like the morning's departure, which was somewhat hushed and secretive – there's almost an air of deliberate boldness, as though they're taking the line that they've got nothing to be ashamed of, they're not the ones to blame for any possible rupture

once indoors it's the usual hasty sorting out, the quick preparation of a supper, the mollification of a somewhat testy PS who fell asleep on the way home and didn't want to be woken up – she whines and clings to Pansy's trousers, provoking her big sister into a slamming-door mood and her big brother into a competitive attention-seeking mood because he's feeling neglected – Martin sails through the turmoil with a calmness that irritates Pansy who, with one hand trying to grill fish fingers and with the other seeking to uncling the tight grip of PS's fingers, doesn't exactly appreciate his detachment – *all together now* may be the watchword and catchphrase of the charmer at her knees but reiterated continuously it's enough to give Pansy the screaming abdabs

none of which is soothed by a knocking on the front door, a firm but polite knock, a knock with respectful knuckles – Pansy doesn't actually yell in case the person outside hears her, but the hoarse whisper which she directs at Martin has all the characteristics of a muted shout – *you go! – and don't let them in!*

when he opens the door, only partly in case it's Josh, who'd be bold enough to walk in without being invited, Martin's taken aback to see Lance

I'm sorry to disturb you says the farmer's son with true apology in his voice – *only I wondered if your son would like this*

in his hands Lance holds a ram's horn, ridged and curved, of a dark grey colour – he holds it out for Martin to take – *it's years old, from a Norfolk ram – I had it when I was a boy and I haven't got a lot of use for it now – perhaps Sean might want it – if he doesn't . . .*

oh, he'll be thrilled, he'll love it – are you sure? – if you've had it for such a long time . . .

honestly, I'm clearing things out anyway – it'll remind him of the farm

well, it's very kind of you

once he's closed the door Martin has every intention of calling out to Sean that there's something for him, but Pansy quickly motions him to be quiet

give it to him now and he'll never go to sleep – leave it until the morning, hide it

very kind of him, isn't it? – not a bad lad, I suppose

it wasn't me who thought he was

with the easy felicity of the detached author [and of you, the equally detached reader] we shall pass over this busy scene to one of a more relaxed nature, using our liberty to fast-forward to the evening when finally, finally, peace reigns because the youngest are now asleep – Ellen, of course, is allowed to read until eight-thirty, but unless someone goes in to check she'll be at it until ten o'clock – Martin and Pansy are relaxing over a bottle of rather pricey Australian wine which they felt they owed themselves when passing an off-licence this afternoon, and it's unlikely either of them will remember their daughter's permit – Ellen **will** ruin her eyes and need glasses by the time she's eleven, which might appeal to her because she could then look more studious than she does at present

just before they pass the half-bottle mark a knock comes at the outside door – to Martin who opens it Beth says *do you mind if I come in for a moment? – I think we owe you an apology for last night*

no matter how strained our feelings, whatever high dudgeon we are currently enjoying, however peeved we may be at the dispositions of others, we civilized beings cannot help but fall into the customary ways of polite behaviour – when Beth's shown in to the living room the first thing Pansy says is – *will you have some wine?*

doesn't go down too well with Martin, not because he isn't civilized and doesn't share that manner of polite behaviour but because he's looking at the bottle and thinking *only a small glass, Pansy, only a small one!*

Beth accepts, and continuing with the same polite behaviour accepts also the invitation to take a seat – she carefully arranges her skirt with the same deliberation that she's no doubt employed in carefully arranging the words she wishes to utter and takes a small sip at the glass – Pansy and Martin smile with fragile attention and wait to hear what she has to say, being only too well aware that she comes as an emissary on her husband's behalf, and not necessarily with his blessing

I'm afraid Josh was a bit out of order last night – he's very embarrassed at what he did, what he said – he really is quite sorry he upset you, Pansy, he didn't mean to – he's a bit

sheepish now and doesn't quite know how to face you, so he asked me to come and break the ice for him – it really was a big mistake on his part

Pansy's unimpressed by this second-hand apology – her face remains serious and unsmiling, she looks straight at Beth with the anticipation of further declarations of remorse

so I hope you can put it to one side, and we can carry on with the holiday

this isn't enough – while Martin shifts in his seat and seems about to say something which would allow bygones to be bygones, Pansy puts down her glass and asks Beth a straight question – *what do you think about it?*

what do I think? – well, he was very silly, wasn't he? – he shouldn't have said what he did

is that all, that he was silly to say it? – what's your view of your husband asking me to go to bed with him? – doesn't it worry you that he was doing that? – don't you care that he was behaving like that? – if I thought Martin was propositioning another woman, especially in circumstances as close as this, and if I thought he meant it, then he'd be booted out of the house – all you seem to be worried about was that he said it, not that he meant it!

Beth's taken aback by the vehemence of this argument – the relaxed, rather beseeching look which her face had worn up till now changes into one of stony offence – surprise at this reception of her apology makes her put down her glass also, leaning forward to deposit it on the coffee table – when she straightens up there's a change of tone in her manner

I'm afraid my relationship with Josh obviously doesn't match yours with Martin – the way he spoke to you is what

I said, a mistake, and he shouldn't have done what he did –
if he was 'propositioning' you like you say, then that's what
he does, that's the way he is

a little silence ensues, during which each of the participants tries to analyse and understand which way the
conversation is going – on Martin's part there seems to be
confusion, whether at the words of Beth or of his wife is not
apparent – he frowns heavily and slowly looks at one after
the other – he licks his lips as if about to say something, but
the words seem not to be available – on Pansy's part there
appears a measure of confusion as well, but different to
Martin's, it's laced with a lack of comprehension that's evident as she stares hard at Beth – for her part, the object of
this stare shows a high level of indignation and defensiveness
– she didn't come here to be attacked when all she was doing
was apologizing for her husband – she stares back at Pansy
and adds *I'm sorry if you feel differently*

the silence comes again, a different sort of character to it,
one that suggests no one knows quite how to wrap this up –
Martin seems the most uncomfortable, fidgeting in his chair,
taking long sips at his wine – he looks towards Pansy, regarding it as her business primarily, nothing much to do with him
– this is two women disagreeing on their attitudes to marriage – he seems surprised by Beth's laid-back attitude towards
the philandering plans of her husband, but probably holds
the view that some women just go through life accepting the
inevitable – when she says that's how Josh is he can quite
believe it

Pansy's expression indicates a greater depth to her
thoughts – where she was leaning forward to question Beth

226

she now leans back, but this does not necessarily mean as a style of relaxation, in fact she's anything but relaxed – her hands in her lap involuntarily caress themselves, a stimulus to reflection – what seems to be affecting her with the same surprise as that of Martin, is that Beth should be so accommodating of Josh's disloyalty, but this surprise is tempered with the ease with which it's done – in Pansy's book Beth should be more angry than she appears to be

the pause lasts long enough for Beth to take it that her presence is uncomfortable for all concerned and she stands up – *I'd better be getting back – I hope you'll accept the apology*

this is formal and with no trace of any apology in it – neither Martin nor Pansy stand up and for a moment Beth hesitates, waiting for something to be said in reply – the response eventually comes from Pansy

do you approve of him having affairs, Beth?

this is straightforward enough for Beth to feel she needs to sit down again, and she perches on the edge of the seat, bites her lip before speaking

there's been a misunderstanding all round, really – well, let's say we misunderstood things, on our side – Josh blundered, of course, he said something he shouldn't have done – the whole thing's his fault, he suggested and arranged the holiday, didn't he? – that was the mistake because he worked on the assumption that . . . that, well, that you would both be amenable

amenable? – amenable to what? – Pansy raises her voice, leans forward again

Beth moves on her seat, her eyes flash from one to the other of her listeners – *well, we often go on holiday with other couples and . . . well, not only on holiday, not always on holiday – you know how it is, what we do is we . . . we change over – we thought that this time . . .*

what do you mean, change over? – you switch partners! – is that what you mean? – and you thought we were like that? – Pansy's on her feet now, Martin follows her action and stands beside her

Beth tries to stand as well but with the other two close in front of her only manages to sit up straighter – *look, it's all been a mistake, I'm sorry, obviously you're not . . . we know now you're not . . .*

and that was the plan, was it? demands Martin – *that I'd let Josh sleep with my wife? – and I was supposed to go with you?*

Beth manages to get to her feet, squirms away from the other two, stands trying to rouse her indignation again – *I'm sorry, it's all a big mistake – we do it all the time, we thought you might be willing to as well, at least on this occasion – I'm sorry we've offended you, but obviously you have different standards to us – Josh thought . . .*

you do this all the time? – there's a sickly horror on Pansy's face – *you sleep with other men?*

it's not as uncommon as you think . . . everybody's doing it

you're a whore, that's what you are, a bloody whore!

once a flushed Beth has gone, having paused, frozen for a second or two at the force of Pansy's words before turning quickly and leaving without uttering another word herself, there's left behind a mood of indecision – though the atmosphere remains so highly charged that neither Martin nor

Pansy can bring themselves to speak, an unconscious unity of view nevertheless unites them – Martin stands by the closed door after letting Beth out, leans against it looking with a face clouded with anxiety at Pansy as she firmly plumps the cushions, throws them angrily into the chairs – each of them have words boiling up in their minds, but each are reluctant to let out the head of steam – with slow movements he crosses over to her, puts his arms round her and apologizes softly for having brought her into the situation

hardly your fault she breathes – *you weren't to know*

no, but I persuaded you – you weren't keen – not much of a holiday now, is it?

what do we do now?

we can't stay

no, we can't – we'll have to go home

I don't want to do that, the children want their holiday – Martin breaks away, catches at her hand and steers her into a chair before sitting down himself facing her – *no, what we'll do is get a bed and breakfast somewhere – we've got three days before we need to go home, we can go along the coast and get away from here*

what a waste of money – we'd be spending more

well, we can't stay here, can we? – I don't want to face either of them

she gives him a sympathetic smile – *and next week you'll be back at work with him, that won't be easy*

don't worry about that, let's finish our holiday – I'll face that when the time comes

how can they ever do it!

I don't know – some people are just . . . he lets the words drift away, unable to think of a suitable ending – *no, I don't know* he sighs

Pansy rises from her chair, stands with her hands on her hips – *well, we can start sorting out, I suppose – shall we get away early?*

why not? – if the Broadfields aren't up I can always just drop a note in – but I agree with you, how can they do it? – how can they . . . again he's lost for words

they must be very sad people, but think of the children – how it affects them

I presume they don't know about it – well, I wouldn't be surprised if Michael knew, he looks a streetwise lad – fancy knowing your parents are like that!

he stands up and once again puts his arms round Pansy, kisses the top of her head – *yes, we'll get away early – get our children away from it*

they are suddenly interrupted by the appearance of Ellen, standing in the doorway, her face serious and concerned

why do we have to go?

in their surprise both parents begin to give different answers, Pansy letting Martin complete the reply with his version – *we think we'd like to go farther along the coast, stay at a guest house – the farm's got a bit boring, hasn't it? – but you should be asleep, we'll be going off early*

and you know what you're like says Pansy – *you'll never get up*

Ellen still looks serious, her frown deepens – *why did you call Auntie Beth a whore?*

11

Thursday morning

even Brewster's not yet in the yard when the door to Stook opens – the Oxfords made an early start, getting the children, even Ellen, drowsy but surprisingly not irritable, out of their beds at six o'clock – PS was the lively one, ready for a game with her breakfast, taking longer than anyone else to eat her toast and smiling exaggeratedly whenever Pansy spoke to her – she's developed a trick which she knows to be regarded as cute, which is to put her head on one side and look under her brows at people, expecting with probably good cause that they'll be happy to oblige her in any way they can – *who taught her that?* asks Josh, looking at Ellen – *not me!* answers the accused – *well, I never did* says Sean – *I think she looks silly, anyway*

most of the packing was done last night, only the most essential items, the nightwear and the catering things left until this morning – Sean is excited that they should be going somewhere but he wants a promise that they'll come back to the farm 'one day', and this Martin has to give him with fingers crossed behind his back – Pansy takes a more cautious view, pointing out to Sean that there are farms everywhere, some of them even better than this one, and they're sure to have another farm holiday one day – to which Martin adds under his breath *without company*

Ellen is very cooperative, helping with the dishes, packing her bag and offering to dress PS – because of the previous night's experience and the subsequent explanation of Pansy's remark, she feels part of the grown-up's world, with almost adult responsibility – because of her avid reading she's well aware of what a whore is, even at such a tender age, and the explanation had to be carefully given that Mummy was using the term in a different way, one that Ellen wouldn't have come across, and really it meant no more than that she thought Auntie Beth was too bossy – it was only to be used very rarely and Mummy lost her temper a little and shouldn't have said it – sometimes mummies can't help themselves, just like Ellen gets furious at some of the things Sean does and loses **her** temper, although whether Ellen was agreeable to this comparison isn't clear, as after all he's her brother and you're expected to lose your temper with boys from time to time – but because her parents sat her down and talked to her in a grown-up way, using the longest words they could think of, she feels more privileged this morning – she did ask if they were leaving because the others were hateful but such was the general melee at the time that the question was conveniently ignored

Martin has a note in his hand as he leaves the sanctuary of the Stook doorway and heads for the farmhouse – he's hoping he can just drop it in and make a quick getaway without having to amplify the reason he's giving – crossing the yard he wonders if any of the Waterfords are up and whether he's being watched, but it's only seven-thirty so he doubts if that's the case – nevertheless he tries to walk as quietly as possible on the shingle, opening the little gate carefully and closing it behind him – the slinking figure of the cat disappears behind the pallets as Martin reaches the door, and much to his dismay the door stands open with Mr Broadfield framed within it

they surprise each other – on Mr Broadfield's part he almost jumps, for his mind had obviously been on something else, but he recovers quickly and asks if he can be of help

I wanted to tell you we'll be leaving today – Martin

leaving? – Mr Broadfield

going home – Martin

going home? – Mr Broadfield

yes, we have to go back for a doctor's appointment for one of the children – we'd forgotten it, you see, and it's rather important – we've had a lovely time, the farm's wonderful, Sean loves it tremendously, so it's a great pity, but there you are

Mr Broadfield – *won't you come back – after the appointment?*

Martin – *we thought of that, but it would mean too much travelling, and it would only be for a day, so . . .*

Mr Broadfield – *we can't give you a refund*

Martin – *no, no, I appreciate that, I wasn't expecting that – perhaps you'd give our thanks to your wife for everything – we've enjoyed it*

as he recrosses the yard Martin reflects that he's lying twice over, for he doesn't think he's actually enjoyed very much of the holiday, particularly this bit, and certainly not last night – he'll be glad to get on the road again and is quite looking forward to motoring along the coast, something we all like to do, don't we, especially when it's fine weather like today – there was a time when this was the prerogative of the wealthy, and of course the roads were emptier then, life was more enjoyable all round – now the roads are full of all the proletariat and their caravans, not to mention motor-bikes – I wouldn't mind having a motorhome, in fact it's something I've always wanted, the convenience of being able to pull in for a night's sleep, be able to cook your dinner in it, go where you will, whatever takes your fancy – or better still perhaps a cabincruiser, or a barge – a houseboat?

when he gets back to the cottage Pansy's there ready and waiting, all the bags and children available for loading – she pokes out her head and looks round towards the Wheatsheaf door, acting as though this is a moonlight flit and everything has to be done secretively – the act of stowing everything away in the car and installing the children takes but a few minutes, and then she's making for the gate, walking as Martin walked, trying to do so silently on the shingle

at the windows of the car two blonde heads can be seen absorbing the last views of the farm, the voice of PS can be heard faintly singing *altogether now* or *all together now*, whichever it is, and the car bumps through the potholes and disappears in the dust

he's up on the wall, Sammy, a bit early for him, the moss giving that nasty damp feel to his haunches, but it's a place he has to be for he suspects that, although it's not Saturday [when his instinct tells him what day it is], this is the last he'll be seeing of these particular visitors – he's not sorry, it means they're taking that horrid little child away, the one that nearly pulled his tail off – as the last of the dust settles he slowly steps down on to the pallets, no point in getting the old rheumatics going, and anyway, there's a bit of breakfast to be had

so that leaves us with the Waterfords, with Beth and Josh, with Abigail and Michael – are they still asleep, did they see the Oxfords go? – the children wouldn't have roused themselves to dash to their windows and look out, they'd have turned over if they heard anything – as for Josh, he still snores, out to the world, you could have brought an army tank into the yard and he wouldn't have heard it – Beth now, she's a different matter, she's been up a long time, since five o'clock actually, drinking endless cups of coffee

if I drink any more I'll be looking like it – but it's either that or the drink, and I don't think I can face any alcohol at this time of the day – so they've gone! – it's the best thing, I don't see how we could have acted normally any more, the whole thing's been busted wide open – he tried to sneak across the yard without being noticed, but I nearly waved to him – no, I wouldn't have fancied him anyway, did at first, but it was only habit – they're the sort who have to hold hands all the time, he's so soft – can't say I envy Josh having to work with him, that'll be fun next week – now, I've been up since five and mooching about and it's the first time I've noticed it – his wallet, just left there on the floor, what's it doing there? – oh God, it's totally empty, what's he gone and done? – I bet he's taken the contents to bed with him, done that before, put it under his pillow like he thought someone was going to steal it in the night – but that's been the whole wallet, not just . . . why's he taken everything out?

and up into the bedroom Beth goes to see where the old fool's put his money, feeling under the snoring man's pillow until he wakes with a start

what you doing? – he's bleary, his words are slurred, the shock's too much

where's your money and things – your wallet's downstairs empty – what have you done with it?

from deep sleep to the appreciation of financial affairs is a huge step to take first thing in the morning when you're so rudely awakened – Josh blinks, rubs his eyes and asks her again what she's doing

you've emptied your wallet – what have you done with it?

I don't know – I haven't done anything with it – where is it?

downstairs, and it's got nothing in it – did you take it out last night?

their evening was an abstemious one when Beth returned from the Oxfords, and Josh recalls exactly what he was doing – *I haven't done anything with it – it's empty?*

very empty

that step to financial acumen is taken, Josh leaps out of bed – *Michael! – I bet he's been looking for money again – he's helped himself, he's done it before – where is he?*

the delegation of two move swiftly from their bedroom to the door of Michael's, where Beth begins to tap politely – Josh is impatient, brushing past her to throw the door open – they both stare at the empty room with a bed that's obviously not been slept in – the only sign that Michael's ever been here is a pair of trousers on the floor and a T-shirt on the bed

where's he gone? asks Beth of a wordless Josh – *where is he?*

and well might she ask – who saw him go? – does Abigail know anything? – a hurried foray into her room to rouse and cross-examine the girl produces blank bewilderment – *how would I know?*

when he gets downstairs Josh fondly caresses his wallet, dreaming mistily of all the goodies that once resided therein – his thoughts of his son are far from fond however, and his temper is anything but tender – the words *I'll murder him* spring easily to his lips, along with other less savoury objectives, and he immediately starts barking his orders – *he'll have gone home somehow, by train probably if he's got all my money – I'll have to get ready, go after him* – and he hurries back up to the bedroom to get some clothes on – *if I'm quick I'll beat the train, he'll have to change a couple of times, it's not direct*

Beth's in a state of distress – she trots up the stairs after him – *you can't just go off and leave us here – what will we do? – you'll be gone all day, all night!*

I'm not letting him get away with it

well, we'll come with you – Abi, get yourself dressed

oh, Mum!

I can't hang around – Josh is irritated now – irritation and anger are not a happy combination and he begins to look like thunder, his black hair out of style and hanging about his face as he dresses

Beth's adamant about things – *we're not staying here on our own, that's for sure – we've no money anyway, have we, you had it all – I've got no more than a couple of pounds, Abi's probably got the same*

well, hurry up then – we'll all go, we might as well take everything with us, we might as well say goodbye to any idea of a holiday – it hasn't been a lot of fun, has it? – come on then, start packing! – hurry up!

a trio of hasty packers then – Abigail's the most lethargic, having to be constantly egged on by her mother who in turn is being urged by her husband – where careful folding and separating and crease-avoiding was the dominant stipulation at the time of leaving home, the return passage is anything but careful – clothes are grabbed, squashed, screwed into rags almost and crammed into cases with the only requirement being the need not to forget anything – only at the last minute, when bags are being taken downstairs, does someone remember to look in Michael's room and sweep into a supermarket bag anything that remains there

Brewster savours all the excitement, running around the sitting room, getting in the way, trying to get up the stairs – when Josh opens the front door he's out immediately, trotting to the nearest wall to say good morning, taking himself off to the small gate to see if Sammy's around – when he sees the bags being loaded into the car he gets extra excited, a couple of barks escape him as he tries eagerly to get aboard so as not to be forgotten

once they're in the car, with Abigail despatched to operate the gate, Beth raises the matter of saying goodbye to their hosts – are they being discourteous by just driving off?

Josh is all man of action – *no time – they'll find out soon enough when we don't come back – have you got your credit card?*

yes – what for?

well, I haven't got anything, have I? – we'll need to fill up with petrol

oh dear, I think I'm near my limit

the excitement and the two barks from Brewster have brought Sammy out of his place of daily retirement to assume his watch from the wall – the moss is still damp but he's able to find a thinner patch which allows him to settle his old limbs – through half-closed eyes he watches the loading, all the comings and goings, and recognizes the signs, as with the Oxfords a little earlier, of an imminent departure – he sees Brewster leap into the car, sees Abigail open and close the gate, sees her climb into her seat, watches the trail of dust as the vehicle speeds down the lane – no, it's not a Saturday, but it feels like one

with gentle motion, as befitting an old cat, Sammy climbs down from the wall, pallet by pallet – behind the little gate he pauses, stares through the rails as if estimating his chances of resuming his normal daily patrol of the property – then he slips through and walks directly to the door of Wheatsheaf, only the slightest of limps indicating the crystallization of his joints – once beside the door he makes a preliminary survey, sniffing the frame and the panels with a delicate twitching of his nostrils, before first sitting and then lying in front of the door, a small version of the previous incumbent, a mimic of the canine beast

lying here, his head resting near his outstretched paws, he
sniffs the ground about him and closes his eyes

in a short space of time, with a hustle and a bustle, speed
bordering on panic, we've lost them then, our visitors, the
holidaymakers whom I clinically introduced as cliques A and
B – they've gone back to where they came from, wherever
that was – I named them the Oxfords and the Waterfords,
and I named their children too, like some ruling patriarch –
I can only say, here and now, that I had no idea how they
would turn out, honest I didn't – I think we all had our suspicions that it would end in tears, didn't we, but I'm as
disappointed as you must be at the Waterfords and their
nasty 'hobby' – we must assume Michael, loaded with his
father's money and credit cards, is hotfooting it to London
or wherever he planned to go, and poor Abigail seems almost
destined to become a carbon copy of her mother – much more
hope for the Oxford children, but I do worry about Ellen's
reading – she's far too young to be on things like *Middle-
march*, and it's very likely she **will** ruin her eyesight

which of course leaves us with the Broadfields – here we
have a disintegrating family that at any moment will split into
several disparate parts, each going their own way – the big
question is when will Lance pluck up the courage to face his
father – according to Mrs B he's tried to do it several times
and always finds some convenient last-minute reason for
evading it – come now, Lance, be brave, take the plunge, you
know it's got to be done, otherwise you're doomed to a life
of misery

I know, I know – don't push me, don't go on about it –

bad enough my mother always carping on, without anyone else joining in

he's standing in the kitchen making himself a sandwich, deftly spreading margarine and slicing cheese, quite a dab hand at it – I imagine Mr Broadfield senior isn't quite so domesticated

him? – I don't think he's ever done a thing in the kitchen, he only dries his boots here – he can't even make a cup of tea for himself, honest, hard to believe but it's the truth – he's always had someone wait on him, his mother, his wife, his children, even Bert – how can someone go through life without knowing how to provide food and drink for himself?

he **has** made provision, in getting married – in employing Bert – it's like some men can't put up a shelf or change a light bulb, useless when it comes to decorating – they make other arrangements, don't they, employ someone else or, as in your father's case, make sure there's always someone to do it for them

I couldn't be like that, dependent – I want to know I can look after myself, be self-reliant – especially when it comes to food

I suppose that shows signs of insecurity, the need to manage without the help of others, rather than independence – there's the residual fear, subconscious, that you'll be all alone, and won't be able to survive

what are you now, a psychiatrist? – I thought you were an author

well, you just pick these things up, don't you – authors think, you know, we can still use our brains, it's not all pen and ink *or a computer keyboard*

well, as I've said before, I prefer to use a pen, type it out afterwards

well, I must go – he's finished making his sandwich, neatly cut it in half and gently wrapped it in cling film – now he's pressing down the lid of his lunchbox, already containing an apple and a banana – and did I see a chocolate bar in there?

yes, you did – you get hungry on a tractor all day

bit lonely too, I imagine

very – there's the radio, but you get fed up with that – early in the season I can spend twelve hours a day, several days in a row, without talking to anyone, being with anyone – just going back and forth, up and down – you wonder why farmers are dull? – in the good old days we'd have had the company of horses, you can talk to them, communicate with them

on that subject, do you think Tilly's decision to give up her riding is something to do with a boyfriend?

oh, you'd better ask her that – she's got her reasons – I'm keeping out of it – I'm off now, got to get going – he picks up the box, turns towards the door – *the visitors went off rather quickly, didn't they? – something to do with a doctor's appointment, Dad said – I thought I saw the others loading up too*

yes, that's right, they've all cut their holiday short – they fell out, had an argument – that's the trouble with going on holiday with another family

well, we've got their money, that's all Dad will worry about

*

when we thought we'd seen the last of the visitors, watched them pull away in their cars, the two families doing so for different reasons, I for one imagined that that would be the end of it – but what is this I detect now, something that Sammy would detect were he on his wall where he should be?

slowly coming back up the lane, very slowly as if tiptoeing, the Oxfords' vehicle creeps into sight – it stops well short of the gate in the lee of the hedge and Martin alights, pushing his door to instead of slamming it – there's obviously stealth being employed here, particularly noticeable in the way he keeps close against the hedge until he's able to look round the end of it into the farm – relief is obviously upon him, for he turns back to the car and puts his thumb up in the air – what he's seen, of course, is that the Waterfords' car is no longer in front of Wheatsheaf – bolder now, but still with diffident step he lets himself through the gate and walks towards the farmhouse – there is no sign of other movement from anyone else in the car – it sits there silent and slightly menacing

across the crisp gravel, across the synthetic cobblestones, Martin approaches the farmhouse kitchen door where he presumes to find Mrs Broadfield, and is surprised as he reaches it to find Lance about to come out

oh, had to come back, I'm afraid he stutters – *we left something behind – that horn you kindly gave Sean, he forgot to pack it – he suddenly remembered and made such a fuss we couldn't go on – do you think I could have the key . . .*

I don't think it's locked – Lance backs into the kitchen to throw a glance at the dresser which stands in a corner – *no, it won't be locked, Debbie'll be in to clean it – did he like it, then?*

well, he wouldn't let us go home without it, that's for sure – I'll just nip over then – thanks very much again, and good-bye once more – I'm sorry we've had to cut it short

the others have left too – not long after you

left? – you mean gone?

they didn't say why – rushed off, they did – the boy wasn't with them so perhaps it was something to do with him

oh yes, maybe – anyway, all the best to you

crossing the yard Martin muses on the departure of Beth and Josh – that will interest Pansy, and reassure her too, she's probably anxious that they'll come back any minute and catch her in the lane – well, well, well, fancy them leaving at the same time

now unfortunately for Lance, before he's had time to leave the kitchen his father enters from the living room

good morning, Mr Broadfield, haven't heard you out with your shotgun the last couple of days

I don't always do it, just once or twice in the week, it's her idea – says they like it, but I think they find it frightening

Lance is fidgeting – he's eager to get away – *better be off, Dad – got that last bit of Hedge field to do this morning*

yes, well – you're not going to be skiving there, are you, reading that paper of yours? – he does, you know, I've seen him, sits there reading the paper – I send him out to do a job and he takes hours because he's wasting time

it's a pretty boring job for a young man

look, one day he's going to be running this place on his own – how do you think I was when I was young? – of course it's boring at times, but it's life, isn't it, you've just got to get down to it

perhaps he doesn't want to do it at all

oh, you're taking his mother's side

well, I'm going, leave you two to talk about me – Lance opens the door, tucks his box under his arm – *I'll see you later*

hang on, hang on – what about the vet, he's supposed to be coming, isn't he?

not till this afternoon

well, you make sure you're here – you can see him, I don't want to

the kitchen becomes a little crowded as Mrs Broadfield comes through, rubbing her hands together as if in preparation for making dough – *you off, Lance?*

yes, I'll be back for the vet, don't worry about it – and I don't have a paper

Mrs Broadfield shakes her head – *you two been at it again? – I don't know, why don't you just get it over with, Lance? – for God's sake tell him*

tell me what? – what have you got to tell me?

oh, it can wait – Lance has his feet outside

no, no – if you've got something to say, you say it now – what's he got to tell me?

Mrs Broadfield shakes her head again, a look of exasperation crosses her face – Lance gives her an appealing look, as if to say 'now look what you've done!' – Broadfield's eyes are hard and challenging, his mouth is set in a firm line as he looks from one to the other – *what you got to tell me?*

oh, it's just that he's arranged a course . . . Mrs Broadfield lifts her arms in the air hopelessly and lets the words tail off

outside the kitchen Lance shuffles his feet, tries not to look at his father

a course? – what sort of course?

journalism – Lance mumbles his answer, looks down at his feet

what?

journalism – in London

London! – what good's that? – what good's London to me? – no, no, you're not going to London for some silly course in . . . in . . .

he wants to be a journalist, not a farmer

course he wants to be a farmer, this is his home, isn't it, it's his farm when I'm gone – course he wants to be a farmer

Lance, perhaps emboldened by being outside, begins to defend his corner – *no, I don't, I never have – I want to do something else*

there isn't anything else, you're a farmer – you come in here where I can see you, come in here

obediently Lance steps back into the kitchen, Mrs Broadfield gives out a sigh as he stands framed against the light – Broadfield waves his finger

don't think you can get ideas of doing something else, you'll help me on this farm until I'm gone, that's what you'll do

you can't make him, Ben

I don't have to make him, he knows what he's got to do – you don't think I can run this place all on my own, do you? – what are sons for, that's why you have children

246

I want to be a journalist, Dad – the words are out, Lance swallows hard and tries to look his father in the eye – *I don't want to run the farm, I want to be a journalist*

that's not a job! – how do you think you'll live, you couldn't get a bus fare out of that, you're only good for farming, like me and my father before me – you want to get these ideas out of your head, that's what you want to do – too much reading of those newspapers, that's what it is, gives you big ideas – now you get out on that tractor, and come back here for the vet when he comes – you can forget all about going to London or anything like that, you get to work, there's work to be done here, real work

if he wants to . . .

nothing about what he wants – and you can shut up too, I've had enough of you encouraging him, you're the one who's put these ideas in his head anyway

he's got his own ideas! – I don't . . .

shut your mouth, I said, I'm not having women telling me what I should and shouldn't do with my own son – get out on that tractor!

Lance hesitates – Mrs Broadfield, red in the face, turns to face her husband – *don't you talk to me . . .*

he ignores her – *you get on that tractor!*

Lance pushes his way between them, white faced, not like his mother, anger coming out differently – *I'm not going anywhere* – and he goes through to the living room

you come here! – Broadfield makes a grab for his sleeve, but Lance twists away, goes on through the room with his father following – his mother trails behind, trying to say something that no one hears *don't you walk away from me!* – Broadfield thunders – *don't you walk away from me! – you come back here when I tell you!*

Lance reaches the stairs, steps up quickly, gets to the landing before Broadfield can reach him, goes to his room and shuts the door firmly – Broadfield tries the handle, bangs on the door with his fist – *you come out here! – don't you hide away from me, who do you think you are? – open this door, you open it!*

behind him Mrs Broadfield paws at his back, alternately shouting and sobbing – *leave him alone, leave him alone – Ben, stop it!*

Broadfield hammers relentlessly at the door – *no son of mine's going to get the better of me! – open this door!*

inside the room there are tears in Lance's eyes as he cowers in a corner by the window

Ben! – Mrs Broadfield appeals in vain – *oh, do stop it!*

Broadfield leaves off hammering the door long enough to push her away, making her stumble against the banister, nearly falling down the stairs – stepping back a pace he raises his foot, crashes it against the door, which shakes but doesn't give

Ben!

Broadfield kicks once more – this time the door threatens to give way – *when I get in there you're going to pay for this!*

Ben!

she's sobbing a bit now, almost hysterically – Broadfield has another kick, the door shakes, just about holds – *bastard!* – he yells – *I'll get you out of there* – and there's Tilly's voice over the commotion, she's shouting at her father to stop, she's

248

calling out – *what about me, don't you care? – only Lance, is he the only one?– all about him, what about me?* – and as a last appeal *don't you care that I'm pregnant?*

it's a dreadful scene, appalling, how can it happen like this? – I didn't expect them to end up in this situation – when I sat down at the beginning of this story, worrying over the characters that were appearing, I thought the trouble would come from the visitors, that's who I thought might be shouting at one another, not the rustic Broadfields living in a haven of bucolic bliss – this is what comes of letting the characters have their own way, developing without an authorial check – if I ever write something again it's going to be planned and plotted well before I start, that's for sure!

Broadfield leaves off kicking the door and roughly pushes his way past his tearful wife to go downstairs – she's nursing her ribs where she fell heavily against the banisters, staring at Tilly who stands beside her with a wild look in her eyes, hands clenched up against her neck – inside the room Lance remains cowering in his corner, eyes glistening, ears attentive to what might be going on beyond the battered door – it's not solely through fear that the tears tremble but in recognition of his timidity, his weakness that prevents him standing his ground against a bully – sons should have more guts, especially a farmer's boy – for a moment all is quiet, a pause in the action ensues

over in Stook Martin's had to search high and low for the ram's horn, which wasn't where Sean said it would be – he's heard the raised voices from the farmhouse which made him search as fast as he could, and now he's got it, clutched tightly in his hand as he quickly steps out across the yard –

whatever's going on he doesn't want to be part of it, and he's on his way down the lane before Sammy's even had time to squeeze back through his gate

you took long enough is Pansy's ungrateful comment

not a happy scene Martin reports – *let's get on our way*

why, what's happening?

a big row by the sound of it – your fault, young man – happy now?

thanks, Dad – I love this – and I think Lance is great!

the sound of the car starting and negotiating a three-point turn in the lane is all Sammy hears as he stiffly climbs the pallets and reaches the top of the wall to observe any goings-off, but dust, just dust, that's all there is to see from here, just dust

and to his attentive ears comes the sound of a child declaiming at the top of her voice *altogether now* or *all together now* whichever it is, who can say for certain

and as for me, I've had enough, I'm going to follow the Oxfords . . .